Three-times Golden Heart® finalist **Tina Beckett** learned to pack her suitcases almost before she learned to read. Born to a military family, she has lived in the United States, Puerto Rico, Portugal and Brazil. In addition to travelling, Tina loves to cuddle with her pug, Alex, spend time with her family, and hit the trails on her horse. Learn more about Tina from her website, or 'friend' her on Facebook.

CONSEQUENCES OF THEIR NEW YORK NIGHT

TINA BECKETT

THE TROUBLE WITH THE TEMPTING DOC

TINA BECKETT

MILLS & BOON

First Published in Great Britain 2021
by Mills & Boon, an imprint of HarperCollins*Publishers*
1 London Bridge Street, London, SE1 9GF

Consequences of Their New York Night © 2021 by Tina Beckett

The Trouble with the Tempting Doc © 2021 by Tina Beckett

ISBN: 978-0-263-29757-7

MIX
Paper from
responsible sources
FSC® C007454

Printed and bound in Spain
by CPI, Barcelona

CONSEQUENCES
OF THEIR
NEW YORK NIGHT

TINA BECKETT

MILLS & BOON

For my husband. Always and forever.

PROLOGUE

KALEB SABAT THUMPED a glass of whiskey in front of his friend without saying a word. The bar was packed with the normal weekend crowd. Singles trolling for some easy company for the night. People celebrating the wins and losses they'd experienced during the day. Kaleb was there for none of those things.

He'd been the best man at his buddy's wedding five years ago, just as they were both finishing up medical school. And now he was here drinking to the finalizing of Snowden's divorce. It wasn't exactly a celebration, but close enough. Kaleb could only be glad he and his fiancée had called it quits before it got to the point of selling a home and dividing up assets.

"Hell," Snow said, then tipped back his glass and drained it in two swallows. "Why did we have to be so young and stupid, anyway? First your relationship crashes. And then mine."

"I have no idea." He took a drink of his own whiskey and gave a slight grimace as the brew bit the back of his throat and traced a path of fire down his esophagus. A good kind of fire.

Friends since the time they were kids, Snow had spent more time at Kaleb's house than he had at his own as they were growing up. Only later did Kaleb find out why. His friend's home hadn't been a very good example of marital harmony. Or any other kind of harmony.

Then again, nothing could really prepare you for finding out your spouse was cheating on you with a colleague. He tipped his glass again and said the only thing he could think of. "At least they're moving out of state."

Evidently Theresa was letting no grass grow under her feet. Snow's ex was busy scheduling another wedding.

"Let's agree neither of us is getting involved with women ever again."

Kaleb laughed. "Define *involved*." He'd pretty much gotten his relationship skills honed to a very rigid set of requirements. No women who had a significant other. No lasting ties. No sleeping over. Actually he didn't have women over at his house anymore period. He went to their place or found other more inventive ways of getting physically close.

"That's easy. No rings. No strings. No walking the aisle. No sleeping—"

Kaleb held up a hand. "We're not allowed to sleep?"

"Funny. You know what I mean."

Unfortunately he did. Relationships were hard. He had no idea how his mom and dad had navigated thirty-five years of marital bliss, but they had. And they were still very much in love. So was his sister, who was expecting her second child. But as much as Kaleb might wish otherwise, he was not like them. His relationship track record was a royal failure with two broken engagements. He was not looking to add a third to that list.

"You were the one who actually got married, Snow, not me."

"Way to rub it in, pal. But whatever you do, don't find out the hard way what marriage is really about, like I did."

Kaleb already had, and it hadn't taken marriage to do that. Just two different women. One who'd insisted they have a baby right away, when he was just starting medical school. He'd said no, even though he wanted a family. Eventually. When things settled down. But no matter how much he tried to explain that fact, she'd kept pushing. When an ovulation tracking chart had fallen out of her purse, he knew the relationship was doomed. And maybe even his shot at fatherhood, since he was now swearing off women.

His second engagement was just as much of a flop. Candice thought a doctor that specialized in facial reconstruction meant having a plastic surgeon at her beck and call. After all, she'd landed a few parts on Broadway and had her sights set on Hollywood. Unfortunately for her, Kaleb had chosen his profession to help people with disfiguring injuries or conditions. She'd found that out when he'd gone on his first medical mission.

Why go there when you could make more money staying home?

That particular relationship had ended on an even uglier note than his first one. He'd broken off the engagement before he left on his trip and had thankfully come home to an empty apartment. Candice had cleaned out her stuff and most of his furniture, as well. It was a small price to pay to get her out of his life. So Snow wasn't the only one who'd learned the hard way.

"I have no intention of ever getting married. Two engagements were enough for me."

"Best decision you'll ever make." He raised a hand to get a second drink. "You want another?"

Kaleb had only taken a sip of his so far. "No. And I think you're going to need a designated driver, at this rate."

"You sure? We could always call a cab. After all, it's a celebration."

Except Snow's face had a hardness to it that belied his words.

"Let's not call it a celebration. How about calling it a resolution." When the bartender set a new drink in front of his friend, Kaleb lifted his glass. "To confirmed bachelorhood."

Snow raised his own. "To being smarter."

"I'll drink to that." And while Kaleb merely tasted his whiskey, his friend drained his second glass.

He had a feeling it was going to be a very long night. And he might just have to revise his no-sleeping-over policy, because his friend was probably going to be sacking out on his new sofa.

But Snow was right about one thing—Kaleb was going to learn from his friend's mistake. And his own.

No more asking someone to move in with him. No more engagement rings. No kids. That one made him take a hard swallow.

And the biggest taboo of all? Walking down a very long aisle. One lined with dying flowers and broken promises, and where the only exit was a very expensive piece of paper—just like the one Snow had just signed.

No, it wasn't worth it.

To bachelorhood. The two words rolled silently through his head. If he got nothing else out of tonight, he was going to carry that thought with him and make it his own personal creed.

CHAPTER ONE

Six months later

KALEB WOKE UP to an empty bed. And sunlight streaming through the window of the swanky hotel.

Where was he? And why was he…?

He sat up in a hurry. Whoa. He'd spent the entire night there? Holy hell.

For him, that was unheard of. It was one of his taboos, along with several other things. The only explanation that made any sense was he'd been more exhausted than he thought last night. After the awful day he'd had, it was no wonder.

Snatches of the previous evening came back to haunt him: the soft, insistent press of kisses on his body. Hands that skimmed pleasure points he didn't even know he had. And an explosion that had taken him down a rabbit hole, where the experience was repeated several times. His body reacted to the memories.

But to spend the night?

Damn. Thank God she hadn't waited around for him to wake up. That might have been awkward, no matter how spectacularly she'd fit against him. No matter how intoxicating her fragrance was. No, he would have just kissed her on the lips and said his goodbyes. He paused. Well, the goodbyes might have come after he'd acted out a few more scenes with…

Nicola.

He murmured the name in his head. Tasted it on his tongue. He didn't know her last name. It hadn't been important at the time. All that had mattered was the way her eyes had touched on him in the bar and then returned several times. There'd been a hint of uncertainty in their depths that had done a number on him. So he'd gone over and bought her a drink. One that she'd accepted. A half hour later, they were out of there and in a hotel room. And what happened next had been…

Heaven.

No. Not heaven. Just another night. Just another woman.

Except he'd slept there—his arm holding her naked form to his—instead of getting up and gathering his clothes, like he normally did. Why? Was it the thrill of being there with a perfect stranger?

Maybe, except he'd had one-night stands before this. And that he was dissecting his reasons for staying made him think that something had been different this time.

Only it wasn't. Maybe it was a good thing he hadn't asked what her full name was.

Avoiding commitment was the best decision he'd ever made. Whatever his reasons for staying over, they didn't change that fact.

He lay back, lacing his fingers together behind his head. He would probably never see this Nicola person again, unless she frequented that bar, and he was pretty sure that was the first time he'd ever seen her there. She'd been alone. No wing person, not that she'd needed one. And that trace of something in her gaze had awoken instincts he'd thought were long dead.

Maybe not dead. But they'd been submerged in a sea of disillusionment.

Hell. He did not want to start tracing the origins of that word.

He pried himself out of bed and strode to the shower, turning it on full blast. He had about an hour before he needed to be at work, so he would change once he got to his office. Soon he would be able to put all thoughts of last night and the mystery woman out of his head, and get back to life as he knew it. Life as he wanted to know it. Without any Candices or Melanies or Nicolas cluttering it up and making him wonder if he'd made the wrong decision about remaining a bachelor. About not being a father. He hadn't. It had been the best thing he'd ever done. And nothing, or no *one*, was going to convince him otherwise.

Nicola's mind was wandering, and her thoughts slid in and out of places that were best left for another time. The hospital was huge and the names of people she'd been introduced to were starting to squish together inside the confines of her skull.

And as the space grew even tighter, something had to give. So squeezing between the cracks came the memory of a night five weeks ago. And the tall stranger she'd fallen into bed with.

She swallowed. She still couldn't believe she'd done that. What had she been thinking?

She hadn't been. And that had been the idea. She hadn't wanted to think, to talk…to remember. She'd just wanted to feel. And, God, had she ever. She'd…

"Kaleb, could you come over here for a moment?" Harvey Smith's voice shocked her back to reality, making her blink. "I want you to meet the newest member of our team, Nicola Bradley. Her specialty is internal medicine with an emphasis on diagnostics. She'll be helping us crack the tough cases."

As the hospital administrator continued to speak, she turned to greet the newcomer, and a wave of shock knocked her flat, setting off all kinds of sirens and alarms.

"Nicola, meet Kaleb Sabat. He's New York City Memorial's chief of reconstructive surgery."

She somehow met the man's cool blue eyes without flinching. How was this even possible? Was this some sort of cosmic joke? If so, the punch line was lost on her.

The man she'd shared a crazy, impulsive night of sex with was NYC Memorial's chief of reconstructive surgery? Oh, God. What should she do? What *could* she do?

Quit? Run down the hallway until she found the nearest exit? No. Nicola was no chicken. At least she hoped not.

She was going to pretend it never happened, that's

what she'd do. And hope that he did the same. Or maybe he didn't even remember her.

Please, God…

"Nice to meet you, Dr. Sabat," she murmured, placing the slightest emphasis on his title.

The man's head tilted sideways for a second, his eyebrows coming together as a host of changes came over his face, the last of which was sardonic amusement.

Oh, no. He remembered. *Remembered!*

They'd both had a little too much to drink that night five weeks ago, and she'd hoped…

If she'd had any idea he'd worked at the hospital she was transferring to, she would have moved off that barstool quicker than anyone believed possible. But she'd been grieving and needed to forget.

Kaleb had given her a few hours of respite…and more.

But it was behind her. Needed to stay behind her.

"You live here in the city?" His sharp eyes were on her. Watching.

She blinked. "I do now. I just moved from a facility in New Jersey." She shifted, hoping he wouldn't see something in her expression that gave her away.

"Oh? Which facility?"

Aware that the hospital administrator was taking in their conversation, she flipped her hair over her shoulder, then regretted the move when Kaleb's eyes followed the gesture. "Grace Central. It's a small private clinic."

"I'm familiar with it. It specializes in research and grants, does it not?"

That surprised her. Most people had no idea Grace Central even existed. But it had been where she'd landed after finishing up medical school. A few years later, she'd branched out, into consulting on cases from neighboring clinics, before her hospital's administrator—a man who'd been like a second father to her—pulled her aside and said that while he knew Nicola loved working there, she could do more good at one of the bigger hospitals, as much as he hated to lose her. But after her brother, who'd also worked there had… Well, she'd needed to leave. Find someplace new. Someplace that didn't have those devastating memories attached to it.

"It does. Why?" She clamped her jaws shut as she felt herself grow defensive. One of her worst personality traits, but it was really none of his business why she'd decided to move to NYC Memorial.

"No reason."

She was very glad he didn't refer to the night they'd spent together or tell Harvey that they'd already met. Repeatedly. In more ways than one.

"Actually a good friend suggested I transfer here, and I agreed with his assessment. It's a wonderful opportunity. One I couldn't pass up."

Something else chased across Kaleb's face—speculation. "Yes, it would be a shame to let opportunities like this pass you by, wouldn't it."

Before she could work through his meaning, Harvey spoke, drawing her attention back to where it should be. "Yes, indeed. I think you'll like working here. Thousands of patients come through our doors every month.

We pride ourselves on trying to give each of them the answers they need. Kaleb had a tough case himself last month. I told him to take some time off, but he wouldn't hear of it. That's the kind of dedication we like to see."

Last month. Was that tough case part of the reason he'd wound up in that bar slugging back whiskey like it was water?

"Positive outcome, I hope."

"I'm afraid not."

Her glance jerked back to Kaleb's face. Not a muscle moved in those hard features, but those piercing eyes had chilled even further.

"I'm so sorry." It was hard to imagine what kind of case a plastic surgeon would find difficult other than some kind of body dysmorphic disorder, but as neither of them offered more details there was no way of knowing.

Had the patient felt lost? Like there was no way out? The way her brother had?

"It's why we're so glad you're here."

Kaleb held out his hand. "Sorry. I've got to run. I have a patient in a few minutes. Nice to meet you, Dr....Bradley." The amusement was back. It was in the way he said her last name. Maybe because she'd purposely avoided telling him her full name.

A hesitation on her part would have given her away, so she slid her hand into his and forced herself not to shudder as the contact set her nerve endings to dancing. It was a reminder of all the other places he'd made her body dance.

Then it was over, and Kaleb was striding down the

hallway away from them. She drew a shaky breath, then released it.

Harvey chuckled. "Sorry. Kaleb can be a little rough around the edges at times, but he's a good doctor. One of the best we have."

She bet. He was one of the best she'd ever had, too. That was part of the problem with seeing him again. It had been a whole lot easier being uninhibited when she'd thought they'd be going their own separate ways. And now a part of her cringed at the explicit things she'd said…and done. She'd never been like that with anyone before. Not even her ex. At the time, she'd chalked it up to the liquid courage the bartender had placed in front of her. But she had a feeling it was the man himself that had drawn those things from her. Things she didn't even know she was capable of.

The only good thing she could pull from her current situation was that it wasn't likely she would be working with Kaleb on a regular basis. It was more probable she'd be paired up with cases from neurology or oncology, or even orthopedics. But reconstruction was, for the most part, cut-and-dried. No sifting among ambiguous symptoms to find a root cause of illness.

And yet, Harvey said he'd had a hard case. Had offered him time off.

She couldn't stop herself from asking. "You mentioned Dr. Sabat had had a difficult case not long ago."

"Yes. Tragic, really. A twenty-five-year-old came in with what was thought to be a deviated septum. She'd always had problems with snoring, and having what she said was clogged sinuses. A sleep study had ruled out apnea, so she and her husband met with Kaleb to discuss surgery. He sent her for imaging to see what he would be working with." The man sighed. "Everyone was shocked when there turned out to be a tumor in her nasal cavity. A biopsy showed primary melanoma, which had spread to her brain. As you know, it's a rare place for melanoma to start. Unfortunately, the patient went home after hearing the diagnosis and ended her life."

A horrified shudder went through her. What were the chances? That had to be why he'd been at the bar that night. They'd both had something they wanted to forget. Needed to forget.

And now, all Nicola wanted to do was forget what her "wanting to forget" had caused.

"I've read about melanoma occurring in the nasal cavity, but have never been involved in a case. It carries a poor prognosis, doesn't it? And with it having already metastasized…"

"Yes. And because she'd always had sinus issues and just considered it a minor annoyance, it took longer for her to get fed up enough to seek help. By then, it was probably too late. It's tragic no matter how you look at it."

Yes, it was. "For her husband, as well."

"She also had two toddlers at home."

"God." She couldn't imagine the emotional pain the woman had gone through. And to leave two toddlers behind? Nicola was about ten years older than Kaleb's patient and had no children of her own. Although she'd always hoped someday…

"How terrible."

"It was a blow to everyone who worked on her case. Kaleb took it especially hard." He shook his head. "Well, let's finish showing you around so you can get back to your day. Are you starting next week?"

"Yes. I've wrapped up all of my cases at Grace Central, so I should be good to start on Monday."

"Perfect."

Showing her around and introducing her to some of the other staff members took another hour. If names and titles had blurred together before, they now had stopped registering at all. Especially after the shock of seeing Kaleb again.

The administrator opened the door to yet another room. "And this will be your office."

"My…?" She blinked. She actually hadn't expected to have four walls and a door to call her own. Grace Central had an open office concept, so there were very few private offices outside of two conference rooms. Most of the staff worked in areas that were divided into sections that, while a step up from cubicles, would definitely not qualify as offices. They were more like wide melamine shelves with a chair underneath. Just to house a computer and maybe a picture or two.

"I really don't think I need something this…big." What Nicola meant was that she didn't really need anything with a door.

Harvey glanced inside and then at her with a smile. "This is one of our smaller offices, actually. I was afraid you might feel insulted."

"Not insulted at all."

He was right. The space wasn't large. It housed a desk with two office chairs in front of it and a bookcase behind. There was a coatrack to the side and a laptop already on top of the desk. As if reading the question on her face, he nodded. "We'd rather you use our computer equipment rather than your personal laptop due to privacy concerns."

She could understand that. "This seems like a luxury compared to what I had before."

He glanced around again, maybe trying to understand her reservations. "You'll be meeting with doctors and patients alike, so it's better to have a place to do that rather than having to keep checking to see if there's a room open on the fourth floor. It's where all of our conference rooms are."

This hospital had one whole floor dedicated to meeting space? It was going to take some getting used to. Grace Central's staff was close-knit and worked well together, probably because of the small size. But after her brother's death, the words of consolation had become too unbearable. She had several friends there that she'd promised to keep in touch with. She had a feeling it would be a lot harder to forge those kinds of relationships in a hospital as large as NYC Memorial, where she knew no one.

Strike that. She knew one person.

Really? "Knew" might be stretching it a little. Although learning about his patient had been a jolt. And it was good to know he didn't normally hang out drinking his troubles away at a bar.

Yikes. Is that what he thought she did? Maybe she

should set him straight at some point. The last thing she wanted was for him to think NYC Memorial's newest doctor had a drinking problem. Or go to Harvey with his "concerns" and ignite all kinds of questions and rumors.

Yes. She was going to have a little chat with Dr. Sabat and set some things straight.

Except she'd pretended not to know him. So that might be a very awkward conversation. She wavered a second or two before deciding to let it drop. If he told on her, she could just as easily tell on him.

And now she was acting like they were both children, ready to retaliate against each other. They weren't. At least she wasn't. Unless his behavior endangered his patients, she wasn't about to say anything to anyone about what had happened. And she definitely wouldn't mention it to Kaleb.

So she was going to put that night into her past. Once and for all.

She decided to speak what she hoped would become a prophetic statement. "I love the office and the hospital. I have a feeling I'm going to be very happy at NYC Memorial."

CHAPTER TWO

NICOLA WAITED FOR the explosion. The one that normally accompanied challenging a surgeon's diagnosis.

Dr. Danvers held up his hand when the intern standing next to him looked like he was going to argue Danvers's point. "So you're saying what we saw on the MRI slides is an incidental finding. Care to explain your reasoning?"

How was she going to convince him that the conclusion from two doctors—that the patient's condition was due to a brain tumor—was really something else entirely? Something a whole lot more simple. Something that wouldn't involve cutting open the patient's skull and digging around with a scalpel. It would be easier to let them go in and send off a sample to pathology and have her idea confirmed, but why do that when she could show them another possibility?

Out of the corner of her eye, she saw someone push through the door to the staff lounge.

Great. Kaleb. Just the person she was trying to avoid.

He made his way over to them, and, of course, Dr.

Danvers had to fill him in on what they were talking about.

Eying her, Kaleb said, "What do you think it is?"

"A bit of fat."

Dr. Danvers stared at her as if in disbelief. "Fat."

"You *know* it happens. You see something on the film that you don't like. Something that looks nefarious and assume that it's the worst-case scenario. We all do it."

"Sometimes it *is* the worst-case scenario." Kaleb folded his arms across his chest.

Was he thinking of his own patient? The one who'd had malignant melanoma? Hadn't her own brother's misdiagnoses over the years turned out to be far worse than anyone believed possible?

Something inside of her turned soft as compassion swirled to life. "Yes. Sometimes it is. But not always. Let's do another scan. With contrast, this time. Surely waiting another day or two won't make a difference at this point. And if, God forbid, it is a tumor, there's no sign of it having spread. But if we take another look, using a different technique, we might be able to know for sure. She's young. Her brain is still developing."

Kaleb glanced at Danvers. "She's got a point."

That surprised her. Especially since his last statement had carried a pessimism that made her chest tighten.

She knew that feeling all too well. But she couldn't let it cloud her judgment about other cases. If she did, the temptation to over test, over treat, would always be there whispering in her ear. Instead, she was somehow able to push her brother's case into a little compartment, one she kept locked tight. Except for that one time—when she'd gone to a bar and let it consume her, hoping by drowning it, she could finally come to terms with it. Only she'd done much more than drink that night. She'd let a moment of impulse direct her to a hotel room. A lapse in judgment that she was having a very hard time kicking aside. Especially seeing that lapse standing here in the flesh.

Dr. Danvers and the intern glanced at each other and Danvers finally shrugged. "Okay. Let's order up another study—with contrast this time—and see what we get. But, I want to be very clear here…if the new scan doesn't look any different, we'll be recommending surgery to her parents."

That was fair. All she'd wanted was a hearing. For them to take a breath before jumping into something that couldn't be taken back.

Like she'd done with Kaleb? Jumping into something that couldn't be taken back?

"If that happens, I'll back you up a hundred percent. But I really feel it's not a malignancy."

"We'll see." Dr. Danvers and his partner in crime retreated, but not before throwing a pointed look at Kaleb that she couldn't quite read.

Once they were gone, Kaleb nodded at a nearby table in the cafeteria. "Still taking advantage of every opportunity that comes your way?"

"Excuse me?"

He shook his head. "Never mind. Do you have a minute?"

She tensed. Was he going to bring up the night at the bar or what had happened after they wound up in a hotel room? Oh, Lord, she hoped not. Especially since she'd been thinking about just that when the NYC Memorial's administrator had been introducing her to people. Then to realize that Kaleb was actually here, at her new hospital… "Sure."

She dropped into one of the lounge's seats before her legs decided to desert her. She'd been pretty successful at steering clear of him, not that it was hard in a hospital this size.

"Coffee?"

"Yes, please. One sugar, no cream." It would give her a minute or two to compose herself after her confrontation with Danvers and his intern. There hadn't been an explosion, but she could tell both doctors had been irritated with her. But they'd come to her with the question, not the other way around. It wasn't like she was some ambulance chaser trying to drum up business. If her time at Grace Central was any indication of how things would go in New York, she wouldn't have to chase anyone. She would have more work than she'd have time for very soon.

He came back with the coffee and set hers in front of her. "So how are things going so far?"

Instead of her tension draining away at the question, it coiled in her gut, squeezing tight. There seemed to be some secondary meaning behind almost everything he said to her. It had to be her imagination. Right? "Things are going fine. It's all pretty new, though."

She'd moved into her office exactly a week ago.

But in that short period of time, she'd had a couple of run-ins like she'd had with Danvers. She considered it part of her job to question things, to be that little devil sitting on someone's shoulder.

"Danvers is a pretty nice guy, you'll find. Quite reasonable, actually."

Was he saying she wasn't? "Really? Why would that matter to me?"

He stared at her for a minute or two. "They're going to be your colleagues, Nicola. Hell, they already are."

The squeezing inside tightened even more. "Ah. I get it. Don't challenge the good-old-boy way of doing things."

"That's not what I'm saying at all." He sighed. "Look, I wish you'd been here when that case I'd had landed on my desk. I'm sure Harvey filled you in on what happened."

"He did, and I'm sorry." Her brother's face swirled in front of her, dredging up the sick feeling of horror she'd had. She forced the emotion back to the pit of her stomach.

"It's why I went…" He shook his head. "Never mind. None of that matters."

She took a sip of coffee. He wasn't the enemy. He was trying to help. "Sorry. My answer just now was defensive. So was the way I approached Dr. Danvers. It's just that it's sometimes hard to get a hearing, especially if I'm not patting someone on the back and telling them exactly what they want to hear. There are times when, instead of letting them go ahead and do the treatment their way, I have to disagree and speak my mind. It's why I was hired. And, believe me, it's not always easy for me. In fact, it's damn hard, so I know I sometimes come across as a—"

"Hard ass?"

She laughed. "Wow, you don't pull any punches, do you?"

"No more than you do."

"Touché. But in the end, my concern has to be for the well-being of the patient, rather than worrying about soothing another doctor's ego."

"Which is, like you said, exactly why Harvey brought you in. But that also means there might be some feelings of resentment, in the sense that some might feel the hospital's administrator is overstepping his bounds—as if he's looking over their shoulders and busting their chops."

She hadn't really thought about it that way. Her opinions had been respected, for the most part, at Grace Central. So to find out there was some animosity toward her at her current hospital was a hard pill to swallow. "What do you suggest I do?"

"Collaborate."

She frowned. "I thought that's what I was doing."

"Is it?"

Looking back at her interaction with the two doctors a few minutes ago, she could acknowledge the brusqueness in her responses. "I guess it's hard to be challenged."

"It is. And that works both ways. People tend to mimic the tone they sense in someone else."

"And my tone wasn't pleasing to the ear?" This time

the words were accompanied by a smile to show she was joking.

He laughed. "Like you said. It's hard to be challenged. And for the record, I hope you're right about the patient."

"Me, too. Especially after what you just said."

"Looking forward to delivering the I-told-you-so?"

"No. Hoping that a little girl doesn't need brain surgery."

He rested his forearms on the table and stared at her. "If you're right and the MRI image was just a piece of fat, what is causing her diplopia? Or did you already share that with Dr. Danvers?"

"I haven't seen all of the tests yet. Just the MRI reading. But I plan to review the case tonight when I get home."

"Why not do it right now? I'd like to see your process."

"Here in the cafeteria?"

"How about in my office?"

She wasn't sure how she felt about having someone watch her. It reminded her of his comment about the hospital administrator looking over someone's shoulder. "My process isn't all that exciting. It basically consists of me staring at a piece of paper for a long time and then muttering to myself. Repeatedly."

"That's okay. I've been known to mutter from time to time myself."

Sudden heat washed up her neck and into her face. She'd been a witness to that muttering. Only what she remembered most were the things he'd said with his lips pressed tight to her throat. Not to mention his...

Oh, Lord. This was the last thing she should be thinking about. Especially since she didn't want him to know she remembered that night. It was a whole lot easier to just sit here and pretend they only knew each other from work.

Because it was the truth. She knew about his lovemaking—and that was some pretty fantastic stuff—but she didn't know him as a person.

She still didn't. And if she were smart she would make sure it stayed that way. Which meant having him watch her work would be excruciating. But if she turned him down, he would wonder why and maybe start asking questions she really didn't want to answer. Like maybe about a certain night. Or her reasons for being in that bar.

So she'd let him watch. And satisfy his curiosity, she hoped.

Then after they were done, she would steer clear of both Dr. Sabat and her memories of that night in the hotel room.

He'd hoped he was wrong. That he'd imagined she didn't remember him. But evidently she really didn't. Once the shock of seeing her had worn off, he'd watched her face for some hint that she was simply trying to hide from Harvey the fact that they'd had a one-night stand. In fact, he'd been mentally rehearsing what to say if she told the administrator they'd already met.

He hadn't needed to say anything. Her "nice to meet you" had been smooth and polite. And totally believable. Even to him. She had him doubting his memories of that night. Until she bit the corner of her lip, the way she had that night. Whenever he'd done something she liked.

Like lick the little hollow at the base of her throat. Or touch...

Don't go there, Kaleb.

But as that firm bottom swished back and forth in front of him with each step she took, it was damn hard not to relive those memories. It was also damn hard to understand why this was so difficult. He'd always been able to keep his professional life separate from his personal one. He'd done it ever since his breakup with his ex.

But then again, he'd never had a woman forget she'd slept with him before.

That had to be the difference. His ego was wounded.

One side of his mouth went up. Isn't that what she'd said? That she wasn't interested in stroking anyone's ego? Well, maybe not, but she'd seemed pretty interested in stroking his...

Hell! Knock it off, dammit!

They got to her office, and she unlocked the door and went in, and he finally managed to remove his gaze from her ass and focus on the interior of the room.

It was as stark and unadorned as her words to Dr. Danvers had been. "I like what you've done to the place. Looks like you're making yourself at home." He couldn't hide the slight irony behind the words.

She swung around to look at him and then glanced at the space. "I wasn't actually expecting to have an office, so I decided to wait and make sure this wasn't some kind of mistake."

It took him a second to realize she was joking. Well, maybe not the part about having an office, but the rest. "I'm pretty sure you're supposed to at least put a family photo on your desk, so your patients know you're not a robot."

Her face changed in a millisecond, a stricken look coming over it. There was a huge pause. "I'm not a robot."

This time she wasn't joking. Maybe his earlier words had stung more than he'd meant them to. "I'm sorry. I never meant to imply you were."

"I know. You were kidding. So was I."

No, she hadn't been. And there was still a strained look at the corners of her eyes. Like he'd said something that had struck a nerve. But he was at a loss to figure out what.

Her lips twisted. "Putting a family picture in here might be a little problematic for me. And my family."

"Oh?"

"My brother passed away recently, so I'm not quite ready to stare at a picture of him every time I come into this room. To see him smiling and full of life would be hard right now."

Shock froze his vocal cords for a second before he recovered. "Hell, Nicola, I didn't know. I'm really sorry."

"It's okay." She pulled in a deep breath, then let it

out on an audible note. "It was so…unexpected, and we're all still grieving. So yes. Complicated to put a picture in here. Do I display one with him in it? Omit him, as if he'd never existed? And if my parents come to visit me at the hospital, it might make things harder on them."

"I can see how that might." He wanted to ask what had happened, but it was none of his business, and like she'd just said, it might make it harder on her. His earlier thoughts about the way her bottom swished seemed way out of line in light of what she'd just revealed.

"Anyway, that's not why you came to my office, right? To admire the decor? Or lack of it?"

No. The only decor he'd admired so far had been her. But that was going to stop right here, right now. It was how he'd ended up in two very bad relationships. It also made him decide not to ask about that evening. Especially since he'd been so shocked to find he'd spent the entire night there. If she wasn't going to bring it up, then neither was he. After all, what good would it do? And she didn't seem worried about him saying anything to anyone, so she probably really didn't remember. Or had her reasons for keeping quiet about it.

"Nope. So how do you want to do this? With me behind your desk? Or you in front of it?"

Her eyes widened. "Pardon me?"

Damn. He was losing it. It had to be the shock of what she'd said. "To look at the scans on your computer."

Her shoulders seemed to relax in a rush. "Got it. Sorry. I don't know what I was thinking."

Well, that made two of them, because he didn't know what the hell he was thinking, either.

"Let's sit in front of it. It'll be easier." She swiveled her screen around and moved her keyboard in front of one of the two chairs, then grabbed a large spiral-bound notebook off her desk.

Well, the paper and pen seemed a little low-tech, but then again, he liked to write his thoughts by hand and then enter them into the computer later, too. "It seems we agree on one thing, anyway," he said.

"What's that?" She came around and sank into her chair, waiting for him to do the same.

"You take handwritten notes."

She flipped her notebook open to a bookmarked page and set it on the desk, then turned it toward him. "I tend to think in linear terms, and since I don't have a whiteboard in my office yet, this is how I'm doing it."

It was actually more of a sketchbook than a note-book, and he saw why. On the sheet in front of him was something that looked like a series of filled-in rectangles with lines going here, there and everywhere.

"This was a case I had at Grace Central." She pointed at the top row. "I write down symptoms in the order they happen and draw a line toward possible causes. I keep going until the lines begin to converge."

Her pen moved to the third row, where some of the conditions had only one line drawn to them, while others had multiples. "Then I move the most likely down a row and start all over again, asking the patient questions about other things they may or may not have noticed. Sometimes, after living with some kind of minor irritation for a period of time, it becomes a type of background noise that gets drowned out by the more pressing symptoms."

He noticed that she'd added hair loss to the new row. He tapped a finger on it. "So this was one of those minor issues she hadn't noticed?"

"Yes. She started noticing more hair tangled in her hairbrush, along with gradual weight gain, which she attributed to menopausal symptoms."

"But it wasn't."

"I didn't think so. So we worked our way down to a group of subsets and ran a more narrow spectrum of tests to see what, if anything, it added to our search."

The test results were added to the graph, and this time the lines all converged on one diagnosis: Hashimoto's, an autoimmune condition where the body's cells attack healthy tissue. In this case, the thyroid.

"Amazing. Okay, so I take back the part about our processes being similar. This goes way beyond anything I do."

"I bet you do other things that are equally amazing," she said, before her face flamed to life, and she suddenly became very interested in switching between her computer screens.

If he didn't know better, he'd think there was something more behind those words. As if she might actually remember...

No. It was probably just like when he'd said something that could be construed a different way. Except she hadn't tried to correct herself and say she was talking about his work.

Good try, Kaleb. It really does bother you that she doesn't remember that crazy sex you had together.

And it had been crazy. The brusque attitude she now carried around with her at work had been nowhere to be seen. Instead she'd been...

Incredibly sexy. Scorchingly hot.

Unforgettable.

And that last word was the one that bothered him the most. Because he couldn't seem to shake it off, no matter how hard he tried. Was it just the juxtaposition between the raw sensuality of that night and the chilly aloofness she'd shown him at work? It made for a combination that intrigued him. Made him want to explore that contrast a little more in depth.

But he wasn't going to. And from her attitude, she would not welcome him asking her out on a date.

And then there was the issue of keeping his personal life separate from his private life. It had been working just fine for him so far. And Snow would laugh him out of town if he knew how he was dwelling on this, especially after that toast they'd made last winter.

Nicola's voice pulled him back from his thoughts.

"So here's what we know about Dr. Danvers's patient so far. She developed diplopia in her left eye about four months ago. Right eye is normal. A trip to an optometrist, followed by an appointment with an ophthalmologist, revealed no structural problems with the eye other than some astigmatism. Before this incident, her vision had been twenty-twenty. It's still perfect in her right eye, but her left eye has double vision. Enough to interfere with her daily activities."

He nodded. "I can see why Danvers ordered an MRI. And why he assumed the shadow was a microadenoma, especially since it's near her pituitary gland. A growing tumor can cause vision problems."

"Yes. The only thing that bothers me is that a microadenoma of that size shouldn't cause as much disruption in her vision as the patient has. Now a macroadenoma, that's a different story."

Strangely, Kaleb was enjoying listening to her bouncing around ideas. It was no different than the back-and-forth he'd shared with other colleagues, wasn't it? Except he hadn't slept with his other colleagues.

"So what else besides a tumor could be causing the problem?" He nodded at the screen. "We have her vision tests from two years ago that show her with perfect vision."

"Lots of things. Multiple sclerosis. Myasthenia gravis. Stroke. Guillain-Barré—"

"Yes, I've seen something as simple as heavy eyelids causing vision changes as people age. But this patient is young."

"Yes, she is." She tapped her pencil on the paper of her sketchbook and then started writing up a chart much like the one she'd just shown him. "I hadn't thought about eyelid weight. Or something else affecting the eyelids. Any mention of chalazions?"

He wasn't sure if the question was directed toward him, but she was suddenly moving through different doctors' reports and tests. "Hmm...not seeing it."

"What does that mean?"

"It means I would like to meet with her and ask a couple of questions. Do you think Danvers would object to me talking to his patient?"

"I can't see why not. Like I said earlier, he's a pretty reasonable guy."

She smiled. "Yes, you did. Right before you told me I wasn't."

"I never said you weren't reasonable."

"Not in so many words. But I'm pretty good at reading between the lines."

He held up a hand. "There was nothing there to read, I swear. I only said that you and Danvers were now colleagues and that you might want to take a more measured approach."

"In other words, be more reasonable?" Her eyebrows went up and she turned to meet his gaze.

"Looks like I'm not going to win this particular argument."

"Do you want to? Win, I mean?"

He leaned back and crossed his arms over his chest. "Not particularly. Especially not this kind of argument. If I'm in it to win, it needs to have a pretty big payoff at the end."

"I totally agree. When that happens, I have a fight-to-win, take-no-prisoners mentality."

He clapped a hand to his chest. "Should I be worried?"

"Not today..." She gave a soft laugh that was very attractive.

He glanced at her face and liked what he saw. It's what had drawn him to her in the bar. That delicate bone structure and the hint of crow's feet at the corners of her eyes. It was an indication that she liked to smile. And although he hadn't seen as much of that particular feature here at work, the evidence was there for all to see.

And she'd smiled a lot that night as she'd sipped her drink.

Then again, so had he. Only his smile had been fake. He'd been shocked by the events surrounding a patient and had needed a drink. Or two or three. By the end of that night, neither he nor Nicola had been under the legal limit, so they'd shared a cab. And instead of having it take them home, they'd made out in the back seat, and then asked the driver to drop them off at a hotel. The rest was history.

Well, his history, since Nicola didn't seem to remember that night.

Her brother had died. She'd said it had been recent. As in before their night together? Or after it?

On impulse, he leaned closer and covered her hand with his. He realized it was a mistake when the softness of her skin reminded him of how much he'd enjoyed stroking it. Kissing it. He cleared his throat so he could force out the words. "Hey, I really am sorry about your brother."

Her eyes met his for a long moment, then she said, "Thanks. I appreciate it. It's been hard. On me. On my parents. He worked with me at Grace Central as a researcher. If we could have known what was coming... Well, maybe things might have been different."

"How so?"

"I don't know. We could have talked to him. Tried to make sure he knew that we would always be there for him. That we wanted him there with us."

A chill went up his spine, a type of déjà vu that never boded well for what was about to follow.

"Had he been sick?"

Her hand shifted under his, index finger hooking over his as if needing to hold on to something. He had a feeling she wasn't even aware of what she'd done. But it was doing a number on his gut—a strange protective instinct rose up, just like it had at the bar.

"He'd been diagnosed with ankylosing spondylitis."

"Damn." Ankylosing spondylitis was a devastating inflammatory condition where bones of the back, or even ribs, could fuse, causing pain and severe loss of motion, sometimes to the point of impeding respiration. "That doesn't normally carry a death sentence, though."

"Not directly, no, but for a man who prided himself on being strong and fit—he loved to windsurf, sail and go mountain climbing—it was a life-altering diagnosis. To him, it might as well have been a death sentence. And it ultimately became one."

"Did he have complications from treatment?"

She gave a visible swallow. "No, Kaleb, he didn't. Danny died before he ever started treatment. He received his diagnosis, then went home and ended his life. My dad found him the next day when I called saying Danny hadn't arrived at work yet. I asked Dad to check on him. Something I wished I'd never done, because…" She shook her head. "Well, it's why having his picture on my desk right now would be so hard."

His throat squeezed at the pain in her voice and a million thoughts and emotions went through him. It was so eerily similar to what had happened with his melanoma patient. The despair and fear that both of them must have felt. Damn. They'd been caught between a rock and a hard place with what seemed like no way out.

"Damn, Nicola. I had no idea."

She let out a laugh that was far from amused and took her hand from his, using it to flip through the pages of her sketchbook. Back, back, back she went, stopping at a page and staring at it. "He told me he'd been having some hip and back pain, and so I did up one of my nifty little charts. When I asked if he was having light sensitivity—never dreaming he'd answer yes—my world shifted. Became a dark hole. I wanted to scrub away everything I'd written down and pretend like I didn't know. Except I did."

Nicola pointed to a box that had the condition listed. The word *no!* appeared as a long silent scream on the page. She'd known it was going to be a devastating blow to her brother, especially with what she'd said about his lifestyle.

"Did you break the news to him?"

"No. I—I couldn't. I referred him to a doctor friend, telling that friend what I suspected. The sooner treatment is started, to knock down the inflammation, the better. Tests were rushed and for once, I prayed I was wrong. I would have given *anything* to be wrong, Kaleb."

"I know."

One shoulder went up in a half shrug, and her chin wobbled. "But I wasn't." Her voice lowered to a whisper. "Oh, God, I wasn't. And Danny…"

He couldn't stop himself from wrapping an arm around her shoulder and drawing her close. "I can't imagine how hard it was to realize his pain wasn't due to simple muscle strain."

"You have no idea."

No, he didn't. His mom had endured a mastectomy and radiation treatments, but he hadn't been the one who'd diagnosed her, so as hard as that had been, it would have been even tougher if he'd had to do what Nicola had done.

She leaned her head against his chest, and Kaleb's hand slid under her hair to support her neck, the honey-eyed strands sliding over his skin like silk. Just like they had that night. The tightening in his throat shifted to somewhere lower, and he cursed himself. Told himself to move away. Now.

But his mind and his body seemed disconnected from each other at the moment.

His ears picked up a sigh, and she murmured against his chest, "Thank you. I'm sorry for blubbering all over your shirt. I'm not sure why it suddenly hit me again."

"Maybe because I pressed you for information, when I shouldn't have."

"It's not that. Every once in a while it just seems to

build up inside of me, looking for an exit. I think that's why I ended up…"

Her words trailed away for a second, and he wondered if she was going to say it was why she'd ended up in the bar that night.

But when her voice came back, she simply said, "I think that's why I seem short sometimes when I talk to people."

It made sense. It also made him feel pretty damn crappy for lecturing her about the way she'd talked to Danvers. A good reason not to assign motive to things he knew nothing about. And she wasn't being short now. In fact, she was being…soft, approachable. And he liked it. Way too much.

And if he didn't move away, he might do something he'd regret even more than their night together.

He shifted sideways a bit, so it wouldn't seem as awkward, then moved his hand down to her shoulder and gave her what he hoped was a reassuring pat or two. She moved back upright quickly. So quickly that it knocked his hand away.

"Sorry, again." She brushed her hair off her forehead, and the movement was probably meant to cover the fact that she'd swiped the area below her eyes. "And I probably need to get ready for my next consultation, which is in less than an hour."

"Got it. I probably need to get going, as well." He pried himself from his chair and stood to his feet. "Let me know when Danvers's patient has her new MRI. I'd like to know where all your little arrows wind up."

"I will." She stood, too.

He moved toward the door, only to have her voice stop him when he gripped the handle to open it.

"Oh, and Kaleb…"

"Yes?" He glanced back at her.

"From now on, I'll try to be a little more 'colleaguey' toward those I work with. Feel free to call me out if I don't succeed."

No way was he going to do that. Especially given how he'd felt when she told him about her brother. But rather than argue, he simply nodded and pushed through the door.

As he walked down the hall, he gave himself a stiff lecture, which he quickly counteracted. *Nothing happened, so just settle down.*

Some good advice, if he'd ever heard it.

The problem was, he'd wanted something to happen. And if he allowed it to, it might be a bigger disaster than that night in the hotel. And she might end up as a third notch on his belt of failed relationships.

CHAPTER THREE

WHY ON EARTH had she told him all of Danny's story yesterday? Maybe it was Kaleb's suggestion of putting a family picture in her office and the fact that she thought of her brother every single day. Agonized over it whenever her head hit the pillow. And Kaleb's hand had felt so damn good on hers in her office. As if he cared. Really cared.

In that moment she'd realized how much she'd needed someone besides Grace Central and her family to know what had happened to him. Someone who understood the devastating loss that suicide brought. Kaleb had lost a patient to it. And she'd lost a brother.

But once she'd said the actual words, a spurt of panic had shot through her, along with a few other emotions she hadn't wanted to dissect. The panic had been chased by a vague sense of nausea over letting someone she barely knew see her like this. But when his arm had gone around her, she'd slid right against his chest with a sense of belonging that had shocked her. Scared her. And when his warm palm had settled on the back of her neck, she'd almost melted. It was sensual and comforting and familiar, all at the same time. It was the same sensation she'd had in the bar all those weeks ago. She'd wanted to look up at him. Had wanted him to kiss her. Make her forget all over again.

Which would have been stupid. Because it hadn't changed anything that night, and it wouldn't change anything if she let it happen again. Thank God she'd snuck out of his room in the early hours of the morning, before he woke up. Better she'd left than him. It was becoming a ritual with her now. To leave before being left. She wanted to be the first one to exit a room. Or be the first one to leave a get-together. That's what losing a fiancé, followed by losing a brother, did. The thought of being left behind had evidently become a crippling force that she couldn't shake.

Because when Kaleb had been the first one to move away from her when they were in her office, she'd squirmed inside. Felt that same sense of fearful dread. Which is probably why she'd been slightly sick after the encounter. Why she'd woken up this morning with that same low-grade churning in her midsection at the thought of facing him again.

She pulled two pieces of bread out of the wrapper and slid them into her toaster, waiting for that warm smell of crisp toast to fill the air. It was weird how much she loved it. Even when she was sick, it was normally the one thing she could eat. A minute or two later, her nose twitched. Ah, right on cue. The toaster kicked the bread into the air with a sharp snap, and Nicola retrieved it, then spread some butter and a spoonful of marmalade onto each slice.

Almost as soon as she bit into the food, her stomach settled and she closed her eyes to enjoy the treat.

"See? I try to treat you right." She leaned against the counter and let the tangy blend of flavors dance across her tongue.

Dr. Danvers's diplopia patient had an appointment this afternoon for the second scan. That was a lot quicker than she'd thought it would be. But it would give her a chance to ask the patient and her parents a few more questions. If she wanted to be there on time, she'd better get a move on. After finishing her breakfast, she went to the bathroom and slapped on a little makeup, frowning at the dark circles under her eyes. Lack of sleep last night?

She shrugged and reached under the counter for the sponge to wipe out her sink, her feminine products catching her eye. Hmm, she hadn't gotten her period yet.

How long overdue was she?

Not more than a week or two. She'd never been particularly regular, so she couldn't really chart it beyond having a vague sense of when it might come. But she was wrong more often than she was right.

She always kept something in her purse just in case. Maybe that's why she'd felt a little off yesterday and this morning—she was getting ready to start. Just what she needed. But the alternative was...

She shuddered. Yeah, not what she needed on top of everything else. Besides, it wasn't like she was having a lot of sex nowadays.

Except for...

She blinked. Don't even go there. They'd used protection and she was still within her normal parameters of a week or two late.

Besides, she couldn't do anything about it right this second. So if another week went by and nothing happened, then she'd let herself worry. But until then, she was going on with her life.

Starting with Dr. Danvers's patient.

An hour later, she sat in an exam room with Lindy MacDonald and her parents, along with Dr. Danvers. This time, his prickly intern was nowhere to be seen, for which she was glad. Lindy was being prepped for the MRI, with the neurologist explaining to the girl's parents what would happen with the contrast. They had to sign yet another consent form. Nicola noticed the mom's hand was shaking. Poor woman, she had to be scared out of her mind wondering if something was growing in her daughter's brain.

If Nicola was going to ask her questions, she'd better do it now.

"Do you mind if I ask you a couple of things?"

She'd been introduced a few minutes ago, and Danvers had given her permission to examine Lindy, as well. She was positive the surgeon had been thorough, so she skipped a physical exam. Instead she asked about any strange symptoms that she might not have attributed to her daughter's double vision, but that had occurred, nonetheless.

"No, nothing I can think of."

"What about her eyes? Besides the double vision.

Any lumps or bumps or eye strain that were out of the ordinary?"

"Mom, what about that spider bite?"

"I'd forgotten about that." The woman shook her head. "But surely, that can't have anything to do with it."

"Spider bite?" Nicola leaned forward. How many times had she heard that before, that a simple symptom couldn't have anything to do with a condition, only to realize it had *everything* to do with it?

"She got this strange bump on her eyelid. I thought maybe it was a mosquito bite at first. It came and went for about six months. Every time I got ready to make a doctor's appointment, it seemed to get better. I used hot compresses and antihistamine lotion on it and eventually it faded to nothing."

"So you never took her to the doctor for it?" She glanced at the chart to remind herself which eye they were dealing with.

"No. She said it didn't hurt or anything. Just looked like an insect bite, or maybe even a sty or something. But it was in the middle of her lid."

"Which lid?"

"Her left one."

Standing next to her, she saw Dr. Danvers stiffen. Then he moved over to the patient. Pushing his glasses onto his nose, he asked Lindy's mom, "Mind if I take a quick look?"

"No, of course not."

The surgeon tilted the girl's chin and looked closely at her. "Close your eyes, please."

Lindy shut her eyes, and Dr. Danvers used his gloved thumb to apply slight pressure to different parts of the eyelid. His gaze came up and fixed Nicola with a look. "I think there's a slight thickening here. How did you know?"

"I didn't. And I don't know for sure. Not without seeing the scans. But I've heard of cases where a large chalazion can exert enough pressure on the cornea to change its shape."

"A chalazion?" Lindy's mom came over and looked at her daughter's eyelid.

"Maybe so." Danvers looked at his patient. "I'm going to turn your lid inside out, okay?"

"Will it hurt?"

"No. It might feel a little funny, though. I want to look at the back of your lid." He quickly flipped up her lid and stared at the undersurface. "I do see a slight scarring here. Look."

Nicola came closer and saw what he did. A whitened portion in the middle of all those blood vessels.

After righting Lindy's lid, he sat on the stool across from her parents. "Your daughter may have had what's called a chalazion. It's a little different than a sty in that a sty is normally on the margin of the eyelid, whereas a chalazion's core tends to point toward the eye itself. So when it bursts, or drains, the opening will appear on the back of the lid, where it's out of sight. You may even miss it when that happens—you'll just notice that the swelling appears to subside. Just like what you described. How big would you say her swelling was?"

"Maybe the size of an M&M. Once it got even larger

than that. But she said it never hurt. She was more embarrassed by what her friends might think than anything else."

Lindy said, "Because it was ugly. I'm glad it's gone."

"I am, too," Danvers said. "I still would like to do the MRI to rule out anything else, but it's possible this chalazion caused her change in vision, which would be much simpler than what we thought."

"Will it be permanent?"

"If the pressure was there for six months, it might be. The best-case scenario would be for her eye to slowly return to its former shape. It may also be why Lindy's vision has seemed to fluctuate in that eye enough to make it difficult to prescribe a corrective lens."

"We thought we were going crazy. It was like every time I took her in, they came up with a different reading. And there were times she couldn't tell which screen was clearer."

Nicola should feel a flare of pride, but that nagging sense of unease in the pit of her stomach was back, and she wasn't sure what to do about it. Could it be the case itself? That she was afraid of being wrong and being shown up? Or have someone say "I told you I was right."

No. As long as they got the right diagnosis, Nicola didn't care who came up with it.

And if it saved a patient from having brain surgery, it was worth all the discomfort in the world.

Maybe she was hungry. All she'd had for breakfast

was toast. Probably not a smart move to eat nothing but carbs. Except she did that all the time with no ill effects.

"Okay, let's get her to radiology and take a closer look at that spot we saw the other day."

Lindy glanced at her. "Will you be there?"

Her face turned warm. "If you'd like me to be. I won't be able to be in the room while you're having the MRI, but I can wait right outside. Will that be okay?"

"Yes."

Nicola glanced at Dr. Danvers, who nodded and gave her a smile. A genuine one, this time. Maybe he believed her.

Why wouldn't he? It's not like she had any skin in the game. She just wanted what was best for his patient.

As did he, she reminded herself.

The contrast went smoothly, and so did the MRI. Fortunately, the patient didn't have claustrophobia, so she was in and out in forty minutes and sent back to a waiting area with her mom and dad. Danvers was going to read the scans himself, so there would be no waiting time. Kaleb was right. He was a good guy. She didn't sense any resentment, for which she was grateful. And, honestly, he would have eventually come to the same conclusion. Or at least agreed that it wasn't a tumor, even if he'd opened her up and sectioned the spot.

Sitting in his office a few minutes later, she waited tensely as he went through the scans on his computer. He pointed out several interesting things as they scrolled through, and she put the information into her mental filing cabinet for future reference.

"Okay, here we go." A slice of Lindy's pituitary

gland came into view and the shadow seemed less distinct now than it had in the previous test. And nothing really stood out as abnormal.

He looked up with a sigh. "I'll have to give it to you. You were right. It's probably not a microadenoma. Just an 'incidentaloma,' like you said. Thank you for not backing down."

Kaleb's words came back to her. "Dr. Danvers, I hope you don't think I—"

"Clint, please. After all, it looks like I'll be calling on you for consults on a regular basis."

She blinked, a sudden warmth going through her system. Was he saying he appreciated her input? He'd thanked her for not backing down, so it certainly sounded like it. She remembered his incredulous response when she'd suggested the image might show a simple piece of fatty tissue. He'd been right to be surprised. According to Kaleb, she probably hadn't helped her case by just blowing past his diagnosis and forming one of her own. Maybe she'd work on that a little. As a woman in medical school there had been times where she'd had to stand up to someone because of her gender—felt like she'd had to be a little bit bolder in order to gain a hearing, even though she'd been in the top ten of her class.

But this wasn't school, and they were all on equal footing here. So she could afford to relax a bit and enjoy the view. She'd made it. And it seemed like even in a hospital the size of NYC Memorial, she was going to swim, and not sink.

"And you can call me Nicola, or Nic, either one."

"Okay, Nic, I should apologize for my attitude yesterday. I'm not used to people second-guessing me."

So she hadn't imagined it.

She gave him a smile. "I've been told by a very reliable source that I can be a bit abrasive at times."

His laugh was warm. "As someone who's also been called abrasive—and a few other things that aren't suitable for work—I can relate. You can be abrasive with me anytime you want. I promise to not be offended. Or at least try to get over it, if I am."

"I promise to do the same." She grinned. "Or at least try."

The door opened and Kaleb came in, glancing from one to the other. "I hope by the giddy look on both of your faces that this means good news for the patient. Was it a chalazion?"

Clint's eyebrows pulled together. "Now how on earth could you have guessed that?"

The scene in her office flew before her eyes, and stopped at the part where her head had been planted on his chest and his thumb had swept across her nape.

"Kaleb happened to be in my office, when I was going over the patient's files."

"But that wasn't in her files, or I would have seen it."

Kaleb came over and looked at the screen where Lindy's images were. "Nicola made a list of possibilities. And chalazion was on the top of her list."

Clint's eyes swung to hers. "So you figured this out, before you even asked the patient whether she'd had any problems with her eyelid."

"No, I hadn't figured it out. I just have this weird

way of connecting lines on a diagram. Wherever most of those lines meet is the place I start looking first."

"And a chalazion fit all the criteria."

"It did. But I couldn't be sure unless the patient connected the dots for me."

Clint's fingers went to the computer screen and traced the small dot near Lindy's pituitary gland. "And if the patient hadn't remembered having that bump on her eyelid?"

"I don't know, honestly. All we can do is our best, using the information we have at the time."

Like telling Kaleb about Danny's suicide? Like going to that bar and sleeping with him? Maybe. She'd done just what she said. Done the best she could to get by.

"So what's the treatment plan? Or is there one?" Kaleb asked. "If the patient's diplopia isn't caused by a tumor, can anything be done?"

"We need to get her vision stabilized so she can at least be fitted with glasses. So I'll be referring her to an ophthalmic surgeon. He may be able to deal with the scar tissue behind her lid and control whatever inflammation is still going on. But for now, we need to give the family the good news."

"We?" Nicola looked at him in surprise. Maybe he meant "we" in the figurative sense. Or maybe he meant for Kaleb to go with him.

He smiled. "I think since you're the one who actually made me second-guess my diagnosis, you should be there. And Kaleb, too, since he vouched for you."

Kaleb had vouched for her? That surprised her. Especially since he'd given her a little speech about playing nicely.

Well, not exactly that, but it was probably what he'd meant.

Her eyes met his and found him looking at her, with one eyebrow quirked up. Ah, so he hadn't meant her to find out about that. But why? She'd do the same for him if need be.

"I'd love to go with you. Thank you."

Clint stood. "Kaleb, you in?"

"Sure. I'm always up for delivering good news."

But didn't he usually deliver good news? Well, the melanoma case certainly couldn't be considered good, but for the most part, he was helping someone feel better about themselves, right? So definitely not bad news, unless he was unable or unwilling to perform surgery on someone.

They made their way to the waiting room, where the family had been asked to stay until after the results were read. Lindy's dad stood first, looking worried. Who could blame him? They'd gone from thinking their daughter would undergo brain surgery, to them saying maybe not.

Clint went over and shook his hand then smiled at Lindy and her mom, who were sitting close together. "Well, I have some very good news, thanks to Dr. Bradley here. She—and I would agree—thinks the bump Lindy had on her eyelid changed the shape of her cornea and has caused her vision problem."

"So there's not a tumor?" Lindy's mom reached for her husband's hand.

"No. We don't think so."

"But the MRI…" she said.

"We're not sure what the image is, but we're pretty sure it's not a microadenoma, like I originally thought."

Lindy's dad sank back into his chair, still gripping his wife's hand. He lifted it to his mouth and kissed it, before looking at her. "This is great news. For all of us."

"Yes, especially since we want to add to our family. We were going to try, and then when Lindy developed double vision, we decided we needed to put it off to concentrate on her. But now I guess it's okay to move forward…?" She glanced up at Clint. "Right? Lindy's treatment isn't going to be complicated?"

"I don't believe so. There's a little pocket of scar tissue behind her eyelid that may need to be scraped to lower its profile, but it will almost certainly be a quick outpatient surgery. I'm going to call you with the number of a great surgeon who specializes in ocular problems. He should be able to do her surgery."

"How can I ever thank you?" Lindy's mom looked at Nicola, her eyes filling with tears.

"There's no need to thank me. I'm just happy it turned out to be something so simple."

"So are we." She hauled in a deep breath and blew it out. "So anything we need to do before we get your referral?"

Clint smiled. "Nope. Go and enjoy your life. And let me know how things go. Good luck on adding to your family."

Lindy's mom gave her husband a knowing look.

"Thank you. And we'll definitely let you know about Lindy's treatment. Thank you again. All of you."

"Let me know if you need anything in the meantime. My office should call you sometime this afternoon with the information on the ocular surgeon. I'll touch bases with him, as well."

With that, they said their goodbyes and left the room.

"Well," Kaleb said. "These are the cases that make everything worthwhile."

"Agreed."

Kaleb looked at her and Clint. "Are you guys up for lunch at Plato's?"

"Not me, sorry." Clint said. "I'm supposed to meet with my wife at noon." He glanced at his watch. "And I'm about to be late. You guys go and enjoy." He left the room with a wave.

Nicola's stomach gave a twinge of protest. She was sure Kaleb hadn't been angling for lunch to be a two-person deal, so she tried to let him off the hook. "Look, I'm sure you have somewhere you need to be, as well."

"Yes, I do."

Nicola swallowed. He didn't have to be quite so quick to find an excuse. "Okay, well then, I guess—"

"I mean, yes, I do, as in I need to be sitting down to eat somewhere. You don't have to come, if you don't want to, but since it's noon…"

Maybe she'd feel better if she had something in her stomach. "That would be great. Is this place close?"

"It's actually just half a block from here. It's an easy walk."

"Okay, great."

They left the hospital and started down the street. It was warm and muggy outside already, but at least the sun wasn't blazing down on them. Still, she was glad the restaurant was close, or she'd be wilting by the time they got there.

"Looks like you and Clint were on the same page this time."

"Yes, thanks to you." Nicola shifted to pass someone on the sidewalk. "Thanks for vouching for me."

He smiled. "I vouched for Clint, when I was talking to you, if you remember right."

That's right—he had. Some of the warm feelings she'd had about it melted away. So putting in a good word for her hadn't been so special after all. He probably did it with all of his colleagues. Part of his whole "collaborating" mindset.

"Well, I appreciate it, anyway, but don't feel like you have to stick up for me. Hopefully my work can stand on its own merit very soon."

"It already can. Except when two stubborn and proud personalities collide. I felt like a little mediation might be in order."

"Mediation. So you're a diplomat as well as a surgeon?" She couldn't totally banish the hint of irritation from her voice. Maybe it was the heat, but what had started off as something positive had shifted to feeling like he'd inserted himself where he hadn't been needed. "You don't think Clint and I could have worked it out on our own?"

He touched her arm. "Sorry. You're right. I wasn't

trying to interfere. Danvers is a friend, but I certainly didn't want him biting your head off, since I felt you were onto something."

Okay, now she felt like a jerk. "I'm sorry. I'm just used to fighting my own battles."

"I know you are. I truly was just trying to help." His hand slid back to his side. "We're almost there. I hope you like burgers. Although they have some other things on the menu, as well."

"A burger sounds good right about now."

Her stomach was still a little rough, but she was pretty sure that as soon as she ate something, she'd feel better. That's what had happened this morning, although it hadn't lasted long.

Something pinged in her head, but she didn't have time to stop and examine whatever it was right now. If it was still there when she got home, she'd deal with it then.

A minute or two later they arrived.

Plato's had an artsy feel, with shiny chrome panels accented with touches of black. She admired the exterior while Kaleb went in to give their names. There were people waiting outside, but then again this was New York, so she shouldn't have expected anything else.

He came back out. "About fifteen minutes. Is that okay?"

"Better than I thought it would be, actually. I've heard of horrific wait times at some restaurants."

"There are a lot of people to feed in the city. You didn't have wait times where you were?"

"We did. But Grace Central was located a little off the beaten track, so it was easier to find an off time there."

He nodded, motioning her to some chairs that had been set outside under some nearby shade trees. "Do you miss it? Your old hospital, I mean."

"Hmm. That's a hard question. I miss the hospital itself. But I needed to make a change. Danny's death just cemented things. I'd also just gotten out of a relationship—with someone who also worked there— a few months before I applied at NYC Memorial. It…" She shrugged. "It was a hard time all the way around. And my hospital administrator felt like I needed to go somewhere with more opportunities. He's actually the one who found out the hospital here was looking for someone with a diagnostic emphasis."

"And you haven't looked back?"

She crossed her legs, searching for the right words. Her breakup, while hard, hadn't exactly been unexpected. But Danny's death…

While she did miss the smaller feel of her old hospital, it now held a lot of painful memories. And she'd come to realize her former administrator really was right. She thought she'd be leery of giving her opinions in a bigger hospital, but that hadn't been the case. She was still the same person she'd been before the move.

Then why didn't she feel the same?

"I've tried not to look back. Oh, I still have friends there that I miss, but I like it at NYC Memorial so far."

"I'm glad."

Was he? Was he really? She wasn't sure why it mattered, but suddenly it did. Maybe a month and a half ago, she wouldn't have cared. But there was something about Kaleb that made her curious.

"I've told you quite a bit about myself. But I know almost nothing about you. How long have you worked at the hospital?"

"I actually came here fresh out of medical school. I can't imagine being anywhere else."

A man walked up, glanced at her with a tilted head and then greeted Kaleb. "Well, well, well. Funny to see you here."

"Hi, Snow. I could say the same about you."

Kaleb turned to her. "Snow, this is Nicola Bradley. She just started at the hospital a couple of weeks ago. She helped diagnose a case that Clint Danvers was working on. We're actually celebrating a good outcome, but Clint had somewhere he had to be, so he bailed on us."

Said as if he was trying to explain away eating lunch with her? Her stomach churned just a bit harder.

"Good outcomes are always reason to celebrate. You and I have had a couple of toasts about that very subject not too long ago." The man held out his hand. "Snowden Tangredi. I'm one of NYC Memorials' transplant surgeons. Welcome to the hospital. You work with Clint?"

"Not exactly. I work in internal medicine, but specialize in diagnostics."

"Interesting. Kaleb and I go way back. You could say we've been through some memorable life events together. In fact—"

"Snow, she's not interested."

Actually she was. Intrigued was more like it, because Kaleb seemed to have known what his friend had been about to say and was anxious to head him off.

"Okay," Snowden said. "Although I'm not exactly sure that's true." The other man gave her a smile.

She had a feeling there was some pointed exchange happening between them that only the two friends could understand.

Nicola said, "We were just waiting to be seated. Do you want to join us? I'm sure we could add another person to our party."

"I'm not exactly sure Kaleb would like that." He shot his friend a look. "Besides, I'm headed to the courthouse to meet a friend—he's a lawyer there."

"Well, don't let us hold you up."

Kaleb's words were a bit sharper than necessary. She was right. Something was going on between these two that she didn't understand. But Kaleb wasn't anxious for his friend to stick around. It was almost as if he was hiding something and was afraid Snowden might spill the beans. But what?

She had no idea. But whatever it was, it was none of her business. So she let the men finish their small talk, only adding something if she was asked directly.

And when Snowden finally headed off in the direction of the courthouse, Kaleb seemed to relax in his seat.

And then they were being called by the hostess to head up front. Their table was ready.

And just in time to save Kaleb from answering any awkward questions. Not that she was going to ask them.

Even if she was dying to know what those life events Snowden mentioned were. And why Kaleb seemed so anxious to keep them quiet.

CHAPTER FOUR

NICOLA'S NAUSEA HADN'T gone away over the last week, and her period was still AWOL. It had put her in full-fledged panic mode. Which is why she'd been locked in the bathroom in her apartment for the last half hour, alternating between a false sense of calm and full-out panic. It was the moment of truth. She needed to know if her worry was justified.

And now she did.

Her professional self warred with her private self, each struggling to handle the news in her own way. Then she forced the diagnostician in her to work on the problem. What possible explanation was there—other than the most obvious one—for the two vertical stripes on the pregnancy test.

She swallowed as she stared at the indicator in her hand. Okay…there was ovarian cysts. Kidney problems… Cancer.

But wasn't the most obvious reason also the most likely one, given the occurrences leading up to it? Especially since the test strip she was holding was the third one. With the exact same results.

She was pregnant.

God…pregnant!

The calmness swung back to terror. It had been almost eight weeks since that night at the bar. The night she'd tried to pretend hadn't happened. Or had at least pretended she'd been too drunk to remember. Situational amnesia.

Was that even a thing? Well, right now, she was wishing the amnesia was very real. Or that she at least had no idea who the father was.

That would be so much easier than what she was facing right now, which was telling Kaleb the truth.

Exactly how did she do that at this late date? Go to him and admit she'd been faking it all along? That she remembered every blasted second of that night?

Well, obviously she hadn't been faking everything. But protection? God, yes, they'd used it. Each and every time.

Lining the plastic tests on the counter, she touched a finger to each one, the matching stripes telling a story she didn't want to believe. She wished she could sweep them into the trash and make this all go away. But she couldn't. She'd never really believed in fate.

Until now.

She was going to follow through with the pregnancy. Because the other option made her stomach churn in a way that had nothing to do with morning sickness. But that meant she wasn't going to be able to hide it from Kaleb. She would need prenatal care, sooner rather than later, since at thirty-five, the chances of chromosomal abnormalities went up, along with a whole slew of other things.

And Kaleb... God only knew how he would react to the news.

Her eyes met her own troubled gaze in the mirror, before glancing down at her body. There would be no disguising the changes that were heading her way. And even if there was, the baby would have to be born somewhere.

Just a week ago, she'd toyed with the idea of starting a family. On her own. With some anonymous sperm donor. But this donor was far from anonymous. Far from a laundry list of defining characteristics with a carefully calculated timeline. And her vision of the procedure had been a hell of a lot chillier than her night with Kaleb had been.

It looked like the universe had taken the decision out of her hands.

Danny would probably find it amusing, that in trying to drown out what had happened that night at the hotel room, she'd actually created a reminder that would follow her for the rest of her life.

The image of Kaleb pushing a stroller teased her with might-have-beens that smacked of forevers and perfect endings. He would send her a look, eyes crinkling at the corners in a way that needed no spoken words.

There would be no looks, though. No spoken words.

Hadn't she gotten involved with a colleague once before? And where had that gotten her? Nowhere, that's where. She'd ended up leaving her previous hospital because of it. Well, not just because of it, but it had certainly played a part in her decision. In fact, Bill had left first, before returning to the hospital a few months later. But by then, they'd both known there would be no going back.

No, Kaleb wasn't going to be in her life forever. But wasn't it okay for it to have happened this way? She respected Kaleb. Probably more than she should. And that laundry list she'd thought about moments earlier couldn't hold a candle to the flesh-and-blood man she could see. Had talked to. Worked with.

And the baby was definitely his—there'd been nobody else since Bill. There'd been nothing traumatic about their breakup, and Bill was a very nice guy. They'd simply decided they were better suited as friends than a romantic couple. The passion just hadn't been there. Soon after their breakup, he'd found that passion with a national-parks employee.

No. There'd been no one else. Hadn't even come close to sleeping with anyone.

She swallowed. Maybe Kaleb was right. Maybe she was too abrasive, pushing people away before they got close enough to hurt her. Ha! Leave before you got left.

Was that why she couldn't find love with someone, like Bill had, after their split? Because she held people at arm's length for fear that they would disappear?

Her hand swept from her neck down to her abdomen and rested there. Kaleb's baby might be growing inside of her, even now. She needed to tell him. Before it was too late and he accused her of keeping the news from him.

What if he'd been some faceless alcoholic, drinking his way to an early grave in that bar? Would she still feel the need to try to find him? To tell him he was going to father her child?

No. She wouldn't. And she was pretty sure if that had been the case, the person wouldn't want to be found.

So was it any more fair to Kaleb to tell him?

"He's going to find out, Nic. There won't be much hiding it, unless you call Bill and coax him to pretend the baby is his." But that wasn't fair to him, either, or his new girlfriend. Her hand pressed harder against her stomach, the earlier option coming back to her.

You could always just...

It would be easier, wouldn't it? No need to tell anyone. Not her parents, not her colleagues and especially not Kaleb.

It would just be...gone.

A knife twisted in her midsection as she picked up the test again and stared at it. Pictured purposely erasing that extra vertical line. Pictured no birthdays. No Christmas celebrations. No future grandchildren.

"I can't. Oh, God, Kaleb, I'm so sorry, but I can't."

She wanted this baby. Already. In a way that defied explanation.

And Kaleb was a good person. People did this all the time, didn't they? Asked a friend or coworker to father their child?

It made for a good plotline in a movie or a book, but did it happen in real life? She had no idea.

But that ship had already sailed. She hadn't asked him to father a child. It had just happened.

And if she told him the truth… Well, would having a child be worth the horror of having to stand there and watch as Kaleb's face transformed from surprise to grim denial?

Yes, it would. That was temporary. Something that was uncomfortable in the moment, but that was adjusted to over a course of weeks or months. A new normal would somehow be forged.

And families were no longer just made up of a husband, a wife and their children. If Kaleb wanted to be involved in the child's life, she would make sure it happened. But for now, she'd explain that she hadn't done this on purpose and that she expected nothing from him in regard to the baby. But she owed it to him to at least give him the choice. The same way she was making the choice to have this baby. She also owed it to the baby to find out if there were any genetic issues that might need to be addressed down the road.

And if there were? Huntington's and a wide assortment of inherited disorders filed through her mind's eye. Well, she'd cross that bridge when she came to it. But first, she wanted to see Bill and ask him to run that test through the lab.

Bill? Was she seriously thinking of asking her ex to play a role in this? Why? Why not just find an ob-gyn at NYC Memorial?

She set down the test and thought about their relationship. Despite the breakup, she trusted Bill. Knew him. Knew he would keep her secret. And he was a great obstetrician.

And since she had no idea how Kaleb was going to react when she finally told him, it made sense to have her pregnancy handled elsewhere. If he had a meltdown, it would be easier to have her appointments offsite, where she wouldn't have to face him and where news wouldn't somehow trickle back to him.

There was also her position at NYC Memorial to take into consideration. The timing wasn't the best, since she'd just started her job, and she was pretty sure Harvey might not be thrilled to find out that a doctor he'd had a hand in hiring might need to take maternity leave less than a year after her arrival.

Ugh! This was not going to be easy. On any front. And she'd have to tell her parents, although, honestly, that would probably be the easiest task of all. They'd be thrilled to be grandparents. She'd probably have to arm wrestle her own mother just to hold her baby. And maybe it would help ease a little of their grief over Danny's death. And hers.

"Well, baby, your timing may stink, but I want you to know you'll be loved. Very, very much. By the people who matter most." And maybe Bill would even consent to be the baby's godfather.

Speaking of Bill. She should call him sooner rather than later. Before she chickened out. So she washed her hands, abandoned the tests on the bathroom counter and made her way to the bedroom. Once there she sank on to the bed, picked up her phone and pushed the button listed by his name.

It rang twice and then a familiar voice answered. "Hi, Nic. Long time, no hear. How's the new hospital treating you?"

There was no awkwardness in the question. No stilted speech. And for that, she was grateful. It would make what she needed to ask a little bit easier.

"It's been good, so far." She gulped and then plowed ahead with her news. "So I think I may need your help with a slight problem. If you're willing, that is."

As soon as the words came out, a huge wave of emotion rolled through her, flattening her. Slight problem? No. It wasn't slight. It was a very, very big deal.

A life-changer.

Without warning, her eyes filled and a hiccuped sob came out of her mouth. In the background she could hear Bill talking, the concern in his voice obvious. "Nic, are you okay? Hey, are you still there?"

But it was almost as if she was paralyzed and unable to respond, unable to do anything but sit there and try to catch her breath as a wave of dizziness swept over her.

Bill came back through. "Do I need to call 911?"

That got her attention. "N-no. No, sorry. Something's happened. Something I didn't plan."

"Don't tell me you're getting married?"

That got a strangled laugh. She was glad they'd been able to remain friends. "Hardly. I was told, in no uncertain terms, that I intimidate people."

Those weren't exactly the words Kaleb had used, but the subtext had come through loud and clear.

"You? Intimidating?"

He drew the word out in a way that made her laugh again, her earlier panic beginning to uncoil. "Okay, so you've told me the same thing. I'm working on it."

"Hmm…I'll believe it when I see it." There was a pause and then he said, "Okay, Nic. If you're not involved with someone, then what's the problem? Trouble at the new job?"

"No, the job's fine." She cast around to find the words. Then once she found them, they came pouring out. "I think I'm pregnant, Bill. And I don't know what to do…"

"Pregnant? Are you sure?"

"According to the three home tests I took, I am."

There was a pause. "You need to come in and have it verified, of course."

"I know."

"You said you weren't getting married, and I assumed you weren't involved, but maybe I was wrong?"

It would be so much easier if she'd been like Bill, able to find true love on the heels of a broken romance. But she wasn't.

"No, you aren't wrong. I'm not involved. But I did have a night of…" Of what? Drunken debauchery? No. It hadn't been like that. "It was after Danny died. I went out and had one too many drinks."

"That's not like you."

No, it wasn't. And she was pretty sure it wasn't like Kaleb, either.

"I know. But it is what it is. And I need to make sure, before I say anything to the man I was with."

"So you're keeping it."

This was her chance to say no, she wasn't—that she couldn't raise a child on her own. And all of the other arguments that had run through her head.

"I think I am."

"And the guy? Do you care about him?"

"It's complicated. I actually work with him at the hospital, although I didn't know that at the time." It would have been so much easier if he'd just been a one-night stand, like she'd meant him to be.

"That makes it hard."

"I know. I'll figure it out somehow, though." She paused. "Will you take care of the testing part for me? I'd rather it not be here at NYC Memorial, if I can help it. I'll need to figure some things out before I tell the man in question. Or anyone else, for that matter."

"Well, congratulations…I think."

"Thanks. Like I said, it's complicated, and it wasn't planned, but I'm happy. At least right now. That may change in a matter of hours."

"Well, let me know when you want to come in. And you know I'll help with anything you need. Cheryl and I both will."

"Thanks, Bill, I really appreciate it." She paused. "How soon can you see me? As long as it won't complicate things with Cheryl."

"She'll be fine. I can do it this afternoon, if you want."

A wave of relief went through her. The sooner she knew for sure, the sooner she could plan her next move. "Thank you. I owe you one."

"No, you don't. The only thing you owe me is to be

happy. If this is what you want, I'll back you one hundred percent. Can you get here around five? I'll just be getting off, so no one should be popping into my area to chat or ask questions."

"I'll be there. Thanks again."

Kaleb headed up the walkway and pushed through the door to the hospital just as someone was trying to rush out. The person almost ran into him and skidded sideways to avoid him just as he realized who it was.

Nicola.

"Sorry," she said, eyes widening as she saw him, color sliding into her face and blazing across her cheekbones.

"You're headed somewhere in a hurry."

"I'm just getting off work and I'm running late. I, um, have an appointment in New Jersey."

His head tilted. She hadn't wanted him to catch her coming out, and she'd mumbled those last few words in a way that gave him pause. "You're not thinking of leaving us, are you?"

"Leaving? Why would I be...?" She shook her head. "Oh, my appointment. I am scheduled to meet someone at Grace Central, but it has nothing to do with my work here."

"Good to know." So who was she meeting? And why was that question even relevant? They'd had a good lunch the other day. Except for when Snow had appeared out of nowhere, looking far too interested in what he was doing there with Nicola. Kaleb wasn't exactly sure himself, and that bothered him. He'd forced himself to carry on like nothing out of the ordinary had happened, and they discussed cases and the differences between NYC Memorial and her former hospital. She'd said nothing about going there for an appointment. Or meeting anyone. But then at the end of their lunch, she'd suddenly gotten quiet, as if her thoughts had turned to something else. Something she didn't want to share. And he hadn't pressed. Because he'd had something he didn't want to share, as well. Namely his crazy pact with Snow, which he'd been fairly certain his friend had been about to blurt out.

She shifted her weight, making him realize he was standing there with the door open, blocking her way. He went back through it, holding it open. "Well, I'd better let you get on your way."

"Okay, thanks. I'll probably see you tomorrow."

Probably? Was she lying about leaving? She'd said she was happy at NYC Memorial, so it would be a sudden turnaround if that wound up not being the case.

"Okay, have fun."

She gave him a strange look before moving away from him. He watched her go, her steps quick and staccato, as if she couldn't wait to get to her destination.

Hadn't she said she'd been involved with someone at her old hospital? And that it had been part of the reason she'd left there? Maybe they were getting back together.

While that should make him feel relieved, somehow it didn't. Especially since they'd spent a pretty passionate night together.

Yes, and the woman didn't even remember it. It also didn't mean she couldn't go back to an old flame.

Maybe they'd had a fight, or she'd caught him cheating and had wanted to retaliate.

None of that made him feel any better.

And if she did leave? That shouldn't matter to him at all. Unless Snow had noticed something that Kaleb had been oblivious to. Maybe he and his good friend should have a little chat.

Except the last thing he wanted to do was discuss Nicola with Snow…or anyone else, for that matter. He'd rather just power through this whole thing as if nothing was wrong.

Because it was true. Nothing was wrong.

Then why had he taken a woman he was supposed to have no interest in out for a meal? Or stuck up for her with colleagues like Clint Danvers? Or sat in her office to "see what her process was"? He hadn't done that with any of his other coworkers. So why Nicola? Was it residual emotion from what had happened between them? If that was the case, he was in trouble. Deep trouble. Maybe Kaleb needed to take a step or two back and observe his behavior with an objective eye. The way Snow had.

And if he saw something he didn't like?

Then he needed to back away, while he still could. Before he found himself in another situation that would end badly, like with his exes.

Nicola was different. Although when he'd first seen her at the hospital, he'd wondered if she'd somehow known he worked at NYC Memorial the night they were together. And planned what had happened.

He'd later decided that wasn't the case. But in reality, he knew very little about the woman. He'd dated his former fiancée for more than a year and look at how little he'd known about her. And look at Snow. He'd known his wife for even longer and look where that had led.

No, he needed to tread carefully. Before he found himself sinking in quicksand, with no way out. And Snow standing on the banks saying "Don't look at me. I tried to tell you, and you wouldn't listen."

CHAPTER FIVE

NICOLA WAS STILL IN a daze the next morning. She'd already known in her heart of hearts that her little test strips at home had given her the correct response. She was pregnant.

Pregnant!

And Kaleb was the father.

Bill had been good enough not to ask about the specific circumstances beyond what she'd told him on the phone. And he'd also referred her to a colleague who was a newer ob-gyn at Grace Central. Treating her himself might be considered a conflict of interest, since they'd had an intimate relationship in the past. She hadn't thought about that, but he was right. So she'd walked out of the hospital with a card, for an appointment with her new obstetrician—a woman she'd never worked with, and who would hopefully ask no questions—next week.

And now she had to figure out when to tell Kaleb. Now, while things were early? Or after the first trimester, when there was less chance of miscarrying?

If she miscarried, it would be a moot point. Even

the thought of that happening, though, made her throat squeeze shut.

She walked into NYC Memorial to start her new shift, heading to the coffee shop to pick up a cup of joe before going to her office and sorting through her appointments and consultations for the day.

Staring down at her phone as she stood in line, she tried to figure out if she should risk getting a bagel. Her stomach had been much better behaved this morning, even if her nerves were still a little shaky. A tap on her shoulder had her glancing back to see the very man she was thinking about.

She froze for a second or two, and she saw him frown as he studied her face. "Did your appointment not go the way you'd hoped it would?"

"Appointment?" Her voice ended on a squeak, then she remembered she hadn't specified whom her appointment was with. She took a breath. Then another. "Oh, that. Um, yes. It went fine."

Fine? Was that really the best word to use, if she was going to tell him about the pregnancy? He might think she'd somehow planned this.

No, that was crazy. It wasn't like she'd had an opportunity to sabotage the condoms they'd used. Plus, she'd never admitted to remembering that night. Although he'd never asked outright, so she hadn't had to make a choice about whether or not to outright lie about it.

And if he asked her exactly what her appointment had been about?

Maybe it was better to do this sooner rather than later.

Her heart became a racing, tripping thing in her

chest. What if word somehow got back to him despite the HIPAA laws that were in place? Hospital grapevines were alive and well in most medical facilities.

If he was going to find out from anyone, she'd rather be the one controlling the narrative, right?

Yes. That in itself gave her the courage to open her mouth.

"Hey, I kind of need to talk to you about something. Do you have any room in your schedule today?"

He looked at her for a second, and then someone behind them cleared his throat. Nicola realized she'd allowed a gap to form in front of her and it was now her turn. She moved forward and gave the cashier her order, then paid with her debit card. Kaleb did the same.

Once they had their orders, Kaleb said, "I have some time now. Do you want to find a seat?"

Oh, great. There was no way she was going to say the words "I'm pregnant and the baby is yours" here in the hospital cafeteria, where anyone could hear her. Where anyone could witness his reaction to the news. "Can we go back to my office instead?"

"That bad, huh?" He paused. "Let's go to mine. I need to check on something, anyway."

What could she say? That it wasn't bad news?

It might not be to her, but for him? Oh, yes, probably not news he would be thrilled to hear. But the sooner she got this over with, the sooner she could put this monster in her head to bed and stop obsessing over how he might react.

Then she could concentrate on the baby and not on the fear that her pregnancy might be discovered by him or someone else. Because he was absolutely going to guess, given the time frame.

"That sounds good. Thanks."

She followed him to the elevator and somehow endured the trip to the third floor. She hadn't realized his office was on the same floor as hers. When they got to the farthest corner of the building, Kaleb stopped to unlock a door.

Walking inside, she could see why the hospital administrator had said her office was pretty humble. Because Kaleb's was twice the size and had a sweeping view of the grounds. She guessed plastic surgeons brought in more revenue than a lowly internal-medicine doctor.

Not fair, Nic. For all you know, it goes by seniority and not specialty.

The office was furnished in dark woods and leather furniture, with a squashy couch flanked by two matching chairs to the left. A large screen on the wall behind the grouping must be to show his patients what they could expect from their procedure. It made more sense to have this in a reconstructive surgeon's office, anyway, since she could offer no before-and-after views. And someone like a urologist probably wouldn't need or want this kind of feature.

She caught him looking at her and realized she'd been staring at the television. "I'm taking it you consult with patients in here. Do before-and-after views?"

It gave her a funny feeling, like she was intruding on something intimate. Did he examine patients in here, as well?

That made her squirm, although she wasn't sure why. Her reasons for coming here flew out the window at the thought of a patient baring her breasts to him... Slowly walking toward him...

Dammit, Nicola, you're being ridiculous. He's a doctor. He's a professional. He has a job to do and he does it. Just like you.

"I do reconstructive surgeries. I'm not interested in face-lifts and augmentations, if that's what you're getting at." His voice was tight. Almost angry-sounding.

She blinked, realizing how out of line her thoughts had been. "It wouldn't matter if you did. You would still be treating patients with a need, whether physical or emotional, wouldn't you?"

"Sorry. You're right. I'm not sure why I felt the need to say that."

"Plastic surgeons sometimes get a bad rap. I can see why it might make you defensive."

"Thanks, but I wasn't defensive. Just...cautious. Have a seat." He nodded at the grouping she'd been looking at.

Cautious? What did that mean? Lord, had he read her thoughts?

She did as he asked, now totally flustered. By his reaction to an innocent question. Oh, hell, she wasn't flustered by any of that. It was him. Just him. Kaleb had this presence that made her want to do exactly what she'd imagined moments earlier.

She'd purposely chosen one of the chairs rather than the sofa for just that reason, and she now perched on the very edge, cupping her coffee as if it could ward off the chill that was growing inside of her.

He sat on the sofa across from her and slid an arm along the back of the cushion, looking totally at ease. His dark-washed jeans and blue button-down shirt emphasized his lean good looks. And when that craggy line appeared in the side of his face... God, he was stunning. A real heartbreaker.

Only Kaleb hadn't broken her heart. Far from it. But at this point in her life and career, she neither wanted nor needed a relationship. If she did, she would have fought harder to salvage her relationship with Bill. They had both been focused on their careers, which had helped when they called things off.

And his biggest complaint had been that she was emotionally cool. Too cool. Maybe she was. She hadn't gotten Danny's effervescent personality and sharp wit. Although looking back, maybe those things had covered up a deep well of pain that no one knew existed. And his diagnosis might have brought it all to a head.

She swallowed and shook off the thoughts. She was at a new hospital, with brand-new opportunities to learn and grow. Even though she'd toyed with the idea of finding someone special, she wasn't desperate.

"So what did you want to see me about?"

See him about?

Her thoughts went completely blank for several frightening seconds, before she blurted out the first thing she could grab hold of. "Um, well, before I came to the hospital, I was pretty sure I wouldn't know any of the staff here."

He leaned back, propping one ankle on his knee. His gaze was on her, sharp and wary. "And did you?"

She nodded. "Yes. It was a shock actually. So much so, that I didn't know what to say. Or how to react. Kind of like now."

"I know the feeling." That damn line appeared on the left side of his mouth. "Is this a confession, Nicola?"

"Kind of."

"So when Harvey introduced us, you did remember?" The words came out slowly, as if pondering the implications.

She nodded, her hands tightening on her cup. What else could she say?

"Hell, you sure had me fooled. I could have sworn you thought you were meeting me for the first time."

She paused, trying to find a way to mitigate some of the damage from her deception. Something that wouldn't present her in the worst possible light. If that was even possible at this point. "I thought it would make it super awkward if during that meeting, I said, 'Nice to see you again. I almost didn't recognize you with your clothes on.'"

"Ah, but you saw me with my clothes on. In the bar."

"Yes, but I wasn't paying attention to…*you*. Not until later."

"So it wasn't my witty dialogue that captured your attention." He leaned forward. "I had a feeling the bar scene wasn't someplace you normally found yourself."

How would he know that? Was it something *he* normally did?

"Definitely not someplace I normally go. Or something I normally do." She swallowed. They'd done some pretty damn sexy things.

"You seemed pretty…what shall I say?" The smile appeared again. "Uninhibited."

"Oh, God." She leaned back against the chair with an embarrassed laugh. "My only excuse is that I don't do a lot of drinking."

"So why were you drinking that night?" He paused, his eyes on hers. That mysterious line suddenly lost its grip on his face. "Ah, your brother?"

She nodded.

"Now it all makes sense. Strangely enough, I was there for the same reason."

"I don't understand."

He set his drink on the glass-topped table between them. "I'd just lost a patient."

"Oh!" Understanding dawned in a second. "The melanoma patient."

"Yes. No one expected her to go home and end her life."

"No one expected my brother to do that, either."

She needed to know. "And did it help? Going to the bar? Going back to the hotel?"

"Actually, it did. It was like it jump-started my system and helped me get back on track."

"Me, too." It hadn't erased the pain of what had happened, but it had helped her slide past it and start living again. Helped her realize there was still enjoyment to be found in life. For that, she would be grateful. "It was exciting. And dangerous. And just what I needed."

"I've never thought of myself as dangerous."

"Dangerous in a good way." The emotions of that night came back with a vengeance, bits and pieces of imagery filtering through her brain and reawakening the need she'd felt that night. Her eyes landed on his.

God. How could the man be so sexy, without even trying!

"My ego was pretty banged up when I saw you with Harvey, and you acted like you'd never laid eyes on me."

She laughed. "Harvey was there. And it seemed like the easiest solution at the time. And then afterward, I decided it was too late."

"So why say anything now?"

She hesitated. "Were you able to just shake off that night?"

"No."

The one word carried a wealth of meaning, and she found herself needing to moisten her lips. Tension crackled in the air between them as his gaze pinned her in place, making it hard to breathe. To think.

And then he stood, and her mouth went completely dry at the intent in his eyes. She suddenly wanted the warmth and sexiness he brought to the game. Needed it with a desperation that surprised her.

"No," he repeated. "I wasn't able to just shake it off. I still haven't."

He tugged her to her feet, his fingertips sliding into her hair.

Yes. This sexiness. This man had made her forget all her problems that night. "Me, either."

Almost as soon as the words left her lips, his mouth was on hers. A slow tasting that was so very different from the whirlwind of grief and need that had gone through her the last time they were together.

All thoughts were pushed to the remotest part of her brain. Because the only thing she wanted right now was to make this kiss go on for as long as humanly possible.

This time she could savor. Could enjoy the slight taste of coffee on his tongue, the friction of his lips as they moved across hers. Could revel in the way her emotions opened up and consumed her.

She should stop. Now. But her willpower was pretty much nil. The fact that he'd thought about her after that night, the same way she'd thought about him, was heady. Delicious.

Almost as delicious as his touch.

She hadn't realized the coffee cup was still in her hand, until she felt him take it. What happened to it after that was a mystery she wasn't interested in unraveling. All she knew was that she didn't want him to quit what he was doing.

With her hand now free, she could wrap her arms around his neck. The move pressed her fully against him, and her mind vaguely wondered how she measured up to patients he'd seen. To women he'd had before.

But it didn't matter. He wouldn't be kissing her like he was if there wasn't something about her that he liked. That made him want to tug her out of her seat and plaster his mouth to hers.

That was okay. Because there was something about him that held her captive, as well.

Suddenly he scooped her off her feet and strode to a small door at the back of his office. "Where are we—?"

"Twist the handle, Nicola."

She somehow coaxed her nerveless fingers to do his bidding, and the door opened to reveal a small bathroom, complete with sink, stool and shower.

"It's a little more private here," he murmured.

He pushed the door shut with his foot, then twisted the lock.

"Doesn't your office door lock?"

"Yes. But two layers of protection are better than one, don't you think?"

The words tickled at something in her head that was quickly forgotten when he set her down on the sink's countertop and cupped her face to kiss her again. He stopped for a second, looking at her. "How adventurous are you?"

He had no idea.

"Right now, I feel pretty damn adventurous."

"That's all I needed to hear, Nicola. Because I want you. Right now." His hands went to the edge of her skirt and skimmed it over her thighs.

She lifted to help, her pulse pounding in her ears. They were going to do it. Right here in his office. That's what he meant by adventurous.

And, God, she wanted him, more than any man she'd ever had.

"We don't have much time right now. But I'll make it up to you later."

Later? Her body turned warm as she imagined all the ways he might make it up to her. "Right now, I don't *need* very much time."

"You have no idea what you do to me."

She kind of did. Because he did the same to her. Only more.

He cupped her breast, thumb finding her nipple with the precision of a surgeon. That thought made her laugh.

"Something funny?" He squeezed lightly, turning her giggle into a low moan.

"N-no. Nothing." A feeling of breathlessness made it hard to think. Hard to speak.

She was drowning in a luscious vat of desire. One that she never wanted to climb out of.

Leaving her breast, his fingers looped in the elastic of her bikini panties and slowly peeled them down her legs.

Not much time. Not much time. The words repeated through her head, willing him to hurry. Because if something interrupted them, she was going to be a wreck for the rest of the day. She might have to find some quiet corner of the hospital and...

The sound of a zipper cut through her thoughts.

She gulped. No corner needed.

His arm curved around her butt and dragged her to the very edge of the counter. He stepped between her legs, so she couldn't close them even if she wanted to. She definitely did not want to. A brief thought of protection came and went, but it was a moot point now.

Until a packet was pressed into her hand, and she felt him nudge her opening. "Do me, Nicola."

Oh, God. The bald words with their double meaning made heat arc through her belly and slide down to where he was waiting. Ready. So hot. So hard.

She used her teeth to tear into the plastic packet and took out the condom. She reached down, unable to touch him without her hand sliding over herself in the process. Her eyes closed for a second in utter ecstasy.

"I like that." His cheek brushed hers. "Here, honey. Let me help."

She felt his hand cover hers, and he sheathed himself. But when she went to move her hand away, he held it in place. "Let me help," he repeated.

His fingers cupping hers, he moved her to where she'd been moments earlier, right at the most sensitive part of her body. He used her fingers to stroke herself, and the utter sensuality of it made her teeth come down on her lower lip. She had to stop herself from crying out. She moaned instead.

"Do you feel it, Nicola? This was what it was like for me that night. You are so soft. So sensitive. It drove me wild."

It was driving her pretty wild, too. His erection brushed between their hands, and he included it in their play, gripping it as he continued to urge her to stroke herself. And when her eyes came up, she found him watching her.

"You are absolutely gorgeous. Your pupils tell me everything I need to know."

He moved her hand for a second and entered her

with a hard thrust that drove the breath from her lungs. He groaned against her ear. "Touch yourself, Nic. I want to feel you."

She couldn't resist him if she wanted to. Wrapping her legs around his hips to hold him in place, she did as he asked, the combination of what she was doing along with the deep purposeful movements inside of her making her world spin out of control. Her lids fluttered closed.

"No, baby. Open those beautiful green eyes. I want to see the moment it happens."

She struggled. Tried and failed the first time. But, somehow, she parted her lids. Focused on him as one hand slid up her back and buried itself in her hair. He tipped her back, supporting her with his arm, and then bent over, took her nipple in his mouth and sucked hard.

"Ah…" This time she couldn't stop herself from crying out as a cliff rushed forward to meet her and whispered for her to jump. His tongue lapped her, the movements in time with her stroking fingers, and suddenly it was too much. She took off over the edge, colors swirling as she sailed out into space, her body spasming around him.

She felt him pumping like a wild man, and then he suddenly stiffened, everything coming to a complete halt for several long seconds.

Then he relaxed, pulling her back up to rest against him, his breathing ragged.

She wrapped her arms around his back and held him there, not wanting to come down. She'd never had that kind of reaction before, had never been so totally lost in the act. Not even last time at the hotel. At the time, she'd thought it was the highest of highs. She couldn't have been more wrong.

He kissed her shoulder. "I really don't want this to be a wham-bam thing, but I have a patient I need to see."

"It's okay." She unhooked her legs to let him move away, which he did, making a face as he slid free.

Discarding the used condom, he zipped himself back in, then reached down to scoop up her panties. When he tugged them up her legs, a strange surge of emotion come over her. Had to be hormones.

Hormones!

Oh, God, she'd almost completely forgotten. Actually she had forgotten during the last part of their time together. She hopped off the counter and pulled her undergarment back into place, tugging her skirt down, as well.

"What was it you wanted to tell me?"

Had he read her mind? She swallowed hard, bile washing up her throat. What had she been thinking? She'd come here to tell him something important, not have sex with him. Again.

But if she didn't say it now, she was going to chicken out and put it off. And it would just get more and more complicated with each passing day. Especially if they slept together again, like he'd hinted.

"I'm sorry, Kaleb. This is a little different from how I'd envisioned this scene, and I'm not sure exactly how to say this." There was a long pause. One in which his carefree attitude seemed to dry up and a wariness infused the muscles of his face.

"So you *are* leaving."

"No. No I'm not, but you might wish I was when you hear what I'm about to tell you." She licked her lips and forced herself to say the words that would change both of their lives. Forever.

"I'm pregnant."

CHAPTER SIX

"No, YOU'RE NOT. You can't be."

"Excuse me?"

He'd heard what she'd said, but it made no sense at all. Unless... "Okay, maybe I missed something. You're pregnant, but who's the—?"

"Don't." She held up her hand, a flash of anger crossing her face. "Don't even try to do that."

His brain hadn't fully recovered from what they'd just done, but of all the things she could have said, "I'm pregnant" had not even been on his radar. "We just now had sex, and we used protection. There's no way you can claim to be carrying our child without sounding totally crazy."

Maybe she was crazy. Had she wanted to meet in one of their offices for just this purpose? To have sex and then say she was pregnant? Why? Did she want something from him?

His ex-fiancée's desire to marry a plastic surgeon spewed back into his mind. But as bad as that was, she'd never pretended to be pregnant to get what she wanted.

It made everything he'd done with Nicola seem

tainted now. When he thought of what he'd said. Of what they'd done…

"Sorry to disappoint you, Kaleb. But even your sperm doesn't wear a Superman cape and make me magically aware of the moment of conception. I did a pregnancy test at home several days ago that came back positive. And my appointment was with a friend in New Jersey to confirm the news." Her lips tightened. "It's from that night at the hotel. Not today."

The pieces fell into place with a thump that made his head rattle. Hell, how could he not have figured out what she was trying to say? That's why she'd seemed so strange when she left the hospital.

She was pregnant. And it was his baby. So why had she had sex with him just now?

Unless she was softening him up. Manipulating him, hoping to get the reaction she wanted.

His ex had used sex, too, right before asking him do a little work on her face.

"Did you plan to have sex with me? Is that why you wanted to go back to your office rather than talk somewhere in the open?"

"No!" She cleared her throat before continuing. "No, of course not. And this shouldn't have happened at all. It's just that I knew once I told you… Never mind. I'm sorry. Truly I am. And I don't expect you to do anything about the baby. I just felt like you should know. And you were bound to figure it out, since Immaculate Conception hasn't happened in a very long time."

"The baby." His brain latched on to those two words. "So you're keeping it."

"I am. I'm sorry if that makes you uncomfortable. I'm not planning on telling anyone who the father is. I'll even leave you off the birth certificate. I just didn't want you to put two and two together and start asking awkward questions."

"This goes a little beyond awkward, don't you think? How did this happen, anyway?"

She gave a laugh that sounded pained. "How does it normally happen? It starts off with a man and a woman doing what we did here in this bathroom."

"Hell. And I need to be somewhere in fifteen minutes. We need to talk. Outside of the hospital this time."

"There's no need. Like I said, I don't expect anything out of you."

He felt like an idiot now. He'd suspected all kinds of nefarious motives that had no place in reality. Who was crazy now?

"Well, *you* might not expect anything, but I expect something from myself. This is my child. And I'd appreciate not being cut out of his or her life." His anger flared, but this time at himself. At the way he'd just dragged her into the bathroom as if he had no self-control at all. Maybe he didn't. Not where she was concerned. After all, hadn't he cuddled her close in that hotel room, as if there was something more between them than sex? And he wasn't quite sure what to do with that thought.

He and Snow had made a pact, dammit. One that he knew was for the best.

And yet here he was, expecting a child with someone he didn't love. It was crazy to be expecting a child with *anyone*, for that matter. He didn't have the picture-perfect marriage that his parents had and probably never would. His track record in that department was so seriously flawed it was laughable. This latest foray just drove that point home.

This poor kid.

But it was what it was. There was a baby, and along with the reality that was staring him in the face came responsibility. A responsibility he couldn't turn his back on. Nor did he want to. If Nicola was having this baby, he was damn well going to make sure the child had a father he could be proud of. No more acting like nothing could touch him. No more dwelling on that damn pledge between him and Snow.

He was going to play a part in this baby's life. A big part. Whether Nicola wanted him there or not.

She told you about it, didn't she? That had to account for something.

"Meet me after work, and we'll go somewhere and talk."

"There's no need to—"

"Yes, Nicola, there is. And if you think otherwise, you're very much mistaken. This baby is going to grow up with a mother *and* a father."

She stiffened. "I'm not getting married."

"Then that makes it easier." He gave a hard smile, ignoring the inference in her words. If she could pretend she didn't remember their first night together, he could damn well pretend he didn't understand. Because she was right. She wasn't getting married. Not to him, anyway.

The vision of her standing in a wedding dress smiling at some man who wasn't him made his gut twist sideways. But he'd better face facts. To marry her without love would only be setting them both up for disaster. Or for an ending like Snowden's marriage. His wife had cheated on him and then filed for divorce. There was no way he was putting a child of his through that. So no marriage. Not today. And probably not ever. But there had to be other ways of making sure their baby knew his father loved him or her.

But would he even be able to love a child?

At the thought of a baby, cradled in his arms, his gut shifted again. Along with his heart. Yes, he would. He was sure of it.

As if reading his thoughts, her eyes moistened and she turned away. "I'm so sorry, Kaleb. I didn't plan for any of this to happen."

Of course, she hadn't. And he had been a royal jerk. He went over and cupped her arms, his thumbs stroking her soft skin. He didn't dare hug her. "I know. I'm not sure quite how this came about, but we'll get through it. We'll figure out how we're going to handle the prenatal appointments, the birth and what comes afterward."

"Prenatal?" Her face went very still. "Oh, but—"

"We can talk about it after work." He glanced at his phone. "I really do need to go, before my patient wonders what happened to me. What time do you get off?"

There was a pause, and at first he thought she wasn't going to tell him. Then she closed her eyes. "I get off at six."

"I get off at five thirty. I'll do a little work in my office while I'm waiting for you."

"You want me to meet you…here?"

He glanced around. That was so not a good idea. Especially after all that had happened. "I think it's better if we do this in a more neutral setting. Maybe one of the parks."

"Okay." The relief in her voice was obvious. "I'll meet you just outside the hospital at six fifteen, okay? It'll give me time to change into some jeans and sandals."

That was probably a good idea, since her skirt had been far too convenient. Plus, seeing her in it would immediately bring up images he needed to file away for good. "All right. I'll meet you at the west exit. The one you left through to go to your appointment." Lord, that seemed like forever ago, when in reality it had been just yesterday. And he'd gone from thinking she might be leaving NYC Memorial to finding out he was going to father a child.

His world was pretty much in shambles right now. But as soon as he had time, he was going to sit down and figure out how to put it all to rights. At least he hoped that was possible. Because if not, it was going to be a very rough nine months. "You can stay in the office for as long as you need to."

Right now, he needed to be anywhere but here. So with a quick wave, he headed out.

Waiting impatiently for the elevator doors to open, he pushed the button again. When they did, they revealed the last person he wanted to see right now.

Snow. And unfortunately, his friend was the only one in the elevator.

"Just the man I've been looking for."

"Not in the mood, Snow. I'm already late for an appointment with a patient." And he definitely did not want to get into why he was late. Not to mention the aftermath of that 'why' with its accompanying revelation.

"That's okay, I'll ride down with you." His friend grinned, completely ignoring what Kaleb had just said. "Interesting woman at the restaurant with you the other day. She's new here, isn't she?"

His jaw tightened enough to send a spear of pain through his skull. "Yes. And don't get any ideas." At least not yet. Not until he'd had a chance to sort through all of this and figure how to best deal with things. And he knew without a doubt that Snow was going to have an opinion or two of his own, once news of the pregnancy got out. Right now, though, he couldn't deal with seeing his friend gloat. Or offer words of condolence that would make him feel even worse about the situation. Nothing was going to make this go away, so right now, he just needed time, and lots of it.

"I'm not getting any ideas. I was just curious about how you met her. I'd never seen her before that day at the restaurant. And you're not exactly a social butterfly."

No, he wasn't. And that was definitely not a story he was going to get in to. "Nothing to be curious about. Harvey introduced us, since I happened to be there when she was getting the grand tour."

That was actually the truth, since Harvey had indeed made those formal introductions. And the less formal ones?

Well, those were not something he was going to talk about. Not to his friend. Not to anyone, if he could help it. Kaleb had no idea what Nicola had told her friends or relatives. And right now, he didn't care as long as none of them knew Snow personally.

The elevator came to a stop and Kaleb got off. Unfortunately, so did Snow. "Any chance we could meet up for drinks after work?" his friend said.

Since he was supposed to be meeting Nicola, he didn't think so. "I can't tonight."

"Hot date?"

That made him stop and glare at his friend. "No date at all. I just have some stuff to do, that's all."

Like figure out how he and Nicola were going to make this whole thing work.

"Okay. No need to get all hot under the collar about it."

"Sorry. It just hasn't been a good day. How about Friday or Saturday for drinks?"

"Either of those works, since unlike you, I don't have any special plans. Then again, we both agreed that was something we wouldn't miss, right? The dating? The relationships?"

"Right."

So how did he explain to his friend that while he might have technically kept the terms of their toast, he'd had sex with the newest member of NYC Memorial's staff? Not once, but twice. And had fathered a child with her. Hell. He couldn't even explain it to himself, much less anyone else. At least not right now. Not until he'd had a chance to sit down with Nicola and come up with a plan they could both agree on.

And right now, he was at a loss as to how that was even possible. How any of it was possible. Other than to say that she'd somehow bewitched him and made him forget that he was a rational man who was supposed to have had a rational new outlook on life. And love.

Not that love was involved here. At all. And when Nicola had mentioned marriage, the feelings of how things had been with Melanie—and then after her, Candice—came roaring back. The slyness. The hints. Thank God Mel had never gotten pregnant, or the split would have been that much harder. And Candice... Well, she'd been looking for something in addition to love.

But Kaleb was no longer under the pressure of medical school the way he'd been when Melanie wanted to start a family. So maybe now wasn't such a bad time to have a baby.

But with Nicola? He pulled up outside of one of the exam rooms. "Well, this is my stop. Let me know when you want to have those drinks."

"How about tomorrow? Seven at our usual place."

"Let's try somewhere new." Kaleb didn't know why, but he didn't want to go back to the bar where he'd met Nicola. Not with the way things were right now.

"Okay. How about that place in east Manhattan. I'm too old to go clubbing."

"Define old." He said it with a strained grin.

"Too old to stay out until two when I have to be back here at five in the morning."

That he could definitely relate to. "Okay, east Manhattan it is. I'll meet you at the bar on the corner of Sunset and Brewer."

"Sounds good." Snowden headed down the hallway.

Giving himself a moment or two to regain his composure, Kaleb finally pushed through the door to meet his first patient of the day. Or he should say his patient's parents, since the person he was actually here to see was an infant who'd been born with a cleft lip.

As he took in the scene, he found a very young man and woman sitting in the two seats in the exam room. The man was holding a wrapped bundle. The sight made his chest squeeze. Why did he have to be dealing with a baby, now of all times?

Kaleb forced a friendly smile. "Hello, I'm Dr. Sabat. You must be Mr. and Mrs. Taylor?"

"Yes. Jim and Terra. And this is Trey."

Trey.

If he and Nicola had this baby, what would they name him or her? Would he even be given a chance to help decide?

He set the chart on the bed and peered down at the swaddled baby, the squeezing in his chest growing tighter.

He needed to get his mind back on his job, for his patient's sake. He tried to look at the baby in terms of the cleft defect, which was clearly visible on the right side of the infant's face. According to the chart, the hard palate wasn't affected, just the lip. It would be a fairly straightforward repair. He would just have to make sure he lined the lip margins up perfectly. It might not be noticeable now, but any deviation would become obvious as the child grew and the skin on his lips stretched.

Trey's mom looked at him. "Can this be fixed? I don't want anyone to…" Her voice cracked and she had to try again. "I don't want anyone to make fun of him."

He could well understand her fear. And it was his job to help quell any fear. And in this case it was easy to give reassurance.

"Babies have a remarkable ability to heal. If all goes well, in six months this will be barely noticeable. Maybe a slight redness as the scar heals. But by the time he starts school? It will be a very narrow white line. Certainly not something his peers will notice when they're out on the playground. On the off chance there is a problem, we can do revision surgery a little bit later."

Jim Taylor looked at him for a long time, a muscle in his jaw working, then he spoke. "Is Trey paying the price for being…unplanned?"

Shock went through him, and Kaleb had to work hard to make sure neither of his parents saw it. "Of course not. This was a simply a glitch that happened during cell division. Your baby is going to be fine." He normally didn't give reassurances like this, because nothing was ever certain when it came to surgery, but the baby's dad seemed so beaten down by guilt that Kaleb hadn't been able to help himself. "I'm sorry if someone told you that."

"No," Terra said. "No one said that, but when I first got pregnant…" She closed her eyes. "I didn't want the baby. It was only a couple of weeks later, when I'd decided against getting an abortion, that I allowed myself to care for him. Maybe my rejecting him ended up doing something to him. Maybe it caused that 'glitch' you talked about."

While there were certainly studies that seemed to indicate that high levels of stress early in pregnancy could play a part in some types of birth defects, cleft lip being one of those, the stress would have to be something sudden and profound to disrupt development.

"That's highly unlikely, Terra. I wouldn't worry about that. And Trey's lip should be easy to repair."

It made him think, though. It had to have been stressful for Nicola to tell him about her pregnancy. Were damaging hormones even now flooding her system? He needed to make sure he didn't add to her stress, even though what he'd said was true, that it was unlikely anything he said or did would contribute to his own baby having developmental challenges. And he was pretty sure she would be furious if he treated her with kid gloves.

Pulling up a stool, he said, "Let's take a look." Taking the baby from his father, he laid the infant on his lap, tummy facing up to do a mini exam of his own. Blue eyes stared up at him, blinking as they did an examination of his own. "Hey there, little one. How are you?" He touched a finger to the baby's nose, a feeling of longing going through him. Would he hold his own baby like this, their eyes studying each other?

Swallowing and trying to corral his wayward emotions, he took his stethoscope and listened to Trey's breathing, and especially to his heart, since sometimes cardiac problems accompanied cleft lips and palates. But everything looked and sounded good.

"He's had an EKG, has he not?"

"Yes. His pediatrician said his heart was normal. His lungs are good, too. It seems to be just his lip and nothing else."

Just his lip and nothing else.

Something rattled around in the back of his head. His melanoma patient had thought she just had a deviated septum. Simple. Easy fix. What if this wasn't as cut-and-dried as it looked? What if he was giving them an assurance that didn't match the situation?

Where was this uncertainty coming from?

Maybe because now he was expecting a baby of his own. What if he was in the situation these parents were? Wouldn't he want the doctors to check and double-check until there was no other possible answer?

Lines that all culminated in a single diagnosis.

Like the ones that Nicola drew for herself. Maybe he should call her in on this case, just to be sure.

"That's good news." Kaleb studied the lip, taking measurements of the length and position of the gap. "Any problems suckling?"

He needed to figure out how to broach the subject of Nicola coming to examine the baby without worrying the parents any more than necessary. Especially since under normal circumstances he wouldn't have asked for another consult. The baby's pediatrician had cleared him. Wasn't that enough?

Not right this second, it wasn't.

"No problems. He seems to have figured out what to do."

Since the palate wasn't affected, there wasn't the problem of having fluid traveling into the baby's nose instead of being swallowed. "That's also good. Once the lip is repaired, nursing will be even easier, on both of you."

"How many stitches will he need?"

"I can't give you an exact number. We'll do the sutures in sections. We can't just sew up the outside, because it would still leave a gap behind the lip. So we normally do the stitching in layers. One layer in the back. One in the middle, and then the final stitches on top, where the repair will be the most visible."

"How soon can Trey have the surgery?" Jim asked.

"Let me look at my schedule. I'd also like to call in a colleague to look the baby over, if that's okay."

"Is something else wrong?" Mrs. Taylor asked.

"I'm not seeing anything else, but I would just like another set of eyes to make sure we don't miss anything."

She glanced at her husband and nodded. "We want that, as well."

"Let me call her and see if she's available. I'll be right back."

He handed the baby back to Jim and stepped into the hallway. Dialing her number, he put the phone to his ear. The second her voice came across the line, his gut clenched. What was he doing here? Was this about Trey? Or about talking to the mother of his child?

"Hi, Nicola, are you busy?"

"Aren't we meeting later?"

There was no irritation in her voice, just puzzlement. "Yes, but I have a patient that I'd like you to take a look at, if you have a few moments."

"Yes, of course. I'm just in my office writing up some notes. Where are you?"

He had no idea. Somewhere between stupid and clueless. "I'm down in Pediatrics, room five."

"It's a child?"

"Yes."

Before he could tell her the details, she said, "On my way," and then hung up.

He entered the room again, still holding his phone. Flipping to his calendar, he saw he was pretty booked up, meaning he might need to put off his drink with Snow until another time. Which didn't make Kaleb unhappy. And at least his friend would understand him canceling due to a patient, whereas if he put off their trip to the bar due to going somewhere with Nicola... Well, Snow would probably ask questions he'd rather not answer.

"My colleague will be here in a few minutes, so let's talk dates. I think I can work you into my surgical schedule tomorrow or Saturday, how's that?" Insurance had already preapproved the surgery, so they wouldn't need to wait for that.

"Would Saturday work? I'm pretty sure my mom

and dad will want to fly in for the surgery." Terra glanced at Jim, who nodded.

"Saturday afternoon will be great, if my colleague concurs. I'll call it in and if there are any scheduling conflicts with the surgical suites, I'll let you know later this afternoon."

A knock at the door signaled Nicola had arrived. "Come in."

She came in, hair now pulled back in a ponytail with tendrils trailing the sides of her face. She looked clean-faced and far too beautiful. This was probably a huge mistake. But he wanted to be sure.

"Dr. Bradley, this is Mr. and Mrs. Taylor."

Nicola shook hands with both of them. When she saw the bundle, her eyes widened.

Mrs. Taylor must have noticed, because she said, "This is Trey."

Lowering herself into the chair next to the baby's mom, the diagnostician reached her arms out for him. "May I?"

Settling the wrapped infant in the crook of her arm, she looked far more comfortable holding the baby than he'd felt.

She looked down at the infant and smiled, and hell, that smile…

It was real and warm, with a softness unlike anything he'd seen in her. The image of her holding their baby like this swam behind his eyes. Gorgeous. Why had he said marriage was out of the question?

Because it was. She didn't love him. And even when love was present, things didn't always work out.

But sometimes they did. Like his parents' marriage. And his sister's.

You're not your parents or your sister. You've tried twice and failed.

"Hi, Trey. You're a big, handsome boy," Nicola crooned, her voice a melodic blend that perfectly blended comfort with reassurance. He watched as Mrs. Taylor visibly relaxed. Kaleb wasn't sure what she expected, but whatever it was, the other woman seemed relieved.

So was he. This wasn't a mistake. At least not as far as the baby was concerned.

How about as far as he was concerned?

Well, the jury was still out on that one.

Nicola's finger traced Trey's lip, then she angled the baby up and uncoiled her stethoscope, doing her own listening before nodding. "I like what I'm hearing."

Unfortunately, so did Kaleb.

She continued, "I haven't studied his chart yet, but I'll do that in a bit, but are you okay if I ask you a few questions?"

"Of course," said Mr. Taylor. "Anything that will help."

She handed the baby back to his mother and pulled out the sketchbook. The one that held her brother's page in it. He was surprised she hadn't started a new book after his death. But maybe it was a reminder of what to look for. What could happen.

She asked about the pregnancy, touching Mrs. Taylor's hand when she talked about not wanting the baby as the woman related the same story she'd told Kaleb.

"That must have been hard. But it's very obvious you love your baby. And nothing you did caused that. That's not what I'm looking for. I just want to make sure that surgery goes as planned without any surprises."

"That's what we want, as well."

Nicola was busy drawing her boxes and filling them in, leaving the extra ones blank. A few minutes later, she closed the book. "I think I have all I need. Let me review the chart and see if I find any surprises, given what you've told me. I'll have Kaleb…Dr. Sabat notify you if I see any areas of concern."

"Thank you. We appreciate you coming down on short notice."

"It's not a problem. I was happy to come." She glanced at Kaleb. "Can I get those charts from you?"

"Yep, let me get them from the nurse's station."

"Okay." She glanced at the parents. "I'll say goodbye for now. And congratulations on your baby. He must bring you a lot of happiness."

"Yes, he does."

With that, Kaleb and Nicola went into the hallway.

"I don't see anything out of the ordinary. Were you concerned about something?"

Did he tell her he was suddenly afraid of missing something? Or just lie and pretend that asking for a second opinion was routine?

He decided to go with the truth. "I find myself second-guessing myself sometimes. Because of my other patient. I just wanted to see what you thought."

"Me, too."

"Sorry?"

She sighed, tucking her sketchbook under her arm. "I find myself afraid of missing something important, too. Especially after what happened to my brother."

She understood. Had felt exactly what he had.

"It's hard."

"I know." She glanced down the hallway. "I didn't realize your patient was a baby."

Something in her voice told him that she was feeling the same thing he had when he'd looked into that infant's face.

"It makes it different when you have one of your own coming, doesn't it?"

She nodded. "It does. It's hard not to put myself in their shoes and wonder what I would do. It makes me want to check and double-check the findings."

"Yes. Which is exactly why I called you in."

"I'm glad you did." She smiled, and although the curve of her lips wasn't quite as high as the one she'd given the baby, it still hit him in the solar plexus.

"I'll email you the charts, if that's okay?"

"That's fine. Are we still meeting after work?"

"I would like to, yes."

"Okay, then I won't hold you up." She hesitated. "I'd like to observe the surgery, if I could."

That shocked him. She wanted to watch him work? Or was this about the baby, more than it was about him. Yes, of course it was. There was no way it came out of any kind of interest over his surgical strategies.

"That's fine. There an observation area over all of the surgical suites except for number three. I haven't called to reserve a room yet, but when I do I'll let you know where to come."

That didn't sound quite right. It almost sounded like he was reserving a hotel room rather than a surgical room.

"All right. That sounds good. I'll let you know at the park if I find something else in the charts."

"Okay, thanks. See you later."

He watched as she turned and walked down the hall, her back straight, hips softly swaying.

He knew one thing. He really hoped he was in any room other than surgical room three. He could handle her watching from a distance, but to be in the same room with him? That would be something he'd rather not do.

To keep from staring at her, he swiftly turned and walked back into the room to say his goodbyes to Mr. and Mrs. Taylor.

"Okay, she's going to call me later and tell me what she thinks."

"Thank you so much. You don't know how much this means to us. One of my coworkers said you were the best in the area. He has a friend who split his head open in a motorcycle accident. You did his surgery, and he said the scar is barely visible."

Kaleb was pretty sure he remembered that case. It had taken over a hundred stitches to coax the skin to cover the repaired skull fracture. But the outcome had been a good one.

"We'll get Trey fixed up."

"Thanks again. We're so happy you were here when we needed you."

Kaleb was, too. Once the shock had worn off over seeing his tiny new patient, working with the parents had helped take a little of the edge off. Nicola's pregnancy revelation coming on the heels of having sex with her had done a number on him. But it was neither of their faults. It had happened. And it was their new reality. Both his and Nicola's. What they did from here would lay the groundwork for all their future interactions. So these first few weeks needed to be carefully managed.

If his parents could survive raising him and his sister, surely he could survive having a baby of his own. Couldn't he? He and Nicola might not be together in the way his mom and dad were, but they could be together in a different way, couldn't they? They could be united in purpose, even if they weren't necessarily united in matrimony. So, yes, carefully managed. That was the name of this particular game.

The shade was heavenly this time of summer. And the walk through Central Park to get here hadn't been bad, either. Nicola had been right. The relief she'd felt for the rest of the day after laying her news in front of Kaleb had been wonderful.

Maybe not quite as wonderful as the sex had been, but that part had been a mistake. It would have been a whole lot less complicated to have told him without worrying about their attraction getting in the way.

And it was attraction. She could admit that. Their

first time together could be blamed on the alcohol and heightened emotions that loss had brought to the table.

But the time in his office? No. That tension had been crackling since the moment they sat down. She'd thought it would be okay. That she needed to feel him next to her one last time.

But the horror on his face afterward—when he finally realized what she was trying to say to him—had been pretty unmistakable. And it had been pretty unshakable, as well. It had followed her into the room when she'd done her examination of Trey. She'd felt his eyes on her as she'd looked over the tiny infant, and tried to hide the shock of tender emotions that had gone through her.

She looked for signs of the horror from earlier in his face now, but she was having a hard time reading him.

"I'm going to get us a couple of drinks. What would you like?"

"Sweet tea. Or lemonade if they don't have that. But I can come with you."

"Why don't you wait here and save our places on the bench. And then we can talk about Trey's case and… that other thing."

That other *thing*? Wow, the horror might not be in his face for all to see, but she was pretty sure it was in his voice. In his thoughts. "Okay."

As he headed down the path to the vendor across the way, she sank onto a nearby bench. At least she had a few minutes alone to try to compose her thoughts. She'd opted to drive here separately so she could go

straight home afterward. And to reduce the awkwardness of being together under these circumstances.

Someone whizzed by on a bicycle, helmet buck-
led in place looking like he had somewhere to be. Or
maybe he was training for an upcoming race. Whatever it was, the rider looked carefree and relaxed. The
opposite of what she felt right now. While she was relieved that Kaleb knew the truth, she wasn't quite as
relieved that he hadn't simply said, "Do what you want.
It's nothing to do with me."

That would have been the easier road. One where
she made all the decisions for her child without any
interference from him or anyone else.

Instead, he'd insisted he wanted to be a part of this
baby's life. *His* baby's life. He did not want to be just a
sperm donor. Which was why Nicola was experiencing
a mixture of dread and excitement. Dread that Kaleb
would be in her life despite the fact that he turned her
insides to mush and made her want to drag him back
to her apartment and eat him up. And not the sexual
kind of excitement that was part of her "dread" statement, but excitement that her baby would have a father
who wanted to be involved.

Those two emotions were vying for top spot, but so
far there was no clear winner. It changed from day to
day, from minute to minute. Right now the needle was
pointed toward the excitement part of the equation.

She saw Kaleb returning. And sure enough, he was
carrying two cups.

He sank on to the bench next to her, handing her
one of the cups. "They did have sweet tea."

"Perfect, thanks. I'll need to be careful with what I eat soon enough. But for today? Sweet tea sounded wonderful. What'd you get?" Since it was illegal to drink alcohol in any of New York's parks, it probably wasn't beer.

"Lemonade."

That surprised her. Although she wasn't sure why.

One side of his mouth quirked. "There was a kid in the booth who talked me into a glass. Said he was raising money for a camping trip with a boys club."

Okay, so that didn't surprise her. But it did touch her. "I would have helped him, too."

"Well, since sweet tea was your first choice, I decided to stick with what I knew."

That just emphasized how little they actually knew about each other. Her earlier optimism faded, the needle swinging back toward dread. What if the more they learned about the other, the more they would come to despise each other?

She couldn't see that happening at the moment, but with the divorce rate in today's world...

They weren't getting married. So that was one thing they didn't have to worry about. And if they hated each other? Well, they could simply do a type of shared custody where Kaleb picked up their child every other weekend. If worse came to worst, they could do the exchange at a neutral location.

And if one of them moved out of state?

Ugh. Too much thinking! She needed to focus on the here and now and leave those kinds of worry for another day.

She took a sip of her tea, letting the cold, sweet liquid roll around on her tongue. She wasn't exactly sure what they were here to discuss other than the case. She was only eight weeks along. There was still a long time before the baby was born. But Kaleb had been in a hurry this morning and had seemed insistent. He hadn't changed his mind when she'd been examining Trey.

She pulled out her sketchbook. "So I've been going over the stuff about the baby."

"Baby? As in Trey or…"

"Trey, of course." She set her tea on the bench next to her and flipped open her book, placing it at an angle across her lap so that he could see. "So I compiled everything we know and everything I asked the Taylors about." She followed the path of the lines down several rows of boxes. "They came to the same conclusion you and his pediatrician did. Unless there's something that's not presenting any symptoms, it looks like Trey's diagnosis is right on target."

Kaleb took a huge sip of his lemonade before making a face.

"What's wrong? You don't agree?"

His throat moved as he swallowed, a bitter look on his face. "I agree that this lemonade doesn't have any sugar. No wonder he offered me packets of sweetener."

She laughed. "I thought you'd suddenly decided the case wasn't as simple after all."

"No. That case is simple." He put his own lemonade on the seat. "And unfortunately I'm stuck with surgical suite three."

"The one without the observation deck?"

"That's the one." His mouth was still making these funny-looking movements, as if trying to rid itself of the sour taste.

"Here, take a drink of mine." She held out her cup.

He glanced at her. "Are you sure?"

"Yes. I think we've already shared any germs we have." Her face heated as soon as the words were out of her mouth.

One side of his mouth went up. "Yes, I guess we have. And they were definitely a whole lot sweeter than that lemonade."

The low tones slid over her, making her belly shimmy with need. A need that was going to have to sit there unattended. She was not going down that road again.

He took the glass and swallowed some of the liquid. "You definitely made the right choice as far as that goes."

Did that mean she hadn't made the right choice as far as keeping the baby? No, if that was the case he wouldn't want to be part of the child's life, would he? She decided to skip that topic for now.

"So if you're in surgical suite three, what does that mean? Can I still come in and observe as long as I stay out of the way?"

"Yes. I just wasn't sure if you would want to."

She blinked. "Why not?" Now that she'd seen baby Trey, she found she wanted to see his case to the end. Maybe it was the look in his parents' eyes when they looked at each other, the love so obvious that it hurt.

What would it be like to have that? She and Bill

had been friends, but what she'd thought was love had turned out to be simple affection. The inferno that raged between her and Kaleb made what she'd had with Bill look like soggy embers. Warm, but with little fuel to keep it going.

At first she thought Kaleb wasn't going to answer her question, but then he said, "It was hard to hold that baby and not think about…"

She got it. Because she'd had the exact same feeling. "And not think about ours?"

"Yes."

"I know. I felt it, too. Especially when I held him. It was hard to hand him back."

"Yes, it was. Which brings us back to the reason why we're here." He settled back, stretching his legs out in front of them and crossing them at the ankles. "I wanted to go through a few things."

The man was tall. Really tall. She was five foot six and wasn't used to only coming up to a man's shoulders. But she did. And when he'd stretched out on the bed, she felt enveloped by him. The memory sent a shiver over her. Would their baby be tall? Would he or she have their daddy's looks?

She hoped so.

"Okay. Go ahead. I'm listening."

"I'd like to go to your prenatal appointments. Be there for the birth."

"What?" Shock speared through her, making her grab a couple of quick breaths. Any thoughts of her somehow doing her own thing until after the baby was born went out the window.

He frowned, turning to look at her. "Is that a problem? I'm letting you into my surgical suite."

"That's hardly the same thing." The thought of him being there when the doctor did intimate exams made her squirm. But why? What they'd done in his office had been about as personal as things got.

Maybe it was because this was in the cold light of day and the time in his office, she'd been…drunk. Again. Not with alcohol, but drunk with wanting him. Needing him.

Parts of her twitched to life, and she hurriedly moved her thoughts to less dangerous territory. "I guess I hadn't really thought about it. Is there a particular reason why you'd want to be there?"

"If I'm going to be a part of this baby's life—and I intend to, don't get me wrong—the earlier I can see the reality of what's happening and bond with him or her, the better, don't you agree?"

How could she not agree when he put it that way?

"B-but what about your job?"

"I'll do the same as you will, rearrange my schedule to fit in with those appointments."

"Are you sure, Kaleb? We could keep this a secret from people at the hospital. Keep this part of our lives private. My doctor will be at Grace Central."

"You've already chosen a doctor?"

"Yes, my ex, Bill, is an ob-gyn over there, and he—"

He stiffened beside her. "A man you were involved with is going to deliver our baby?"

She wasn't sure why he was getting upset. "Bill and I are still good friends. But, no, he's not delivering the baby. He did the initial pregnancy test and then referred me to another doctor." She smiled. "Who happens to be a woman, although that doesn't matter."

He was still frowning and a small thread of tension went through her. "Listen, this baby may be yours, but access to my private life is not. I'll do what I want, with whom I want."

After she said it, she realized how it sounded, but there was no way to take back the words. And she wouldn't even if she could.

"I think you've made that perfectly clear."

The chill in his voice made her cringe. "I won't do anything to harm the baby. I need you to know that. But we're not a couple, Kaleb. You don't have the right to try to direct my life."

He muttered something under his breath that she didn't catch. She was beginning to feel like this was a mistake. Maybe she should walk back a couple of steps and tell him he wasn't welcome in the exam room with her. But that didn't seem fair. Or maybe it did. She wasn't sure of anything right now. On some plane, she'd realized this was going to be complicated, but she hadn't realized how complicated until this very moment.

She kept her voice as calm as she could. "Do we need to lay down some ground rules?"

"I don't know about that, but…"

Just then a teenager on a hoverboard glided by, his phone to his ear as he argued with someone. A girlfriend, judging from the heated tones. Nicola spied the bicycle from earlier coming back down the trail in the opposite direction. He, too, was on a phone. Except he wasn't talking. He was looking down at his screen driving with one hand.

"Kaleb!" She stood in a hurry.

He realized, too, and just as he opened his mouth to yell at them, the kid on the hoverboard saw the bike and used his weight to swerve out of the way. It worked, except he'd overcorrected, and before anyone could do anything, his board turned and plowed right into a nearby tree, knocking him backward onto the concrete. His head hit the hard surface with a dull thud. And then he was still.

Too still.

CHAPTER SEVEN

KALEB AND NICOLA jumped up from their bench, drinks and conversation forgotten as they rushed to the teen's aid. The bicyclist had already driven by, oblivious to what both of their distractions had caused.

Nicola dialed 911, while Kaleb kneeled down beside the downed kid. The operator answered, and she quickly relayed what they knew, telling her there were two doctors on the scene of a suspected head injury, and that they needed an ambulance.

"I'm going to put you on speaker, while I help." Nicola set down the phone and took vitals of the unconscious kid. He was breathing, at least. She glanced at his pupils. One was blown. Not good. "Kaleb, look."

He glanced over and swore softly.

The emergency services operator said, "Central Park's medical unit is en route. They're about five minutes out."

"Okay, thanks." She gave the dispatcher the boy's vitals so she could pass them on. "His right pupil is blown. And there's a small amount of blood coming from the ear on that side."

Possible skull fracture. Her argument with Kaleb seemed so ridiculous now. Of course, he could come to her appointments. Could be a part of his child's life. Unlike her brother, who would never be anything more than a few stories told around the dinner table. The ache in her heart almost floored her, almost made her miss the dispatcher's next words.

"Can you secure his head and neck?"

"He's unconscious, so we can keep him still for as long as possible, but neither of us has any medical gear with us."

Nicola got up to direct another cyclist to the other side of the road. "Can you go down a ways and warn people that we've got a medical situation here and ask them to use a different route?"

"Sure. Is he going to be okay?" The woman's eyes were large. "He looks so young."

That had been Nicola's thought, as well. "We hope so. Thanks for your help."

She might not have been able to help her brother, but she could do something to help this boy. That's why she'd gone into medicine. To save lives.

The woman pedaled about fifty yards down the path and stopped, parking her bike sideways to make it more difficult for anyone just to zoom by her.

In the distance, Nicola thought she heard the sound of sirens, but she couldn't be sure. Just then, the boy moaned, his eyes fluttering. Kaleb put his hands on the boy's face. "You need to lie very still, okay?"

"My…head…" The words were slurred, trailing off at the end.

"I know it hurts. You've had an accident. Help is on its way, but for now we need you to lie here and rest, can you do that?"

"Think so."

The ambulance arrived on the scene, the vehicle emblazoned with the words Central Park Medical Unit. Two emergency services workers got out, one pulling a gurney from the back of the vehicle. It didn't take long for them to do their own assessment and get a neck brace and backboard in place.

"Thanks, you guys. We'll take it from here."

"Where are you taking him?"

"NYC Memorial," said one of the EMTs. Five minutes later, the patient was loaded up and headed back to Kaleb and Nicola's own hospital.

Nicola called ahead to let them know a trauma case was one the way. She waved at the bicyclist down the path, thanking her and letting her know she was free to go.

Kaleb took her arm. "You okay?"

"Yes, why wouldn't I be?" She paused, wondering if he was saying what she thought he was. "I'm going to work, Kaleb. For as long as I can. I love my job and don't plan to give it up, even after the baby's born."

"I know. I wouldn't expect anything different. But that doesn't mean I won't worry about the stress of what we do and how it might affect you and the baby."

She should be really irritated with him, but instead, she found his words touched her. Even if the concern wasn't for her so much as it was for the baby—at least it showed her that he would be a caring father.

So maybe they wouldn't end up hating each other after all. Maybe she'd find he had some really good character traits. Character traits that might make her start to...

A quick thought flitted through her head, and she dismissed it immediately. They'd both been working under the influence of adrenaline for the last bit of time. Coming down from it meant her thoughts were suspect right now. So were his. So she needed to extinguish any ideas that weren't based on reason.

Sitting back on the bench and taking a long drink of her sweet tea, she let the sugar course through her, hoping for a jolt of energy. "Well, I think I've had my excitement for the day."

"Yes. Me, too."

Ha! Well, Kaleb had had even more to deal with today than she had. She'd had a couple of days to get used to the idea of being pregnant. He hadn't. He'd had a matter of hours. Hours that he'd spent working cases like Trey's.

"So as to the question of my appointments, if you really want to come to them, I won't stop you. But please don't feel like I expect it." She paused. "I really don't expect anything out of you, Kaleb. My only reason for telling you was that I felt I owed it to you. Plus the fact that you were probably going to figure it out, once I started showing, anyway."

Something like a snort came from beside her. "Well, I appreciate you not making me find out that way."

"It wouldn't have been right. No matter how tempting that might have looked yesterday."

"So you thought about keeping me in the dark. It was the fear of getting caught that made you do the right thing?" There was a tightness to his voice that she didn't like.

"I hope not. But I have to be honest and say it went through my head before I finally decided to tell you." She licked her lips. "Saying that, I'd really rather not tell anyone at the hospital. Not for a while. Maybe not at all. If my appointments are at Grace Central that might make it a little easier to contain."

"Any particular reason you want it kept a secret?"

Her eyebrows shot up. "You *want* people to know?"

He stared off into the distance. "I hadn't given it a lot of thought. But I do have a friend who is bound to figure it out. I'd like to tell him at some point. Just to make it easier on me. Not that that will be a fun conversation."

"I understand. And I'll tell my parents, of course. They'll probably want to meet you." She couldn't imagine a more awkward scenario than sitting there while her dad grilled Kaleb on whatever questions came to mind. But if Kaleb truly wanted to be a part of this baby's life, he was going to meet them at some point. Better to do that sooner rather than later.

"That's fine. So when is your first appointment?"

"In about a week. I'm thirty-five, so they're going to want to monitor me a bit more closely than their younger patients."

He smiled. "You say that like you're ancient, Nicola. I'm thirty-eight."

"Wow, you really are an old man, aren't you?"

When his lips curved, bringing that deadly craggy line in his cheek into play, she gulped and quickly added, "Speaking of ages. Anything on your side of the family I should know about? Genetic conditions?"

His smile turned sober. "No. Not that I'm aware of."

"Okay, nothing on mine, either, except a general absence of luck, I guess. When you said something about a double layer of protection that day in your office, it almost made me laugh. I'd thought if only we'd pulled out two packets instead of just one, this might not have happened."

"Remind me to never use you as a good-luck charm then, while gambling."

For some reason, that stung and she wasn't quite sure why. As if realizing it, he put a hand on hers. "I was joking. It was a simple defect in the condom or packaging. It had nothing to do with luck, bad or otherwise."

"Sorry. I know I'm on edge right now. I'm hoping my hormones don't suddenly decide they're not going to play nicely anymore. I'll do my best not to boo-hoo on your best shirt or anything."

Except she'd already done that. When she'd talked to him about her brother's death. But that hadn't been because of hormones. That had been because there'd been an actual tragedy in her family. A tragedy that was still taking its toll on her and her parents.

She sucked down a deep breath "Okay, so anything else we need to go over?"

"I can't think of anything. Let me know how things go with your parents when you decide to tell them. I'll have to tell my mom and dad, as well. And, like I said, I'll need to tell Snow."

Snow. The man she'd met at the restaurant. The one who'd given her a funny look. "Sounds good. I want to wait a couple of weeks until after my first exam before saying anything to them. Just in case something goes wrong."

Just saying those words made her heart cramp. What if they found something that shouldn't be there. What if her pregnancy hormones really were due to something awful, like a molar pregnancy.

No. She was pregnant. Something inside of her had whispered in her ear even before she'd taken the home pregnancy test. She'd known.

And now, so did Kaleb. The hard part was over. At least she hoped it was. Because if it wasn't, then with the exception of her brother's death, these might be the hardest nine months she'd ever have to endure. As she watched Kaleb pick up their trash and take it to the nearest waste receptacle, she sucked down a deep breath. She needed to be on her guard. Because those pregnancy hormones might not simply cause weepy moments here and there. What if they deceived her and made her think she had feelings for Kaleb? Like she'd had when she'd thought of his character traits?

Any feelings like that would be traitorous, and likely to disappear as soon as the baby was born.

Oh, Lord, had that already happened? What if that incident in his office had been dictated by the baby chemicals that were coursing through her veins? If that was the case, she'd have to be more careful from now on. Any mushy feelings she might develop for Kaleb she was going to attribute to hormones, plain and simple. She'd just have to wait it out and ignore them as much as she could. Then once the baby was born, she could sort out what was and what wasn't real. She held on to that thought as they walked out of the park and each got in their separate cars, and continued to hold it as she took the exit that led to home. And it remained on her mind as she drifted off to sleep later that night.

Saturday found Kaleb in surgical room three waiting for Nicola to get gloved up and in the room. Her last case had run over by fifteen minutes and she said she was on her way. He had a schedule to keep, but he didn't want to start this without her, and he wasn't sure why.

He hadn't seen her all day on Friday, but that was probably just as well. He wasn't quite sure why he'd insisted on being there other than it seemed strange to just ignore the baby until after it was born and then suddenly start making appearances in the child's life. What if Nicola decided during that time that she wanted to do this on her own?

Not happening. So it was better to be there than to sit on the bench and pretend he didn't want to be in the game.

The door to the room opened and Nicola entered with her hands held out for her gloves. She wasn't taking an active part in the surgery and now that she was here, his nerves were acting up.

"Okay, we're ready to start." He glanced at the anesthesiologist, who nodded and adjusted his instruments to deepen sedation.

"Go ahead."

His eyes found Nicola's, before his glance dropped to her stomach. How would he feel if this was his child and Nicola was watching him work?

Ridiculous. There is no way he could work on his child or any other relative.

Choosing his first tool, he studied the baby's lip. He would make the repair using the rotation-and-advancement method, where the side of the defect nearest the nostril would be rotated down to join the lips together and the other side would be "advanced" to fill the hole created by the rotation.

Clearing his throat, he began to talk his way through the procedure to document each step. Out of the corner of his eye, he saw Nicola take a step closer so she could see.

"Could someone turn the screen on?"

Someone flipped a button and the screen on the wall across from him flickered to life. It wasn't just for the diagnostician's benefit. It was also to help the entire team see exactly what Kaleb was seeing through the little camera mounted on the side of his lighted loupes.

"Making the rotation incision. Scalpel, please."

He held his hand out and the surgical nurse placed the tool on his palm.

The first cut is always deep.

The words to a familiar song whispered through his head. It wasn't just the deepest. It also had to be the most accurate for Trey to have a natural appearance.

He gauged the space he needed to cover with the flap. Normally, Kaleb was only minimally aware of the rest of his team in the room. He got into a zone where no one existed except for him and his patient. Only this time, there was a third person in his little circle. Nicola.

He could feel her gaze on him, feel the tension crackling off of her in waves as she followed his progress. If it had been him watching, his hand would be curling around an imaginary scalpel, planning how he would make the incisions. Where he would place each suture. But those were things he couldn't think about right now.

"Rotating the flap and moving it into place. Could someone adjust my loupes a bit to my right, please?"

Hands moved in to do his bidding, then backed away to get a fresh pair of surgical gloves. They had to make sure the surgical field was as free from contamination as possible. This child would not get another chance at this if infection ate away the repair.

With the loupes adjusted, he could see without having to compensate and he moved the flap down to where he'd prepared one side of the lips. It was just a bit tight. So he modified the incision he'd made to help ease the tension.

He secured the innermost part of the repair with dissolving sutures, continuing to describe what he was doing, both for the surgical record and for Nicola's benefit. She'd said she had never seen a cleft repaired before. But that wasn't the only reason she wanted to be here. They'd both talked about how moved they'd been by this child and how it was probably due to the fact that their own child was growing in Nicola's womb at this very second.

Right now, he was glad his expressions were hidden by both the mask and the loupes, because he wouldn't want Nicola to see his eyes. His tension was probably tighter right now than that flap's had been. Only unlike what he'd done with his scalpel, there was no easing this particular tension.

When he got to the outermost part of the repair, he made his stitches as tiny as he could without compromising the strength of the sutures. He adjusted the fit so that the Cupid's bow on the repair side matched that of the other side.

That was about as good as it was going to get. "Rotation completed. Starting the advancement procedure."

He eyed his incision site, using the measurements he'd taken during the baby's exam. His notes were displayed on the screen along with his camera's view. He moved his scalpel a little more to the right.

This should be like second nature to him by now. He'd done a number of these repairs, including volunteering with a medical unit overseas to help impoverished areas. Those children were all equally important, but somehow his performance right now wasn't by rote. He was considering each and every move he made.

Maybe he needed to be doing that with Nicola. Not just coasting along and hoping for the best, but considering every move and its ramifications.

A sound caught his ear. A little blip that stood out from the rest of the background noise. The steady rhythm that always accompanied his surgeries. When they were going well. He ignored it. His scalpel hovered over the incision site just as it came again. A syncopated sound that made him look up and lock eyes with his anesthesiologist. "What's going on, John?"

"Not sure. He's just thrown a couple of PVCs. I'll let you know if they become concerning."

PVCs weren't uncommon during surgery, and normally he just took them in stride unless they became frequent. But right now, his ears were super tuned to the sound. He waited a beat or two and then forced his muscles to relax, wondering if Nicola were as tense as he was at this moment.

"Making the incision."

His scalpel sliced true, freeing the skin to move forward. As if fitting a piece to a jigsaw puzzle, the flap filled the hole perfectly, just as another off-rhythm blip hit his ears. Every muscle in his gut tightened. "Do I need to stop?"

"No. We're still okay."

Forcing himself to ignore the monitor, he sutured the flap in place, his hand surprisingly steady as he molded the baby's new lip.

When the last suture was in place, he looked at the repair with critical eyes, searching for any puckers in the baby's skin that would cause problems later. But the little zigzag-looking line was smooth and even, and the bows on the baby's lips looked symmetrical.

Another blip. A double this time.

Hell. He needed to call it before this turned into something worse. "Okay, the last suture is in place."

He dropped the instrument into the stainless steel

bowl on the table and glanced at his anesthesiologist. The man looked totally unconcerned. As well he should. Kaleb was the one who was having a fit over it.

"Easing back on the sedation."

The cramped muscles in his stomach were starting to ease as he took in the cardiac monitor that was now beeping with nice steady points of sound. Nothing bad had happened, except in his mind.

What if their child had an emergency? Had to have surgery? Was he going to turn into a basket case while in the waiting room, imagining every possible thing that could go wrong?

Judging from his emotions right now? Probably.

He glanced over at Nicola and saw her eyes were glassy as if she, too, had been riding the same emotional roller coaster as he had.

But now it was over and he could get off the ride. He looked around. "Good work, people. We just helped a little boy lead a more normal life."

The atmosphere in the room turned gleeful as people clapped and congratulated him. He didn't want it, any of it. He had just wanted to do his best for this boy.

He went over to John Laroby and nodded. "Thanks. Sorry for pointing out the PVCs."

In reality, John was one of the best anesthesiologists the hospital had. If anyone was aware of the tiniest nuances of sedation it was him.

"I understand. It's a baby. I always get keyed up when we work on them."

"Yeah. Me, too." Except he didn't. Not usually. And he wasn't sure he liked being this involved in one's care. It had to be due to finding out he was going to be a father.

Nicola made to leave the room and gave him a quick wave. He moved to join her, waiting as she discarded her mask and gloves, and then joined her once he'd gotten rid of his.

"How'd it look?"

She nodded with a tilt to her head. "I was impressed."

"Hey, I wasn't looking for accolades, just wanted to know if the repair looked okay."

"You know it does." She smiled. "I have to tell you, I was a nervous wreck, though. I don't know how you do it."

"I was a little nervous on this one, as well."

"Because of the baby?" she said, probably not realizing she'd hit the nail on the head.

"Yes. It was hard not to imagine how I'd feel if Trey were mine. I really wanted to do right by him."

"And you did. But I have to tell you, I'm glad it's over. Especially when you heard his cardiac sounds change. It was hard for me to just stand there."

"John's a great anesthesiologist. I'm sure he was on top of it."

"I'm sure. It doesn't change how I felt, though, when I heard them."

He leaned a shoulder against the wall, noting how tightly her hands were clasped. "Hey, he's fine. It worked out just the way it should have."

Sudden moisture appeared in her eyes. "I know. And I'm just being silly. It's hormones, I'm sure."

"It's the reaction of a human being that is hoping for a good outcome."

She touched his hand, her smile doing something to his insides. "And there was a good outcome, wasn't there? I'm so glad for Trey and his family."

"Me, too." He sucked down a deep breath and decided to tackle a question that had been at the back of his mind all day. "Do you have your appointment date yet?"

"Are you sure you want to come?"

"Absolutely." He was more sure now than he'd been when he'd started the surgery. He wasn't sure why, other than the fact that he needed to be there. No matter how hard it would be when she took the baby home and left him behind.

"It's on Friday."

"Okay. Do you want me to pick you up?"

She hesitated, moistening her lips. "Do you want to?"

"It might not be a bad idea, just in case we need to talk about something."

"Okay. That sounds like a plan." Her smile had faded and something he couldn't read replaced it. "Good job again. Thanks for letting me watch."

"You're welcome. I'll see you next week, then, if not sooner."

CHAPTER EIGHT

NICOLA'S APPOINTMENT WAS the same day the hoverboard accident victim was scheduled to be released from the hospital. Both Kaleb and the diagnostician had peeked in on the boy, since Nicola had been called on to assess some of the test findings. He'd had a skull fracture, like they suspected, but he'd been very lucky not to have any neck or back injuries to go along with that diagnosis. If bad things came in packages of three, he hoped that good things did, as well.

So all that was left on today's agenda was Nic's prenatal appointment. He'd taken the rest of the day off, just so he didn't have to hurry back if there were any problems.

Problems.

Like those blips on Trey's heart monitor during surgery? What if they found something when they did the ultrasound?

Strangely, Nicola was as calm as he was keyed up. Maybe it was an act. Kind of like the performance she'd given when she pretended not to know who he was, when she first came to the hospital. That seemed so long ago now. So much had happened since then.

Actually it had happened even before that first meeting at the hospital. The gears had already been set into motion. Except neither of them had realized it at the time.

He was going to be a father. Heaven help them all. His lips curved in a smile. And he and Nicola had actually come to some kind of a truce, or an unspoken understanding or something, because things were going fairly smoothly. Maybe a little too smoothly.

Would he meet her ex while he was there? He wasn't sure why, but it bothered him that a past romantic interest was involved in any way, shape or form with the birth of his child. It was ridiculous. If Kaleb's ex showed up on the scene, he would be surprised if Nicola gave her a second look. And maybe that bothered him, as well.

His suspicions that she'd slept with him the second time as a way to tell him about the pregnancy had begun fading away. And when he'd seen the emotion on her face while holding baby Trey, any remaining doubts had died completely. She'd had no way of knowing how he'd react to the news about the pregnancy. But she would have equally not known how he'd react after they'd finished making love.

Right?

Men were supposed to be more mellow after sex. But...

No, don't go there again. It won't help anything. Now if she makes a habit out of sleeping with you and then bringing up difficult subjects afterward, then you might have reason to be suspicious.

Not that they were going to sleep together again.

He was on his guard. And he suspected she was, too, if the way they avoided touching the other was anything to go by.

He'd had to cancel his plans to have drinks with Snow—again—but he promised they'd get together sometime next week.

His phone buzzed and he glanced at the readout, frowning. It was Nicola. Hopefully she wasn't going to change her mind about him coming to the appointment. "Hello?"

"Hi, um, it's me, Nicola."

"I know who it is." He smiled. Being pregnant hadn't softened her crisp matter-of-fact tones. So far, the only thing that had had the power to do that had been...

Sex.

"Oh. Well, um, Cade is asking to see you to say goodbye. So are his parents."

It took him a moment to filter through who Cade was and then realized it was the hoverboard victim. "What time?"

"Well...now. I told you about it yesterday."

She had? Oh, hell, she had. They'd passed in the hallway and she'd asked if he was coming. But he hadn't written it down. "Okay, tell them I'll be there in just a few minutes."

"Sounds good."

They were supposed to go to her appointment

in about a half hour, so hopefully Cade's discharge wouldn't take too long. He somehow doubted she'd want to skate out early.

It didn't take him long to get to the pediatric ward on the second floor. Decorated in bright colors with pictures mixed in with paintings of animals in humorous poses and clothing, this ward was the only part of the hospital that had large blocks of color in the linoleum flooring. Everything about it spelled fun and health, a subliminal message to heal and get better. He stopped by the nurses station. "Hoverboard accident victim?" Sometimes it was easier to go by a patient's condition than try to remember all their names.

"Room two-oh-one. They're waiting for you, Dr. Sabat."

"Thanks." He headed down the hallway, hearing laughter coming from the distance. One of those voices belonged to Nicola. How he knew that he wasn't sure. But somewhere along the way, his brain had learned to recognize her throaty tones. His brain immediately retrieved a facial expression to go along with that laugh. When had he memorized that? He wasn't sure, but he had. It was a smile that made tiny crinkles stand out on either side of her nose…making her eyes light up.

Not something he should be focusing on right now. He was here to keep a promise to a patient. Nothing more, nothing less.

He gave a quick knock on the door and then walked in. Cade was sitting on the side of his bed, struggling to put on his socks. A woman hovered nearby, concern clearly chiseled on her face.

"Are you sure I shouldn't—?"

"Mom, I can do it. Just give me a minute or two."

He wasn't sure what they'd been laughing at a second ago, but Nicola's face didn't have a trace of the smile he'd just drawn up from memory.

He turned his attention to the patient. "How are you doing?"

Cade looked up. "Dr. Sabat, you came! Nicola wasn't sure you'd be able to. She said you might have an emergency."

So she'd covered for him. Because he'd forgotten something important.

His jaw tightened. And once he had a child, was he going to forget important events in its life, too? Would Nic have to cover for him? Make up excuses for why he didn't show up for a ballet recital? Or a high-school graduation? Or the birth of a child?

The reality of what was coming suddenly made itself known to him. He would need to reset some of his priorities.

He glanced at Nic, who still wasn't smiling. Was she thinking the same thing he was? That she might need to prod his memory at every turn? Send him text messages, then have to apologize for nagging him? It wouldn't be nagging. And he was going to make it a point not to forget.

"Sorry I'm late." He smiled at Cade. It was funny how the boy called Nic by her given name and yet used Kaleb's title. Maybe there was more softness to her than he gave her credit for. Or maybe she just showed it to people other than him.

That made him wince. Did he bring out a side of her that other people didn't see?

"My dad says I need to lay off the hoverboard for a while."

"That's probably not a bad idea, until your balance is back up to where it should be." Hopefully the kid had learned his lesson about talking on the phone while trying to guide it. The same with the bicyclist who'd been texting at the time, although Kaleb doubted that person had even been aware of what had transpired. Hopefully he saw it in the news and realized...and changed his priorities.

Just like Kaleb needed to do.

"I was on the phone when it happened, you know." Cade said it with a touch of shame in his voice.

"I know. It's a good lesson, don't you think? You were very lucky you weren't injured worse than you were." Kaleb left out the fact that the boy could have died. But somehow he bet Cade was well aware of how lucky he'd been. Or maybe his parents had laid down the law. Maybe that was part of the reason the hoverboard was on hiatus.

"I promised my mom and dad that I'd never do that again. And when I start driving I won't do it, either. I'd heard about what could happen, but I never really thought it would. I know better now."

"I'm glad, Cade."

Just then a nurse came in with some papers. "Are you ready to get out of this place?"

"Am I ever."

Cade's parents came over to Kaleb. "Nicola told us what you did. We are so grateful."

"She had just as much to do with it as I did. I'm just glad we were there, and that he's going to be okay. There's a bicyclist who was just as much at fault as Cade was."

"Yes, Nicola told us. Thank you again for everything."

Well, it seemed like Nicola had everything under control. As usual. He was beginning to think Grace Central had lost more than they realized. Hopefully they didn't suddenly look around and decide to woo her back. Because if that happened, he might just need to…

To what? Do some wooing of her himself?

Uh, no. There would be no wooing or anything else. He was done with that. Once and for all. Wasn't he?

Cade's parents signed the papers and with their son in a wheelchair, they were seen out and into the car.

Nicola came over and bumped his shoulder with hers. "Well, that was certainly a happy ending, wasn't it? I honestly didn't think he was going to be that lucky."

"Nor did I." He glanced at her jeans and thin T-shirt, and realized she'd already changed in preparation of going to her appointment. "You look like you're ready."

"I am…but…"

His chest tightened. Was she having second thoughts about him going with her? "But?"

"If you don't want to come, please don't feel like—"

"I want to. I haven't changed my mind."

She nodded. "Okay, then, if you're sure. I can't wait

for you to see my... I mean, the hospital I used to work at."

He blinked. Maybe it wouldn't be Grace Central that would come looking to win Nicola back. Maybe it would be Nicola who would decide that NYC Memorial was not what she'd been looking for and would decide to head home to New Jersey.

And if that happened?

Well, if it did, he'd let her go and do his best not to watch her as she walked away, taking their baby with her.

CHAPTER NINE

NICOLA WAS LYING on the cold table, her nerves in knots, clammy hands clasped together on her stomach. Why had she let Kaleb come in the room with her? Or thought it a good idea for him to come with her at all?

She'd needed moral support, that's why.

The door opened, and Bill came in, letting it swing closed behind him. "Dr. Banks has been called to do an emergency C-section. So sorry, Nic. You're stuck with me. This time, anyway."

"It's okay." She swiveled her head to look at Kaleb. "This is Dr. Sabat—Kaleb. He's…a friend. He agreed to come with me."

"That was nice of you, Kaleb. Nic could use a friend right now, I'm sure. I'm Bill. I'm one of her friends, too. From a ways back."

"Sorry," she said. "I should have introduced you, too."

A frown came over Kaleb's face. Had he not wanted her to tell Bill his name? Well, what was she supposed to do? Just pretend he didn't exist?

Like that first night they were together?

Looking back, it seemed kind of silly. But she'd been mortified over what had happened—had been afraid that he'd judge her for having a one-night stand.

But what about him? She could have just as easily judged him for sleeping with her.

Bill glanced at the chart. "So it looks like you're starting week nine. We should be able to get a look at that heartbeat today on the ultrasound."

Nicola hadn't even thought about that. She'd be able to see her baby's heart?

Kaleb cleared his throat. "You're going to do the exam, then?"

"Yep. Just the ultrasound part, though. Don't worry." He smiled at Nic. "I take it he knows about us."

"He does. But it doesn't matter. I just want to make sure everything is okay with the baby."

Bill nodded. "Well, then, let's get started."

Nicola unzipped her jeans and parted them, then glanced at Kaleb and was surprised to see his face had taken on a dull red hue that she'd never seen before. At least not on him. Surely he wasn't embarrassed. Not after what they'd done together.

She didn't have much time to think about it as icy lubricant plopped onto the bare skin of her belly. "Yikes, could that be any colder?"

Bill laughed. "Sorry about that."

Dipping the wand of the ultrasound machine in the stuff, he drew the instrument over her stomach. The machine came to life in a series of dark-and-light images that she couldn't make heads or tails of. She thought 3D was supposed to be clearer than the older versions.

"Okay, here we go, so pay attention, Nic."

She stared at the screen, not sure what she was looking at. Then she saw it. A tiny C-shaped object. She could make out a head, a chest...

"There it is. We have a beating heart."

She caught sight of a flickering on the screen and realized that was it. Her baby's heart was pulsing inside of her. "Oh, God."

All of a sudden the cold table and the even colder lubricant were forgotten.

This was real. Very real. Her baby's image was on that screen.

Up until now, the readings on those pregnancy sticks had been some abstract thing that she knew existed, but couldn't see. That couldn't affect her, except for the brief bouts of nausea she'd experienced. But to *see* it. To see that steady flickering light in the object's chest.

"Kaleb..."

"I know. I see it." Something in his voice dragged her attention from the screen, and she caught him leaning forward in his chair, his gaze intent on what was happening on the screen in front of them. It reminded her of how he'd been as he'd operated on baby Trey.

He was invested. Truly invested in this child's life. She wasn't sure it would be as real for him as it was for her when the time came. But it definitely was.

A lump formed in her throat, and she turned her attention back to the monitor. "Is the baby's heart rate normal?"

"A little quick, but stress can do that. Probably feeding off some of his or her mama's energy."

Energy was right. Her nerves were jumping here and there and there was no way she could calm them. Nor did she want to. She wanted to savor this moment, to commit it to memory forever.

Kaleb's voice came through. "How much is 'a little quick'?"

"Only about five beats a minute faster than the norm. It's perfectly okay. If I didn't know better, I'd say you're as nervous as a new fath…" Bill's voice trailed off, and he looked at her, asking a question with his eyes.

He knew. He'd always been intuitive. She gave him a nod.

"Wow, congratulations, then. To both of you." Bill did something with the screen and then pushed some buttons. A paper slid from a slot on the side of the machine. "Just a little something to take home with you. Do you have a name picked out yet?"

"No. I… We haven't even talked about that part yet."

"Well, there's still plenty of time for that," he said.

Kaleb had been oddly silent. "Are you okay?" she asked.

"Just not what I expected to see."

What wasn't? A baby? *His* baby?

She wanted to take his hand and squeeze it. To feel his fingers in hers letting her know everything was going to be okay, but that wasn't appropriate. They weren't a couple, despite what Bill might be thinking. They were just two people who happened to have exchanged some DNA and mixed up a child in the process.

Bill nodded. "It can be overwhelming the first time."

Said as if she and Kaleb were going to have other times. Other babies. But they weren't. This was it. The only baby the two of them would ever make together. And that gave her a funny, queasy sensation that was very different from her light bouts of morning sickness. This had a more permanent feel to it. There was a finality that didn't go down as easy as it should.

After retrieving the piece of paper from the ultrasound machine, Bill handed it to her.

She stared at the first picture of her baby and took in the tiny precious features. And, yes, they were precious. Already. "So he or she does look okay, right?"

"Yes, like I said, so far, so good. We'll keep an eye on that heart rate, just in case, but I suspect it's just a one-off thing. Just take care of yourself. Don't overdo the caffeine and no alcohol. But then you know all of this."

"I do, but thanks. When do I need to come back?"

"Let's see you in a couple of weeks. Hopefully you'll be able to meet Dr. Banks next time."

Kaleb had gone quiet. Lord, she hoped he wasn't regretting coming, or worse, everything that went along with it. Well, if he was, she would make it clear that he could back out at any time. At least up until the baby was born. If he didn't want to do this, he needed to speak up. And soon. Because the last thing she wanted was for her baby to have a dad for three or four years and then have him disappear once he found someone he loved and they started a family of their own.

She swallowed as a shot of reality made its way through her system.

She hadn't thought about what would happen if Kaleb fell in love with someone. But maybe she should. Because the odds were very good that he would, eventually. Kaleb was a gorgeous man that any woman in her right mind would be lucky to have.

Well, any woman except for her. She wasn't in the market for a man, whether it was Kaleb or someone else. She had too much on her plate right now.

They said their goodbyes and made their way out to Kaleb's car. Once he got in, she turned to him. "What's wrong?"

"Nothing."

"Don't give me that, Kaleb. If you want to opt out, just say so, and it will be fine."

He stared out of the windshield for a moment before glancing over at her. "Is my being here with you upsetting you?"

"Upsetting me? What do you mean?"

"The baby's heart rate. Bill said it's higher than it should be, and it made me wonder if it's because I was there with you. He talked about stress and—"

"No. It's not that." She stopped to think about how to put it. His presence had made her nervous, but not in a bad way. It was more of a feeling of guilt for him having to come at all. "Bill also said it was probably nothing. I *was* nervous. I admit it. But more because this was my first appointment, and I was afraid maybe something would be wrong with the baby. What if my brother's illness is somehow bound up in this baby's genetic code? So, yes, there were plenty of things for me to be nervous about. But your being here is not one of them. At least not in the way you're thinking. I just don't want you to feel trapped."

He reached over and gripped her hand for a long second, the way she'd wanted him to in the exam room. "I don't feel trapped. I feel…a sense of awe. I can't believe that baby is something we did together. I mean, what we did was great—more than great, don't get me wrong—but I never dreamed it would result in… A baby. A tiny human being."

"I know. I felt the same way."

"I want to be at your next appointment. And all the rest of them."

She smiled. "Thank you. It helps me to feel like I'm not so alone in all of this."

"You're not alone. And you won't be through any of this."

For the first time since her brother's death, she actually believed those words—believed that maybe this time she wouldn't have to be the one who left.

"My parents want to meet you." The words were said hesitantly, softly, as if they'd been dragged from her.

They were standing outside of the hospital entrance, off to the side, speaking in hushed tones.

"I thought you were going to wait a couple of weeks to tell them."

"I was. But then my mom saw Bill in the grocery store, and he congratulated her on becoming a grandma, without realizing she didn't know. He clammed up immediately when she questioned him on it, but it was too late. The damage was done. So then, I had to field a call—on speakerphone, of all things—from my mom and dad demanding to know why they had to hear about the baby from Bill. Why hadn't I at least called them to tell them personally." She rolled her eyes. "This was so not the way I wanted this to happen."

He could imagine. Because it wasn't the way he'd imagine this would go, either. He hadn't expected them to want to meet him. But, honestly, his parents were going to do the same as soon as they found out. And how could they not? They were going to want to be involved in the baby's life, just like he did. How much easier would it have been if they were a couple?

But they weren't, and pretending to be just for their parents' sake was far beyond the scope of what he was willing to do. Because it would come crashing down around his ears. There was no way around that.

Best just to make the introductions and then just keep things low-key after that. Nicola wouldn't be with him on days he kept the baby. They could just do a pass-off at a supermarket or something. He'd put the baby in his vehicle on his days and hand him or her back when it was Nicola's turn.

And if that seemed complicated and a little cold-blooded, well…it was. But there was no way around it. And it was how it had to be if he wanted to be involved in his child's life.

"I can understand them wanting to meet me. Do they know the situation?"

"They know we're coworkers and that it just…happened. I didn't have the heart to tell my mom I'd gotten pregnant as the result of a one-night stand with a man I met at a bar. And that my grief over Danny precipitated it."

It would be pretty hard to face her dad and look him in the eye, if she had. Somehow that ideal no-commitment ritual he'd built in to his dating habits didn't look quite as appealing as it once had.

Don't spend the night? Ever? It actually seemed pretty selfish looking back at it from where he now stood.

But to try to change now would be to risk falling into another relationship and trying to make it work. Something he wasn't quite willing to do. Not yet, at least.

"So other than surprise, how was their reaction to the news?" He could imagine his parents might be a little disappointed in him. And maybe he was a little disappointed in himself. But even Nicola had said she didn't want marriage. She'd said it before he even had a chance to bring it up.

"It was awkward. And I think they were in shock. But once that wears off, I hope they'll be happy for us. I mean as far as the baby goes."

"Any idea when they want this meeting to take place?"

She rolled her eyes. "They want me to invite you to dinner. Soon." She touched his sleeve. "I'll understand if you don't want to. My parents will just have to understand that while you want to be in their grandchild's life, you don't necessarily want to be in theirs."

He could understand their concern. This was their

grandbaby. They felt protective and wanted to check out the baby's father for themselves. His parents were probably going to want to do the same with her, although he was definitely going to put that off for a while, if he could. Especially since he was still a little worried about stress hormones and Nicola's health, despite her reassurances.

By refusing to go to dinner, would he be opening her up to more stress? Or would he be relieving stress? Maybe that was the question to ask.

"Would my going make it easier or harder on you and your relationship with them?"

"Do you want my honest answer?"

"I really do."

She bit the corner of her lip. His insides immediately took notice. "I think it would relieve some of their worry that you're…say, a sex predator or something. I—" she smiled "—*vouched* for you, like you did for me once upon a time, but I think they want to see it with their own eyes."

It was pretty much what he'd thought. "Well, then I'll go to dinner. How hard could it be?"

"You haven't met my parents." She batted her eyes at him. "So now that we have that out of the way, what are you doing tonight? Inquiring moms want to know."

"Tonight? You said soon, but wow." He laughed. "She's not letting any grass grow under her feet—or mine—is she?"

"My mom is pretty much always ready for company. She keeps a freezer full of entrées that she's cooked ahead of time, so it's just a matter of pulling one out and whipping up a salad to go with it."

His eyebrows went up. "I think I see where you get your organizational skills."

"If you think I'm organized… My mom is over the top. But you'll like her. You'll like them both. They're not going to grill you or make snap judgments. They just want to meet you. No pressure, okay?"

"I'll take your word for it. So what time does she want us there? I'm off at six."

"I'm off early, so I can meet you at their house." She pulled a slip of paper from her purse and scribbled something on it. "This is their address. And, like I said, don't worry. It will be a snap."

It wasn't a snap. From the moment he put their address into his GPS and started heading for the Bradley household, his nerves were pretty much toast. She might think they'd be nonjudgmental, but when he looked at it from the standpoint of his own upbringing, he was pretty sure his parents would be asking him some hard questions. Not about the pregnancy, since those things happen, but over the fact that he'd slept with her with no intention of ever seeing her again.

Hadn't Nicola said she left out that part of her explanation to her parents. So it wasn't just his mom and dad who'd look askance at that. Of course, his parents had been disappointed over his two broken engagements, too. Especially since his sister was, by all accounts, very happy in her marriage. Her second child was due in about a month.

How did they do it? How did his parents, his sister, make that kind of commitment?

Maybe the same way he was making a commitment to be there for his child. No matter what happened. The thought rolled around in his head for a while looking for someplace to lodge.

He crossed the Jersey line at about six thirty. They didn't live very far from the place where Nicola and her brother used to work, so he had five or six more minutes before he arrived. Dinner was planned for six forty-five, so he should be right on time.

Grace Central was on his right-hand side. Was Nicola's ex working tonight? He wondered what her parents had thought of him. The man was like a saint compared to Kaleb.

And he really needed to stop thinking about this or he was going to take the next exit out of town.

Commitment, remember? It's not always going to be easy.

Another two minutes and he was on their street looking for the house number. He saw a brick two-story structure with two rocking chairs on the porch. Red pillows were propped perfectly on each one. He pulled into their driveway and turned off the car.

As soon as he did, the door burst open and a woman stood there, her dark red locks almost the exact same shade as Nicola's. Speaking of Nicola, he didn't see her car here. Hopefully she was inside.

He climbed out of his vehicle and started up the walk, carrying a box containing her parents' favorite wine, according to Nicola.

"Hello. You must be Kaleb. I'm Margaret. Dan is cooking steaks on the grill." She pulled him into a quick embrace, then let him go.

Dan. Nicola's brother must have been named after his father. That had to make things even harder. Something else she said caught at his attention. Didn't Nicola say her mom would just pull a premade meal out of the freezer and heat it up? "You didn't have to go to any trouble."

"No trouble, of course. And a good excuse for Dan to use his grill."

"I brought some wine."

"Why, thank you. Come on in."

She stepped aside to let him in to the house. Walking across the threshold, the scent of freshly baked bread tickled his nostrils. "Is Nicola here yet?"

"She's helping her dad, so yes. She's around back. Her car is parked in the garage."

That's why he hadn't seen it.

Following Margaret as she led the way through a living area that had an airy and open feel, he glanced around at the interior. Unlike Nicola, they evidently didn't have a problem with having their son's pictures displayed on the walls, since there were family portraits in several different places. Danny and Nicola looked a lot alike. If he didn't know better, he'd think they were twins. Continuing to follow Margaret's lead, they arrived in the kitchen. It was large and sprawling without losing that inviting feel that the rest of the house had. "It smells wonderful in here."

"Thank you." She glanced over at him. "So you work with Nicola?"

He hadn't expected the question, and it took him a minute to shift gears and think of a suitable reply. "We don't always work directly together, but we do work at the same hospital, yes." He decided to explain further, and added, "I've consulted with her on a case or two. She's very good at what she does."

"She is thorough. Always has been."

Margaret pulled the wine from the box and stooped to put it in a wine cooler under the cabinet. "Let's join the others outside."

Actually, Kaleb was glad to oblige, since if any questions got awkward, he'd have an excuse for sweating. When he went through the sliding glass door, however, he saw that her idea of outside and his were two different things. While they were technically out on a patio, they were under a covered pergola, where a lazy ceiling fan spun in circles. Sweeping layers of mosquito netting were artfully gathered around the supporting poles and tied with white ribbon. The grill was no metal prefab deal, either, but had been constructed from bricks that matched the ones on the house. It was vented through a chimney that went through the top of the pergola.

Nicola came over and nudged his arm. "Everything okay?"

"Yep, just fine."

"No trouble finding it?"

"Nope."

"Good."

The rapid questions made it hard to gauge her mood. But she didn't seem nervous or irritated.

She smiled at her mom. "It looks like you two introduced yourselves."

"We did," Margaret said. "Why don't you take Kaleb over to meet your dad, while I get the bread out of the oven."

"Okay."

He leaned closer to her ear. "I thought you said dinner would be something simple."

"I thought it would be. It's the way she normally does things. I guess they decided to go all out today. Sorry." She went around to the side of the grill. "Daddy, I want you to meet Kaleb Sabat. Kaleb, this is my father, Dan."

Dan laid his tongs across the grill's grate and reached out to shake his hand. "Nice to meet you, Kaleb. We're hearing a lot about you."

Was there a *finally* implied in that phrase?

"You as well, sir."

"You're just in time, because I think these are about done." He forked up thick steaks and laid them on a platter. "Not sure if you're a medium guy or a well-done guy, but medium will be on the left and well is on the right."

Right about now, Kaleb was feeling pretty well-done, and dinner—and the questions—hadn't even started yet.

Dan set the food on the table in the middle of the patio and hit a switch on the wall. Tiny white lights flickered to life all around the space.

"Is there anything I can help with?" Kaleb said.

"Nope, you're our guest. And I think we're about ready. I told Nic not to let you come too early, for that very reason."

Soon plates of food were being passed around amid the conversation that was as light and easy as the fan overhead. Most of it revolved around Dan's position as an architect at a prestigious firm. It explained why their home was so fastidiously designed.

If he ever had a family, maybe Dan could...

Scratch that. There was no way he was going to ask Nicola's father to design a house that he lived in with someone other than his daughter.

Except the person he'd just pictured in front of this imaginary house had been Nicola, standing outside in bare feet with a white straw hat on her head and a flowing white dress. She was cradling the swell of a baby bump and smiling.

At him.

"Kaleb?"

He glanced up and realized everyone was looking at him. "Sorry. Did I miss something?"

Margaret smiled. "No. I was just congratulating you and Nic on your upcoming arrival."

"Thank you. It was a surprise, but a good one."

And it *was* a good one. Once the shock had worn off, he realized he was happy—in a way that felt strange and yet very right. Things were changing, and surprisingly it wasn't the disaster he'd imagined when Nic first told him about the baby.

"I guess so. Nic said she was going to wait a little longer to tell us, but a mutual friend spilled the beans."

Mutual friend. That was one way to put it. Were they unhappy that Nicola's ex wasn't the one who'd fathered her child?

He decided to let them know that he wasn't going to abandon her. "Her first prenatal exam went well. The baby had a slightly elevated heart rate..." When he glanced at Nic, she was staring at him in a way that... Okay, so he evidently wasn't supposed to have told them that. He tried to fix it. "Bill said it wasn't far out of the normal range, though. And probably due to excitement."

Or stress.

"*Bill* did her exam?" Dan chimed in this time, and lo and behold, Nicola was giving him that look again. One he had no problem reading. He'd intercepted the same kind of looks between his parents and realized they had a secret language where no words were needed.

Was that what they were doing?

"My obstetrician was doing an emergency C-section, Dad. She couldn't be there."

"How's he doing? Bill, I mean?"

Margaret spoke up. "Dan..." Her voice held a warning note.

"He's fine. We don't really talk very much anymore, for obvious reasons."

Dan evidently liked Bill. Maybe his earlier thought about them wishing Dan had fathered this child wasn't so far from the truth after all.

Kaleb cut into his steak, and as he did felt pressure

against his thigh. He glanced over at Nicola and realized she'd put her leg against his. This time not to chastise him, but to reassure him. And it did.

"So, Kaleb and I were in Central Park a little while ago and actually had to help a boy who'd gotten hurt on a hoverboard."

"Oh, wow," Margaret said. "Is he going to be okay?"

"He is, but he fell pretty hard."

"Good thing you were there." She smiled. "Nic said you're going to be involved with the baby's life. That makes us so happy."

The quick change in subject threw him for a minute, but Margaret's voice rang with a sincerity that washed away the discomfort he'd been feeling over being here.

"I wouldn't have it any other way."

"Well—" she reached out and took her husband's hand "we want you to know that you're welcome in our home anytime. Nic speaks very highly of you."

"She told me she'd vouched for me." He sent Nicola a smile that carried hidden meaning. Her leg pressed against his again, letting him know that she'd gotten it.

He liked it. This secret communication that went on between two people. He'd never done this with either of his exes or with anyone else he'd dated.

The mood was warm and festive, and Nicola's parents helped carry most of the conversation, which took the burden off of Kaleb and Nic. He could just sit back and enjoy the evening, which was a far cry from how he'd expected this night to go. He glanced over and caught Nicola laughing at something her dad had said about a client who wanted a house shaped like the international space station. "You're kidding!"

"Nope. I told him that was beyond my skill set and referred him to my least favorite competitor."

They all laughed.

Nic's eyes met his and an urge to take her hand came over him. He made a fist in his lap to keep from acting on the impulse. He'd told her the truth in his office. She was beautiful. And it wasn't just on the outside. The woman's beauty went clear down to her bones. What he'd once thought abrasive, he now realized was passion. A passion for her patients. A passion for finding out the truth.

"What?" she asked.

He realized he'd been staring at her. "Nothing."

Dan and Margaret shared a look, Dan giving her a quick wink. He wasn't sure what that was about, but the warmth in his chest spread. These two were going to make wonderful grandparents. Their love for each other was plain to see even after all these years. Much like his own parents. They seemed to be in the minority nowadays, which was one of the reasons he'd discounted marriage for so long. After striking out twice, he just assumed he didn't have it in him to stick around for the long haul, since he was the one who'd broken off both of those engagements.

But Nicola was different. She was who she seemed. No hints of subterfuge in her manner. And he'd looked for it. Expected to find it. And was dumbfounded when it wasn't there.

When she said something, he could trust that she

meant it. Even the way she dealt with patients was honest. She didn't make fun of them behind their backs or show impatience. Instead, she listened. Really listened.

Just like she'd done with him.

Maybe Snowden was wrong. Hell, maybe Kaleb himself was wrong. Maybe relationships *could* weather the hard times. His own parents and Nicola's had.

They'd just needed the right partner in life.

Could it be done? Well, looking at Nicola, he wondered. Her last relationship hadn't lasted, but he'd watched her treat Bill with respect, and he'd responded in kind. He smiled. His last ex had stolen half of his furniture and made no apologies for it. And he'd been okay with it, because it meant she had cleared out of there. And the one before that? Well, her wish of having a baby had come true. A few months after they broke up. Only it hadn't been with him.

And here he was about to father a child with someone else. But he was more settled now than he'd been back then. He'd thought maybe he wasn't cut out to be a father or a husband, and yet seeing that heart beating on the ultrasound had made him realize he did. The timing just had to be right.

And the woman?

While her parents continued to talk, he used Nicola's tactic and nudged her leg with his. She smiled at him, a tiny dimple appearing at the corner of her mouth. Making her smile was a heady thing. He nudged again.

She responded back, this time using more of her upper thigh. It brushed along his, awakening nerve endings that weren't in his chest, this time.

Secret communications. Oh, yes. He liked them.

He then pressed his whole leg against hers, his foot hooking around her ankle and exerting slow pressure, until her legs parted slightly. Then he smiled at her. A smile that carried a completely different meaning from his earlier ones.

The tip of her tongue came out to moisten her lips. Then she blinked and sat upright. "I think I just heard my phone ping. I'll be right back." Pulling free, she pushed her chair away from the table and headed for the other side of the patio, where her purse was.

Hell, he guessed he'd gone too far. Of course he had. They were at her parents' house, for God's sake, and here he was trying to seduce her right there at their dinner table.

Nicola pulled out her phone and glanced at the screen. "Oh, no, Kaleb. We need to go. There's been an emergency."

That was weird. He couldn't remember being texted about a hospital emergency before. It normally came in the form of phone call.

So maybe she hadn't been trying to get away from him after all. Maybe something really was wrong at the hospital.

"Okay." He glanced at her parents. "I'm sorry to leave like this."

"It's fine. Go ahead," Dan said. "I hope you can come back again. Before the baby arrives."

He smiled. "You can count on it."

And he meant it. The evening had been entirely different than he'd imagined it.

He waited while Nicola got her stuff together, and they headed out the door.

"What's the emergency? Did they say?"

"Who's they?"

He blinked at her. "Whoever texted you."

"I didn't actually say the *text* said there was an emergency. That was spam. I get it all the time."

"What? I don't understand. What's the emergency, then?" Had she not wanted him to stay?

"The emergency was that your leg tugging on mine was starting to elicit some dangerous reactions. Those reactions were soon going to make themselves painfully known. And I don't think my parents would have appreciated me slamming you down on the table next to the bread basket and having my way with you."

Relief poured over him. "So I'm not the only one it was affecting." What had started out as something playful had taken on a life of its own. He'd heated himself up, but he hadn't been sure about her. "So what are we going to do about this so-called emergency?"

"We're going to figure out whose place is closer, and we're going to put out a fire."

He leaned over to kiss her, right there in the front yard of Nicola's childhood home. "What if I want to start a few more fires, before I put any out?"

"I know of at least one fire that is already burning. And there's only one thing that can put it out. And that's you."

CHAPTER TEN

KALEB'S HOUSE WAS CLOSER. As soon as they got through the front door, her mouth was on his, her hands grabbing at the sides of his shirt as he walked her backward. "I don't know where we're going."

"Do you need to know? I just want to enjoy the journey."

"Mmm. That sounds good."

So she let him kiss and touch and caress her as they inched their way through his home. She didn't have time to look at anything. Didn't need to look at anything. All she wanted was his hands on her.

Through a door they went and the next thing she knew, her legs were against the mattress of an unmade bed. She swallowed. He'd slept there last night, his body pressing deep into this mattress the way she wanted him to press into her. Her mouth went dry.

She was never going to forget this night.

His arms slid up her back, and he pressed her against him. "Do you trust me, Nic?"

A frisson of excitement went through her. "Yes."

His lips curved, a slow, knowing smile that touched

parts of her that were already aching with need. He turned her around until she faced the bed, fitting himself against her back, that long hard part of him pushing into the softness of her behind.

She shuddered. Everything about him was a study in sensuality. He knew how to use his voice, his hands, his body, to make her writhe with need. And each time had been different. The first time, boozy and free. The second time, naughty and rushed. And this third time... Oh, God, she had a feeling he was going to take her places she'd never gone before. Things between them were changing. And he seemed okay with it. Willing to sit in the driver's seat, even.

His palms slid down her arms, until one hand reached her breasts. He cupped one, while his other hand trailed down her stomach, holding her in place while he pushed rhythmically against her. His lips were next to her ear. "Can you spend the night?"

What? How was he even forming complete sentences? Her brain was mush.

Somehow, she replied, "Yes."

"Good." He nipped her earlobe. "Because once isn't going to be enough. Not nearly enough."

The hand at her stomach slid lower, curving over her mons and exploring what he found there. Continuing to hold her against him, he released himself and guided his engorged flesh between her legs. "Close them."

Excitement bloomed when she realized what he was going to do. She squeezed her thighs together, his groan rumbling against her ear as he thrust, pleasuring himself and her, while she bit her lip until it hurt.

All too soon, he slid free.

"No…"

"Shh, I'm not done, honey. Not by a long shot."

He pulled her shirt up over her head, hands going back around to squeeze her breasts, before finding the front clasp of her bra and releasing it. He then slid the straps down her arms and let the garment fall to the floor.

When he cupped her again, her breath exited in a hiss. They were so sensitive—the nipples seeking out his palms and the decadent friction they could give.

"I love that you like this, Nic. So soft. I could touch you for hours. But first…"

He pulled back again and unbuttoned her trousers, sliding the zip and then pushing them and her undergarment down her legs. Behind her, she could hear his own clothing rustle as he discarded it.

Then he was still for a minute. But only a minute.

His hands went to hers, pulling them forward, even as he used the weight of his body to bend her torso toward the bed. She shivered, realizing what he was going to do. He pressed her hands into the mattress.

"But I want to touch you," she said.

"Next time. I promise."

His words wrapped around something inside of her and made it sing.

His fingertips skated across her shoulders, skimmed down her spine, smoothed over the curve of her backside. He pressed his lips into the middle of her back. "Spread your legs for me."

Her breath caught as she slowly walked her feet

apart, the cool air in his apartment flowing over her in an intimate caress that made her moan. Then his hands were on her hips, holding her still for what she knew was coming. For what she needed to come.

He was at her entrance, slowly pushing inside, stretching her in a way that was too delicious for words. He went deep, straining into her. Like her nipples, everything he touched was unbelievably sensitive. It was like her whole body's nerve endings were tuned in to his every move…each awaiting their turn to be stroked.

He eased back and drove forward again, going just as deep, holding tight against her. She tried to increase the pace, her need rising up, but he held her still, shushing her when she made to protest. "It's okay. I need to feel you. All of you."

He wasn't touching her anywhere else, but she didn't need it. Her whole being was focused like a laser beam on that single point of contact. His movements stayed slow and deliberate. She would say lazy, except he seemed to be keeping a razor-edged level of control, pushing his limits—and hers—to the very brink.

Then his hand came around and touched her. Just a light flick. Then another, all as he held still inside of her. There were no boundaries between them. There was no need for them anymore, since she was pregnant. She felt the smooth pull, like a rubber band being stretched, further and further, waiting to be set free.

His finger tapped and released, tapped and released.

She wanted him to move inside of her. Wanted him to thrust hard and fast. But he was so very still, his breath coming in gusts against her neck, making her skin prickle.

What had been a light tap got heavier with need. The silence in the room added another layer of expectancy to what was already happening inside of her. She wanted to moan, to scream, but didn't want to break up what was happening. She realized what he was doing. He was setting a scene, readying it for the inevitable climax. Her body's nerve endings had shut down everything in her body except for one tiny set, which was shuddering a little closer with every tap.

Tap…pause. Tap…pause. Tap…pause.

She could feel herself shifting to another plane, her nipples tightening, belly tensing.

The tapping stopped. No. No! *No!* She hung there for a second, then felt the wave beginning to flicker in preparation for receding from the edge. She clawed to stay there, didn't want to leave this place. Not ever.

Then without warning, his thumb and forefinger gripped her, squeezing in quick pulsing motions that rushed her with lightning speed back toward her goal. And then she was flying over it, Kaleb's arm wrapping around her midsection to hold her in place, when she tried to pump. He kept her there, her mind bending as wave after wave of pleasure tore through her. Still motionless, Kaleb suddenly groaned against her ear and she realized he was climaxing without even needing to move.

I want to feel you.

God. Literally that's what he'd done.

He kissed her neck. Nipped her shoulder. Traced

her upper back with his tongue. He took a deep breath and then let it blow out. "Thank you."

He was thanking *her*? He was the one who'd done all the work.

"I don't know what you just did to me. But I don't think I'm ever going to recover."

He suddenly tipped her face to look at her. "Are you okay?"

Oh! He thought he'd hurt her. "No. I meant, I have never experienced anything like that in my life. It was…" She chuckled. "There are no words."

"Mmm. Same here." He kissed her lips, then pulled free. "But we have a lot more fires to deal with before the night is over."

He was right. It was just after midnight, and every fiber of her being was satiated. She was bone-jarringly tired. And happy. And…all kinds of other things.

Kaleb leaned back against the pillows, his hands behind his head.

The other two times she'd been with him, things had been rushed and hurried. She'd never gotten to see the "aftermath Kaleb." As she studied him, she liked what she saw. Wouldn't mind seeing a whole lot more of this side of him in the future.

But was that what he wanted? She wasn't sure.

She turned onto her side and propped herself on her elbow to get a better look. "I vote we don't tell my parents why we needed to leave their house so quickly tonight."

"I think your dad might hunt me down and throw

my carcass on his grill. Medium on the left, well-done on the right."

She laughed. "Are you worried?"

"It depends on whether you'll vouch for me if and when he does."

"Always."

As soon as she said the word, Kaleb rolled over, taking her with him. His forearms bracketing her face, he ran his fingertips over her cheeks and slid down to her lips. "Always?"

"Yes." There was something about the way he said that word that made her shiver.

He kissed her. A long slow kiss that seemed to go on forever. Despite how tired she was, her body flickered back to life.

"I think your parents would like to see us married."

"Mmm…probably. But they'll get used to it the way it is."

"Maybe we should."

His statement came out of nowhere, shocking her. "Should what?"

"Get married?"

"Are you serious? Why?"

There'd been nothing to ever suggest he wanted to get married. In fact, they'd both been pretty adamant that they didn't.

"Why not? It would make everything so much easier."

"What things? You mean the baby?"

"The baby. The situation with your parents. With my parents. Our coworkers. It would take care of all the awkward explanations. People have married for worse reasons."

Her eyes widened. Maybe "they" did, but she didn't. And the fact that he was willing to uproot his life—change everything—just to make those "awkward explanations" easier to handle was horrifying. Unimaginable.

For one thing, her parents would see through the ruse in no time. Pretending to not know him was one thing. But to pretend they loved each other in public, while in private they both knew it was a lie, that in reality... God!

And he was okay with that?

Well, she wasn't. Wasn't willing to put their baby through the eventual meltdown that was bound to happen over time, when Kaleb realized he couldn't keep up the charade anymore. When he eventually walked out on them...

The fear she'd had right after she realized she was pregnant came back to haunt her. That thought that he might want to marry her just for the sake of the baby. Back then she'd blurted out that she had no intention of getting married. He'd agreed with her at the time. And yet here he was, knocking on her door and saying the complete opposite.

There were worse reasons, he'd said.

Except she couldn't imagine anything worse than what he'd just offered her. A marriage of convenience. Of necessity, to avoid awkwardness.

She closed her eyes. She'd always thought if she eventually married, it would be the real deal. It would be because someone loved her. That they couldn't imagine life without her. But Kaleb felt none of those things.

Even Bill had loved her for…her.

In his office, she thought of how sexy Kaleb was, how he could end up being a real heartbreaker, but that he hadn't broken her heart.

She was wrong. Because he just had. She recoiled away as a terrible realization swept over her, swamping her and pressing her flat. "Absolutely not."

"Why? Give me one good reason why it wouldn't make life easier for both of us. For the baby."

Why? Because as she'd been lying here staring up at him, the truth had dawned on her. A truth so tragic that it made what he'd just said to her feel obscene.

Somewhere during the ten weeks they'd known each other, an astounding thing had been growing inside of her. Something that had nothing to do with the baby.

And everything to do with love.

She loved him.

She wasn't sure exactly when or where it had happened, but it had.

He was right. Marrying her would make everything easier. Would make everyone happier.

Everyone except for…her.

Oh, no—*please*, no.

And explaining to him her reasons for turning him down was not an option. She couldn't do it. And she definitely couldn't stay while he continued to list all the reasons why she should say yes.

Because she couldn't. Couldn't say yes.

Not now. Not ever.

Those two phrases repeated over and over in her head until she thought she might vomit.

"I… I'll, um… I'll let you know." She would. But not right now. Not when the burning behind her eyes was about a minute away from turning into a very real flood.

Right now, all she wanted or needed was to escape. To get away before he realized she'd just become the biggest fool on the face of the planet: a woman who'd fallen for a man who only wanted to marry her to make things easy.

Well, it wouldn't. They would make her life hell on earth. Because he was bound to find out the truth, and when he did…

She pushed him off of her and sat up, dragging the sheet around her. "I need to get going. I have an early shift and Danvers wants to run another case by me."

Kaleb frowned, then levered himself up, too. "Are you okay?"

The question almost broke her in two. It was the exact question he'd asked her after they made love tonight. And her answer now was the polar opposite of what it had been then.

"I'm fine. I—I had a good time tonight, thank you. And thanks for coming to my parents' for dinner. See you tomorrow?" No, he wouldn't, but she was not going to let him know about the plan that had just crystalized in her head—a plan that was based solely on a survival instinct she didn't realize she had. Emotional survival rather than physical.

"Do you want me to drive you home?"

"No, my car is here. It'll be easier in the morning if it's at my house."

She hopped out of bed and started dragging on her clothes, trying not to make it look like she was hurrying, but with the way her hands were shaking, it was hard. She threw him a smile just to make sure he didn't follow her outside. "We'll sort out appointments and so forth sometime next week."

"Okay." He got out of bed and caught her wrist. "Are you sure you're okay, Nic?"

"Yes. Just exhausted." She gave a short laugh. "You wore me out."

The correct phrase would have been that she was emotionally wrung out, but that might have made him ask more questions.

"Stay the night, then. You said you would."

"No." She casually lifted her hand to her head to force him to release his grip. She then dragged her fingers through her hair as if straightening it, when really, she didn't care how she looked. "I don't have a change of clothes here, and it'll be so much easier to just…" Too late, she realized she'd parroted his earlier words back to him. It wouldn't be easier. Nothing would be easier for a long, long time.

She could figure everything with the baby out later, but right now, she just needed to get out.

"Okay. Call me to let me know you made it home."

No way was she doing that. "I'll let you know." She'd send him a one-word text, and that was it.

She grabbed her handbag and headed for the front

door, just hoping she could make it to her car and onto the street before she broke down.

And then tomorrow, once she'd composed herself, she was going to put her plan into action. Before anyone—especially Kaleb—realized what was happening.

CHAPTER ELEVEN

ALL HE HAD was a text. One saying that while he could be in the baby's life, Nicola didn't want to marry him. Didn't even want them to continue seeing each other. He'd tried calling her and texting her back, but he'd gotten no response.

And coming out of Harvey Smith's office two days later, he felt shell-shocked. She was gone. Back to her old hospital without saying a word to him as to why.

According to Harvey, she wanted to try to work at both hospitals, consulting at NYC Memorial only when there was a specific case that needed her input. And most of those consultations would happen via a telemedicine link. She wouldn't even need to physically come to the hospital.

The administrator had been fine with that, telling her if she changed her mind or if her caseload got to be too heavy to let him know, and they'd put her back on NYC Memorial's schedule.

What on earth had brought this on? They'd had a sexy evening that she'd been totally into, after leaving her parents' house. Hell, it had been her idea to go back to his place and make love.

She'd been absolutely fine.

Until he mentioned marriage. And then she was up and out of there in a flash. It was almost like she'd been expecting him to ask and was already poised to turn him down. Which she had. In no uncertain terms. Except at the very end, she'd said she would think about it. He guessed she had. And her answer was still no.

His thought after she'd left his apartment was "well, at least she didn't take my furniture." But it had been in a funny sense. He hadn't seriously thought she was walking out of his life for good. Her text had said he could be part of his baby's life, but she hadn't said exactly what that would look like.

His question of marriage had been half joking, but if she'd said yes, he would have gone through with it. He really had thought maybe they could make a go of it.

The one thing missing had been love. But he'd gone the love route twice before and had flamed out. This time, he'd thought if he could go into it with more thought and build it on something other than fickle emotion, it might work. He cared about her. And he'd been pretty sure—until that text—that she might care about him, as well.

Well, hell. Maybe she'd just saved him from one more failed relationship. He should thank Snowden for suggesting they make that toast.

He'd give Nicola a week or so and then try to approach her about the part he was going to play in his child's life. She didn't want to get married? Fine. But he hadn't changed his mind about wanting to be a father in a very real sense of the word.

Okay, he'd give it a week. And then he'd try to call again, and if that failed, he was going to march over to Grace Central and have it out with her in person. If she didn't have him thrown off the property the way she'd thrown him out of her life.

Snow met him at the bar. Their bar. His and Nicola's, where it had all begun. She still hadn't answered his calls, and now he had a decision to make. Over a drink, he told his old friend what had transpired in clinical terms, letting him know that he was going to be a father.

"I knew something was up. I just didn't know what. For supposedly just having met her when Harvey introduced you, you two seemed to know each other a little more than I would have expected. But I had no idea, she was already pregnant."

"I didn't know, either. At least not then. She took a pregnancy test a week or so after you saw us, and it came back positive."

"So if she agreed that you could be a part of the baby's life, and you met her parents, what happened?"

"I don't know. I said her parents probably wanted us to get married and suggested that maybe it wasn't such a bad idea. She took off like a bat out of hell."

"You did what?"

"Yeah. I didn't realize I was that bad of a catch."

"Exactly what reason did you give her for wanting to get married?"

Kaleb took a drink of his beer, wiping the foam from his mouth with the back of his hand. "I said it would make everything easier."

"Easier." Snow laughed. "Man, no wonder you were willing to make that toast. You wouldn't know how to catch a girl if she was placed on your hook."

"I caught two of them just fine, thank you very much. They just weren't what I was looking for."

Snow smiled and leaned forward, thumping his un-touched whiskey glass on the bar. "And just what were you looking for, Kaleb? Something that would make everything easier?"

"No, of course not. I was looking for lov…" He swallowed. Damn. No wonder she'd taken off. No wonder she'd sent him a text that had basically said thanks, but no thanks.

"Right. And don't you think this girl—Nicola—might have been looking for the same thing? Not a man who thought marrying her would make every-thing easier. For him."

"Hell. I thought I was playing it smart this time. Thinking it through without letting my heart or my—" his eyes fell to his lap before coming back up "—lead me around."

"And that, my friend, is the biggest mistake of them all. Not that I'm looking for love anytime soon. Whether or not you choose to, I'm sticking to my vow." He pushed his glass around the polished surface of the bar. "I only have one question."

"What's that?"

"If you married this girl, would you be marrying her for love? Or for the convenience of it?"

Kaleb frowned. "I'm not sure I under—" Suddenly he got it. Realized how far off base he'd been in asking her that question. How insulting it had probably sounded. And it had been a lie. Marrying her wouldn't make things easier.

His throat closed up as he ran through all the things he and Nic had shared in such a short period of time: Collaborated at work. Laughed over drinks. Stood over a baby's bed as he recovered from surgery. Made love like there was no tomorrow.

And he realized his answer to Snow's question was yes. He would have been marrying Nicola for all the right reasons. He just hadn't understood it at the time.

He loved the woman.

"Yeah. You're right. And I'm a damn fool."

"Then forget about our toast and go find the woman and tell her you're not marrying her to make your life easier. In fact, it's about to get a hell of a lot harder. But whatever you do, don't leave out *why* you want to marry her. If that doesn't change things, call me, and we'll go out and get roaring drunk. But if it does…then don't call me until you set a date."

He clapped Kaleb on the back. "Good luck, old friend."

"Thanks. Thanks for everything. Including that toast. Because it led me right to where I needed to be." And with that, Kaleb climbed off his barstool and headed for the door. He knew exactly what he needed to do.

CHAPTER TWELVE

NICOLA STARED AT her computer screen without really seeing it. So far she'd only been over to NYC Memorial two times in the last three weeks. And both of those times, she'd snuck in and out by doors she didn't usually use. It felt stupid, but seeing Kaleb under these circumstances would be unbearable.

She hadn't been able to believe he'd asked to marry her because of the baby. Because of their parents.

To be fair, she hadn't asked him if he loved her. But they say if you have to ask…

Who are "they"? And what kind of data are "they" using to come to that conclusion?

Conclusion.

How did someone come to a conclusion?

Well, she knew how *she* normally did. And it wasn't by sitting around and moping and wishing things were different.

So why not do what she was good at? What she'd trained herself to do?

Taking out her sketchbook, she opened it to the first blank page. Then she got to work, drawing her boxes and meticulously labeling each of them. Then using the data from things she knew to be true, she began to draw her lines. Phrases that were said. Experiences that were had. Each thing made her line slide to one of two possible conclusions at the bottom of her page.

She touched her belly when it growled. Someone was getting hungry. "I know, sweetie. But there's just something I have to do first."

Tapping her pen on her chin, she went day by day, remembering little things. It wouldn't be an exact diagnosis because there was no blood test known to man that could measure what she was looking for. No MRI that could find and pinpoint the truth. This would be purely circumstantial evidence that wouldn't hold up in any court of law. But it would be enough to draw an inference from.

Two more lines trailed down to their spots on the chart. Three more. Ten. And an hour later, when she was done, she tallied them up and wrote her conclusion—a single word—at the very bottom of her page and underlined it three times.

Then she closed her sketchbook and held it tight to her chest, fear and hope warring with each other. Until one of them won out. She climbed to her feet in her little work area and tidied up her desk…straightened her chair. If she was right, this would be the last time she would sit here.

And if she was wrong?

Well, she wasn't handing in her notice—again—quite yet.

Turning around so that she could walk to the exit,

she staggered to a stop when she spotted someone striding toward her. A phantom who had haunted her days and nights ever since she'd walked out of his house. The person she'd been getting ready to go see.

"Kaleb?"

He'd called her repeatedly, but she hadn't been able to bring herself to answer. Not until this very moment.

He approached her. "Hey."

"Hey."

"I've been trying to reach you."

"I know."

God, why did they have to go through all of this stupid small talk in order to get to what was really important. What would make or break the next seven months of her pregnancy.

He took a step closer, seeming encouraged when she didn't walk away from him. "Is there somewhere we can go to talk?"

"Yes. Let's go to the courtyard out back." Leading the way to an area that was more of a paved outdoor faculty lounge than a garden, she found a table at the farthest side of the small space, and laid her sketchbook on top of the melamine surface.

"Nic. I owe you an apology. A big one."

"You do?"

He nodded, starting to reach for her hand before evidently thinking better of it. "I never should have asked you to marry me the last night we were together."

Shock went through her system. And horror. Maybe she'd been wrong. Maybe she should tear that page out of her book and put it through the shredder before he or anyone else saw it. "You shouldn't have?"

"No. Not until I understood what was really driving the question."

She pulled air into her lungs in rhythmic intervals so she wouldn't pass out. "And you think you understand it now?"

"I know I do. And I hope you'll hear me out." This time, he did take her hand, lacing his fingers through hers. "I love you, Nic. The way I've never loved anyone before."

She blinked. Tried to process what he'd just said.

"But you said… You told me you wanted to marry me for all that other stuff. Stuff that has nothing to do with love."

"I know." He let out a sigh. "I'd been down that road—meaning love—a couple of times before, and it always ended disastrously. I thought if I could just be analytical about it this time and give it a name *other* than love, then maybe it would work. Because I desperately wanted it to work, Nic. I still do."

"You do?" Shock turned to laughter, the sound pealing forth until tears streamed down her face, even as he tried to scoot his chair around to console her. She shook him off with a hiccup. "Oh, God, Kaleb. Do you want to see what name I came up with when I tried to be all analytical about it?"

"I'm not sure at this point."

She riffled through her sketchbook until she came up with the right graph and flipped it open so he could see. "Look."

Watching as he worked his way across the page, slowly moving down and reading the words, box by box. Finally, when he'd studied it for what seemed like hours, his fingers traced the lines down to their final resting places and the underlined conclusion.

"Love." His gaze came up and speared her. "You love me?"

"I didn't do the graph to figure out how *I* felt. Read the name at the top."

He looked at where she pointed. "It's my name."

"Yes. I already knew what my feelings were, but I didn't know about you. And your marriage question that night wandered around so much, that it made me wonder if the word you were so afraid of using lay smack-dab in the center." She squeezed his hand. "I was right. Wasn't I?"

"You were. Hell. I can't believe I put both of us through that. But I thought if I said the word *love*, I might jinx it, just like I did those other times."

"You didn't jinx it. Those other times just weren't meant to be. But I think we are. I think what you sensed about my parents was right, as well. They saw it before even we did."

He leaned his cheek against hers, breathing deeply. "Don't throw that page away, Nicola. I want to keep it. Frame it. I want it on the wall in our bedroom so that through the bad times and the good, we'll see those lines leading from where we were to the spot we both want to be." He tapped the word she'd written in the box at the bottom. "Love. That's where I want to stay. With you. Forever."

She cupped his face and looked into his eyes. "I do, too, Kaleb. I never want to step outside of that box. But if either of us does, all we need to do is follow those lines, until they lead us back to this place. Back to where we belong. Those lines will lead us all the way home."

* * * * *

THE TROUBLE WITH
THE TEMPTING DOC

TINA BECKETT

MILLS & BOON

PROLOGUE

SNOWDEN TANGREDI STOOD at the front of the church and adjusted his bow tie. It didn't work. It still felt tight—constrictive—and made him aware of the pulse that pounded in his neck. In his head. In his chest.

The front of a church was definitely not a place he ever saw himself standing again. But at least this time the officiant wasn't there for him. No, the victim this time was his best friend, Kaleb Sabat.

Then again, Kaleb said he'd never walk this path, either. In fact, they'd made a boozy pact to that effect almost a year ago. And yet here Kaleb was, waiting on his bride-to-be.

Some people might have said Kaleb had no choice—that having a baby had put the stamp of fatherhood on his head—but Snow knew his buddy well enough to know that he didn't do anything unless he wanted to. He was one of the most stubborn men Snow knew. But he was also one of the most upright and honest. And loyal to a fault.

His friend glanced his way and gave a half grin that said everything. Their pact to remain bachelors for life was about to be ripped to shreds. And while there was a rueful element to Kaleb's look, there was not an ounce of regret accompanying it. The man was head over heels for Nicola and his new baby girl. And Nicola seemed to love him just as fiercely.

But for how long? How long before reality set in and the newness wore off?

Snow's one jaunt down an aisle very much like this one had been full of the same air of expectation and hope. And healing. Or so he thought. If only he'd known then what he knew now. That the healing he'd hoped for had never materialized. Instead, a gnawing fear had crouched in the background, waiting for him to become the slightest bit irritated or angry. Then it came out to play, claws unsheathed. He soon realized he wasn't cut out for married life. His now *ex*-wife had evidently figured that out, too, since she'd gotten out of Dodge, cheating on him with a colleague.

Emotionally unavailable. Too cold and distant. That's what Theresa had claimed when she confessed she'd fallen in love with someone else. That she wanted a divorce. The sooner, the better.

And she was right. He hadn't been "there" in a very real sense of the word. Oh, he'd loved her in the beginning, but there had been a nagging difficulty in showing that love outside of closed bedroom doors. The same padlock that kept angry emotions imprisoned deep inside of him had evidently trapped the more tender feelings, as well. The strain had taken its toll day by day, and as hurt as he'd been at the time of her confession, he couldn't blame Theresa for looking else-where for what she needed.

Hell. Staying a bachelor was the best thing he could do for himself…and for any other woman who might catch his eye. Not that one had. He now knew the stakes and was playing it smarter this time.

A sudden burst of sound from the pipe organ to his right punched through his thoughts, forcing his mind to circle back to what was happening around him. Everyone stood and turned toward the back of the church. And there was Kaleb's bride, her shining eyes fixed on the man beside him. Nicola had her arm through that of an older man, who had to be her father. And in the crook of the man's other arm was his four-month-old granddaughter.

The pounding in his head increased exponentially the closer the entourage got to the front. Right now, all Snow wanted was to get out of the church and head back to the hospital, a world through which he moved with ease. A world he understood and could relate to.

A world that never cheated on him or expected what he couldn't deliver.

He only hoped his friend didn't find out the hard way that marriage was not as easy as the world made it seem.

Although, the fire and passion in Nicola's eyes gave him pause. Evidently Kaleb didn't suck in the emoting department the way Snow did. Then again, Kaleb's childhood and his own had been poles apart.

Maybe, just maybe, this was one marriage that

would survive. One romance that would continue to burn bright.

And if Kaleb found happiness here in this place, who was Snow to question that?

All he knew was that the toast they'd shared at that bar had been just as binding to him as the solemn words his friend was about to exchange with his fiancée.

Till death do us part.

That was a promise Snow was never going to make again. So while Kaleb and Nicola concentrated on their happiness, Snow was going to stand here and mentally renew a different vow. One he'd made years ago, when he was just a child. A vow he'd broken when Theresa had come along.

He was going to stay alone.

The sins of Kaleb's father were not going to be visited upon his son. Not now. Not ever.

Of that, he was sure.

CHAPTER ONE

Three months later

KIRSTEN NADIF WAS LOST.

Damn. She'd been at the hospital for almost a month now, and she still couldn't seem to find her way around some of the floors. NYC Memorial was massive. Her previous hospital, where she'd started her career, was a quarter of the size of this hospital. So it was understandable that she might feel a bit discombobulated.

She laughed. Discombobulated. One of those fun English words she'd learned years ago in her ESL class in Lebanon. She tended to use that word. A lot. Just for that reason. It helped tie her to her roots and reminded her of her purpose for remaining here in America, even after her father had moved back home.

Not for the first time, she questioned her decision to transfer from Ohio to New York. But it had been for the right reasons. Lately, she'd begun thinking of moving back home to be near her father, and to do that, she would need all the experience she could get. And NYC Memorial was on the cutting edge of pulmonary treatments, including transplantation, a stage her mom had never reached before her death ten years ago. Her dad's decision to move back to Lebanon last year had not been an easy one, and she found she missed him terribly. Never had she felt more alone and out of place than she did right now with people streaming around her.

Just give it time, Kirsten.

She'd already made one friend. Nicola Sabat had seen her wandering down a hallway on her first day at the hospital and had stopped to help, and then invited her to lunch, since she said her husband was at home on "daddy duty"—thanks to a sick babysitter—and Nicola could use the company.

They were on their way to becoming fast friends.

Only today, Nicola was nowhere to be found, and she was late for an appointment with a patient and the hospital's head of transplant surgery.

She spied a sign on the corner of the wide hallway. Critical Care. Finally! Glancing at her cell phone, she saw she was ten minutes late, and now there was a missed-call notification. Her phone had been on silent. Perfect.

Heading in the direction of the arrows, she pressed redial to call the number. It rang once.

"Tangredi."

She blinked at the unfamiliar name before realizing it was the doctor she was supposed to meet. "Hi, this is Dr. Nadif. I'll be there in a minute or two. I got lost. Sorry about that."

There was silence for a few seconds, and Kirsten's chest tightened. Had he hung up on her? She pulled

the phone away from her ear to look just as his voice
came back through. "Then I guess I'll see you in a
minute or two."

Then the phone went dead.

Oh, Lord. Despite the softness of his tone, she
sensed he was irritated. Rightfully so. She should have
probably called, but figured the process of finding out
how to get in touch with him would make her even
more tardy. And she'd had an emergency case in Pediatrics that she'd needed to see to. The ten-year-old had
had persistent bronchitis, and after a troubling X-ray
she'd ordered an MRI of her lungs that was scheduled
for next week. She was probably overreacting, but after
her mom…

She shook her head, dropping her cell phone back
into her pocket. That was the last thing she needed to
think about right now. This was her first time meeting this particular doctor, and their brief interaction
on the phone did not bode well for their developing a
chummy relationship.

Not that she was looking for "chummy." Or a relationship of any kind, for that matter. Been there, done
that and it didn't bear repeating. Then there was the
huge move she was contemplating in the next year or
two.

She quickened her pace, looking toward the U-shaped
bank of white laminated desks, which meant there was
a nurses' station just ahead. Faster to ask than to try to
find the patient's room on her own.

She approached a male nurse who was standing on
the outside of the desk talking to one of the other nurses

and stopped. "Excuse me, can either of you tell me where Tanya Latimer's room is?"

The man's head turned toward her, revealing eyes the color of blue, chipped ice. They perched over cheekbones that were just as hard and severe. She suppressed a shiver.

The nurse behind the desk glanced at her lanyard and spoke to the man. "I think this is who you were waiting for, isn't it, Dr. Tangredi?"

Dr. Tangredi.

Ya ilahi! He wasn't a nurse. He was the doctor she was supposed to meet. Having this embarrassing introduction done in front of an audience was not how she'd envisioned this happening. "Oh, um, hello." She stretched out her hand. "I'm Dr. Nadif."

When his skin connected with hers, it was not what she'd expected. At all. Unlike the rest of his forbidding demeanor, his fingers were warm as they curled around hers. Goose bumps—having nothing to do with the overly cool temperature of the hospital—broke out along her arms.

"I know who you are."

That comment startled her before she realized the nurse wasn't the only one who'd glanced at the lanyard hanging at chest level. Swift heat washed into her cheeks, and she wasn't sure why.

"I'm sorry again for being late."

"I let the medical students go on to lunch."

"Medical…oh, right." This was even worse. It hadn't been just the doctor who'd been kept waiting by her lateness—there had also been a group of students. She could explain that she'd had an emergency, and that she hadn't simply been caught up in some romance novel for the last fifteen minutes.

Not that this man knew anything about romance, if the empty ring finger and his chilly tone were anything to go by.

Unfair, Kirsten. He probably has a girlfriend waiting somewhere. After all, he was gorgeous, despite his less than winning personality. She forged on ahead, deciding she was not going to let him intimidate her. "I can always come back, if that's more convenient for you."

"No, the patient is waiting. I'd rather get your assessment now, before we make any other decisions about her treatment."

"Of course." She straightened her back. "Lead the way."

He nodded a goodbye at the nurse behind the desk, and Kirsten threw the woman a quick smile before following Dr. Tangredi down the hallway, catching up to him in a few strides. "So can you tell me a little more about the patient?"

"Tanya Latimer, female, midtwenties. Primary pulmonary hypertension. Her condition degraded until she was placed on the transplant list. Yesterday, she got a new pair of lungs."

He made it sound like something that happened every day. Like you simply went to some parts superstore and picked out what you wanted. In the real world, lungs and livers and hearts were not so easy to come by. It took time—and, often, another family's tragedy—to make it happen.

And that time sometimes ran out before a donor organ became available. She knew that firsthand.

"How's she doing?"

"Blood oxygen is better than it was before the transplant, but not quite where we would like it to be at this point."

"Any signs of rejection?"

His eyes focused on her again. "No. And we're hoping there won't be."

Hoping there wouldn't be signs? Or that the lungs wouldn't be rejected?

The latter, of course.

"Once the inflammation from surgery settles down, that should improve as long as the donor had no underlying health conditions."

"I screened him myself."

Meaning what? That he was infallible? Well, she hated to break it to him, but even the finest doctors in the world couldn't always halt the progression of disease. Her mom was a case in point of that.

"Okay, but I'd like to read your notes, if that's possible, just so I can see if there's…"

She was going to say "to see if there was something you missed," but something stopped her. And that was crazy. Since when had she been afraid to speak her mind? She wasn't. She was just being cautious.

"I'll have them sent to you. But right now I'd like to have you put eyes on her and actually look at her, and not just go by a set of notes or give her a cursory glance."

Kirsten stiffened. She always looked at her

patients—*really* looked. Why was she feeling so defensive all of a sudden? Maybe because he'd gotten prickly when she'd questioned him, and now he was doing the same to her.

"That's why I came down here."

They stared at each other for a long moment before Dr. Tangredi did something that shocked her. He smiled. It was a smile that floored her with its sudden infusion of warmth. Even his eyes had been transformed into a deeper hue of blue. She struggled to catch her breath for a moment.

"Call me Snow. Please. Most people do."

It wasn't just the change in his demeanor that threw her, but the abrupt change in topic did, too. She felt...

Don't say it.

Her mind filled the blank, anyway. She felt discombobulated.

You really are going to have to find a new favorite word.

Snow. Man, the name fit him. But as long he didn't try to launch any more ice spears at her, she could deal with the name.

"I'm Kirsten."

"All right, Kirsten, let's go see our patient, then."

He pushed through the door of the room, and the first thing that met Kirsten's ears was...noise. Lots of it. During her pulmonary workups she was used to listening closely, whether it was to note subtle changes in lung function through her stethoscope, or to ask a patient to blow through a peak-flow meter. She was used to an asthmatic wheeze and other sounds of oxygen being moved, but the cacophony of an ICU room was always startling to her senses. Cardiac monitors beeped and ventilators hissed, along with the sound of other machines.

The patient's eyes were open, watching them. She followed Snow over to the bed.

"Hello, Ms. Latimer, I'm Dr. Nadif. I'm one of Dr. Tangredi's, er, colleagues. I'm a pulmonologist. And I'd like to check to see how you're doing, if that's okay."

The woman nodded. It had to be a frightening experience to not be able to control your respiration, or speak…to be totally at the mercy of the machines and caregivers. A wave of compassion went through her.

Kirsten went over to the dispenser on the wall and sanitized her hands, then snapped on gloves. Next, she took the woman's hand in her own. "Dr. Tangredi is going to help me examine you, but if anything hurts unbearably in the process, I want you to squeeze my hand, okay?"

Another nod.

She glanced at Snow. "Can you put my stethoscope in my ears so I don't contaminate anything? I can't do it one-handed. It's in my pocket."

Snow's head tilted, but he did as she asked, coming closer and sliding his gloved hand into her pocket. A wave of some weird emotion slid over her as his fingers curled around the instrument, sliding across her hip for a second. But before that emotion had fully registered, he'd pulled out her listening device, uncoiled it and stood in front of her to slide the earpieces in place. He was so close, she could smell the light tangy scent of his aftershave. His hands brushed over her cheekbones as he adjusted the fit. For once she was glad for the noise in the room. It would help mask any changes in her own breathing. And she knew there was a change. She could feel it. Feel it in the sudden heat that flared in her face, in the pulse that thumped in her neck.

"Thanks, that's good." She should have tried to do it herself, rather than risking having him come so close. But, after her breakup with Dave, she'd thought she was immune to men, and had no idea she was going to react to Tangredi the way she had.

Fortunately, he moved back several steps, eyes clipping hers, before he glanced again at the patient.

She took a second to compose herself, then addressed Tanya. "I'm going to listen to your lungs. This might be a little chilly." Still holding the woman's hand, she adjusted the hospital gown so that she had enough room. She wouldn't be able to listen through the patient's back unless they sat her upright, and Kirsten didn't want to do that unless absolutely necessary. She was pretty sure they had already moved her around a lot. Tanya didn't need yet another set of hands causing her pain.

Avoiding the drain tubes and the incision down the middle of her chest, she gently placed her stethoscope on the patient's sides and under her collarbone, listening to bronchial sounds and the inflation of the lungs themselves.

She didn't detect any crackling, which was good. The patient's heart sounded good and strong, as well, and the sides of her neck indicated she had good blood flow to the brain. "Everything sounds the way it should. What's your pain level on a scale of one to ten? You can either squeeze my hand that many times or hold up fingers."

There was a pause and then she lifted her other hand and held up four fingers. So her pain level was a four. She glanced at Snow. "Is that what you'd expect at this point? Or does she need something more?"

Snow checked the chart, then looked at Tanya. "You have another dose of meds coming in just a few minutes. Are you okay until then?"

The woman nodded.

"Good," Kirsten said. "It won't be long, okay?" She gently palpated the woman's belly and then let go of her hand in order to move to her ankles. "No peripheral edema that I can see."

"Yes, I noted that, as well."

"I think she looks good. Good color. So my opinion would be to monitor to make sure her oxygen levels don't drop further, and I would expect to see an improvement tomorrow or the next day." She glanced at Tanya. "And some of your pain should start subsiding a bit in a week or so. Once your incision starts to heal, it will go a long way toward making you more comfortable."

Tanya nodded again. Something pulled at her, though. Something in the woman's eyes that made her want to stay here with her. But she couldn't. Kirsten gave her a smile and then checked her IV bags, noting the medications and the drip. "Can I come back to see how you're doing tomorrow?"

The woman seemed to relax into herself, and her eyes closed, almost as if she was relieved. Kirsten had been right. When she looked at Snow, however, he didn't look nearly as pleased. Afraid she was hijacking his patient? Not likely. He was the transplant expert, not her. She just knew lungs. And from the sounds of them working, this woman had gained a good set of them. But there just seemed to be something...more. Something she couldn't quite put her finger on. Her instincts weren't often wrong.

"Can I see you outside?" Snow smiled at the patient, but the chill was back in his eyes. "I'll check in with you later this afternoon, Ms. Latimer."

Kirsten stripped off her gloves, dropping them into the waste receptacle as she went outside, then coiled her stethoscope again and stuffed it back in her pocket.

Before Snow could lay into her—which is what she suspected he might do—she decided to explain first and leave her uneasy feelings out of the mix, since those were harder to explain. "Seeing her today gave me a baseline of comparison for what's going on. I'd like to check for improvement over the next twenty-four hours in order to predict how she's going to do. That's why you called for the consult, right?"

"Yes. I just didn't realize it would take more than once to satisfy you."

She shot him a glance, then realized he'd meant nothing by those words. It was her own weird reaction to him that was putting thoughts in her head. Time to get back to her reasons for coming to New York. "Is pulse oxygen normally higher than the eighties when you first perform a lung transplant?"

"Pretty much. There's usually a dramatic improvement right away, but considering where most of them start, almost anything is better than where they were before surgery. Over the next couple of days, there should be a steady climb. But these patients are normally in a hypoxic state by the time they're approved for transplantation. And then there's the wait time."

"So why were you concerned with this particular patient?"

He paused before answering. "I've noticed what I think is some apathy, lately, about the process. Transplant candidates go through a rigorous screening process before they're placed on the list. She passed it, but…" He shrugged. "I would say it's a gut feeling more than anything, but my gut's track record has been known to have its weak spots."

She couldn't imagine Snowden Trangredi being anything less than totally self-assured and confident with his decisions. But she guessed anyone could have a bad day and get something wrong. But to admit it? That surprised her, after his attitude earlier.

So what had he been wrong about? A patient? Something else?

"What makes you think she's not fully on board?" She'd had an odd feeling about Tanya, too, so it helped knowing she wasn't the only one.

"Not sure. Like I said, it's just a gut feeling, but she's shown neither excitement nor fear in the hours leading up to surgery. Something just didn't feel right, but since she'd already been approved, it was almost too late to send a concern up the chain to the transplant board. And if I sounded the alarm and was wrong, then a person who desperately needed a transplant might end up overlooked. Or worse, die. And I didn't want that to happen."

Snowden's light hair was just a little too long, the natural curliness very much in evidence at the ends and across the top. It fell down over his forehead in a way that made her tummy heat. And those eyes seemed to see everything. It unnerved her. And it also made her take a mental step back.

Leaning a shoulder against the wall beside her, he glanced at her. "So you've been at NYC Memorial how long now? I know Dr. Billings retired, but I wasn't sure who'd taken his place."

She'd arrived two days before Billings officially left, so there'd been almost no time for him to show her the ropes. They'd been too busy going over his patient files and explaining the rationale behind his treatment methods. They'd been very different from what she'd done at her former hospital.

"I've been here almost a month. I guess it took them longer than they expected to find someone who was qualified to take Dr. Billings's place, although I'm not quite sure why I beat out the other applicants. So I'd barely skidded in before he left. It left me feeling kind of discombobulated."

He blinked. "Discombobulated."

Too late, she realized she'd actually used the word in a sentence. That's what she got for reciting it in her head one too many times. She rushed to cover her blunder.

"It means—"

"I know what the word means. I just don't think I've ever heard someone say it. Out loud."

One side of his mouth curved up in that same smile he'd given her earlier, and that mental step back she'd taken earlier all but disappeared. The problem was, while his smile relieved one kind of tension, it caused another to sprout up in its place. And this one was a bit wilder, a bit more unpredictable.

She did not need wild and unpredictable. Not at this point in her life.

She cleared her throat. "Well, it's just one of those fun words. It helps me not take myself too seriously. I think the world has a habit of doing just that. Being too serious. Too…distant. We don't make the connections we need to."

Connections? What the hell was she talking about?

Snow must have wondered the same thing because his smile faded, and he seemed to stiffen. "As a doctor, I've found it's better to maintain a certain distance with my patients."

This sounded like an argument he'd had before. The explanation seemed to come too quickly. Maybe she wasn't the only one who'd thought his name fit the man. Except she'd seen a crack or two in icy coating. "Yes, of course."

He shoved back that stray lock of hair, dragging his fingers through it as if making an effort to keep it back.

Was he used to it being shorter? She hoped not. She

kind of like it that length. It was the only thing about him that didn't seem to be under some kind of tight control. It was wild and unpredictable.

Ya ilahi! The curse rolled through her head as she clamped down on that observation. Those were the exact words she'd come up with moments earlier.

She certainly didn't need to stand here thinking about the length of his hair or how much self-control the man had. "Well, thanks for asking me to come see Ms. Latimer. You're sure you're okay with me coming back tomorrow? I can come while you're doing rounds if you'd prefer."

"Not necessary. And I think she'd like it if you visited again. She seemed to perk up when you stood beside her. Held her hand. I don't usually get that kind of reception during her appointments."

"It's probably a programmed response." She didn't want him to get back on the subject of maintaining a professional distance, since she was having a little trouble doing that with him right now.

"A what?"

She shrugged. "She probably associates you with pain or discomfort…or fear. I'm not there to do a procedure on her, so she doesn't view me as threatening."

"Threatening." The way he said the word was ominous and not at all what she'd meant.

She was digging herself in deeper. Time to back out of the hole. "I don't mean in a physical way. It has nothing to do with you personally, I'm sure. It's kind of like some people being afraid of the dentist. It doesn't matter how nice they are, sometimes it's associated with something unpleasant, even though it's necessary."

"And you're not associated with that."

"Nope. I'm only there to examine. Not to perform any kind of procedure, and subconsciously Tanya knows it."

"Guess I never thought of it like that."

"I'm sure she's grateful for what you're doing." She hesitated. "Would you mind if I tried talking to her about the surgery and what it means for her? Maybe what you're seeing as apathy really is fear."

"Fear. Hell. Not what I wanted." He took a deep breath and blew it back out. "Okay. I want to be kept in the loop, though. So no secrets, even if she asks you not to tell me something. This is her life we're talking about. I don't want there to be any misunderstandings or hiding of information."

That stung. "Of course. I realize she's your patient, not mine. If she says something I think is important, I'll let you know. You have my word."

"Thank you. I appreciate that."

He paused. "Could you give me a call as soon as you see her? I'll schedule her in my afternoon rounds rather than morning, so I can check any areas of concern you may have. My number should be in your phone, since I called you."

"Yes. I'll add you to my contacts." Did she really need to do that? It's not like they were going to work together on a daily basis, but if she didn't, she'd have to guess which one of the numbers was his. *Sure, Kirsten. That's the reason.* She gave an internal eye roll.

"Sounds good." With that he pushed away from the wall and walked down the hallway. It wasn't quite a swagger, but his lithe body had a loose-limbed way of going that made him seem completely at ease with himself. And why wouldn't he be? He had everything in the world going for him. Looks, skill, personality... She paused at that last one. Well, maybe he had a winning personality. If he chose to show that side of himself. She had a feeling he could be a formidable enemy, though, if provoked.

Well then, she would do her best not to provoke him on purpose, but if he got his feathers ruffled over nothing, she was certainly not going to apologize for the sake of mollifying him.

Kirsten was pretty strong-willed herself, so that could go both ways. Hopefully neither of them would see fit to test the other's limits.

Because she was pretty sure neither she nor Snow would like the outcome, if that happened.

CHAPTER TWO

SNOW WAITED MOST of the morning for her call.

It galled him that he had spent more time than he should have sitting in his office, replaying the sound of her voice in his mind. Her slight accent had a different rise and fall than what he was used to hearing. Although in a city the size of New York, he'd heard a lot of different accents. And a lot of intonations. Until she'd used the words *threatening* and *fear* in relation to his patient. And then he'd been transported back to another world, a world where those two words held a very different meaning.

At home as a child, he'd learned to read voices well and knew when it was time to flee the vicinity. There was a certain blurring of words—the way they ran together in a string of nonsensical phrases—that never boded well for those who lived in his household. So he'd normally chosen that time to grab his bike and ride to his friend Kaleb's house.

The only tone in the Sabat household had been calm. Controlled. Snow had internalized those softer voices and magnified them into a type of self-protection that he'd used at home during the worst times. He'd learned it was possible to keep his emotions in check.

At least he hoped he could. He'd been able to do it with Theresa, keeping a big portion of his childhood a secret from her. But if that fail-safe ever came tumbling down?

He'd decided a while back he was never going to let himself get into a situation where he might lose control of his emotions. The divorce had been a godsend, actually. He no longer had to fear losing his temper, never had to feel his way around every discussion looking for a way to keep things from escalating into an outright argument.

He'd heard a hint of irritation in Kirsten's voice at one point of their conversation, but no real anger. No sharp temper that could wound his patients. Instead, he'd been the one who'd gotten a little testy, and he didn't like it. Didn't like that someone he barely knew had been able to get a rise out of him, when Theresa never could.

"Just get angry, Snow!" she'd insisted toward the end. "Don't freeze me out."

She'd never understood that anger was one of those emotions he'd banished from his vocabulary. That had probably been the last real conversation he and his ex had had, before she found what she'd been looking for in someone else's arms.

It had been his fault. He was enough of a realist to admit it. And he'd been reading the signs—just like he had during his childhood—for a long time. He just hadn't been able to, or wanted, to do anything about it.

He had not wanted his past to rise up and overwhelm his defenses.

Was that what his dad had felt every time he picked up a bottle? Every time he lifted his hand in anger?

Snow didn't drink much anymore. He could remember a couple of times he'd gotten roaring drunk as a way to escape. One of those time was when he'd gone to the bar with Kaleb to celebrate his divorce. And once when he'd realized his good friend might have found what Snow hadn't been able to find: love. He wasn't an alcoholic, like his dad, but he'd decided about six months ago that he was done with the stuff—a twinge of fear that there might be a genetic component to his dad's problems that might eventually catch up to him.

That's probably why Kirsten's offhand comment had burrowed deep and stayed there.

He glanced at the phone on his desk. Damn. Time to get up and get some work done. He'd told Kirsten he would check on their patient later this afternoon, but maybe he would go early. Wait. *Their* patient? He'd used that term yesterday, too, when talking to Kirsten.

His jaw clenched. Tanya Latimer was *his* patient. He'd done the surgery. He'd done the lead-up. Ultimately, what happened to her was on him. There would be no one to swoop in and rescue her if he wasn't on his toes. Just like there'd been no one to swoop in and rescue him and his mom.

Just as he pried himself out of his chair, the desk phone went off. His nerves immediately kicked into high gear. He took a moment to calm himself before picking it up. Despite his efforts, he practically growled a greeting before catching himself.

Hell, what was wrong with him?

"Dr. Tangredi—Snow?"

"Yes." He recognized her voice immediately, sinking back into his chair. "How is she?"

No asking her how she was or how her day was going. He was turning into a first-class jerk.

"I did talk to her." There was a long pause. "Could we, er, meet somewhere to discuss it? I feel like this is better said in person than over the phone."

A sense of foreboding went through him. Maybe Tanya had decided she wanted to stop the process or get a new doctor. Hell, if that happened he was not going to be happy. Not with his patient and not with himself, for ignoring his gut.

"Is now a good time? I can meet you here in my office, or in the staff lounge, whichever is better."

Another pause. "I did get permission to share what's going on with you, but just barely. I think it might be better done in a private place to respect her wishes."

A private place. He liked the tiny differences in the way she phrased things. Like when she'd used the word *discombobulated*. It was unique to her, and…

Damn attractive.

Except he didn't need to find anything about her attractive. Not her raven-colored locks. Not the blue eyes that were such a contrast to her skin tone. "How about here in my office, then?"

That was about as private as it got.

"Okay. Which number?"

"Four-oh-three."

"I'll be up there in a few minutes."

For a split second he wondered if it would have been better to go somewhere for coffee outside of the hospital. He could have found someplace where they would be unlikely to run across anyone he knew. There were other ways to assure privacy without it needing to be a place where it was only the two of them.

Too late now. He'd already invited her up.

He straightened his desk, then got up and moved over to a small seating arrangement in the far corner, consisting of a leather sofa and two matching chairs. He stopped himself. It didn't matter what the space looked like. He wasn't entertaining her. He was having a professional discussion.

Still, he closed the door to the bathroom across from the chairs.

Just as he did, there was a knock on his door. She'd been close. Maybe she was coming from her own office, since they were all on the fourth floor.

He went behind his desk and sat down. "Come in."

Kirsten poked her head in as if to assure herself that she had the right office, then entered the room, shutting the door quietly behind herself. "Hi. Thanks for seeing me." She glanced at his door, her head tilting.

"I wondered if you'd forgotten about calling me this morning." Damn. If that didn't sound like he was sitting here wringing his hands as he waited for her call, he didn't know what did.

She lowered herself into a chair and glanced again

at his door. "Is there something I should know about the hospital?"

He blinked. Was she worried about being alone with him? That thought gutted him. "Such as…?"

"You have an extra lock on your door. Mine only has the one on the doorknob."

He stiffened, even as a wave of relief went through him. It was the door she was worried about, not him. And she was right. He'd had a dead bolt installed. Another habit that he hadn't been able to break. But this one was harmless. "No, there's nothing other than the fact that we're in a big city."

"Do I need more locks?"

Hell, he hoped not. "It was an option when I started at the hospital. You have to do what you feel most comfortable with." It hadn't actually been an option, but they'd asked him if he needed anything specific in his office, and he'd asked about the extra lock, since he did periodically sleep on the couch when he had an especially critical patient. "I sometimes have to spend the night here."

She nodded. "Ah, okay, I see."

He had a feeling she didn't really, but this was one subject he didn't want to dwell on or pick apart. "You didn't come here to discuss the lock on my door, though."

"No." She leaned forward. "Did you ever talk to your patient about her future plans?"

He went back through the various conversations he'd had with her, her husband and her parents. "She was pretty ill by the time I met her. She was in the last stages of primary pulmonary hypertension and if she didn't have a transplant, she would die. Her heart was already enlarged and threatening to fail. They all said transplantation was what she wanted. Including Tanya." He was explaining a lot more than he needed to. Maybe because he wasn't sure what Kirsten was getting at. Could he have missed a concern during one of their conversations? Was she planning on doing something else that required a pristine set of lungs? "If there was a concern, she should have discussed it before agreeing to the transplant."

"It has nothing to do with the transplant. Well, it does, but only indirectly."

"What is it, then?"

"It has to do with her antirejection meds."

He leaned back in his chair, dragging his hand through his hair, his fingers snarling in it for a second. He needed to get the damn curls cut off. He made sure his voice was very steady when he said, "Not taking them is not an option. It will *never* be an option. She knew that up front. It's a lifetime commitment. If there are problems with cost or insurance coverage, we can work through them, and the hospital has a program that—"

"It's not the cost. At least that's not what she relayed to me."

She shifted in her chair as if dreading whatever it was the patient had told her. He probably wasn't helping by reacting every time she said something. Sure, he hadn't raised his voice and his tone had been low, soft even, but maybe she was just as good at reading undertones as he was. Because what he was reading from her was off the chart. There was empathy, a trace of pity. And impatience. He was pretty sure that was directed at him.

Well, he was getting pretty damn impatient himself, despite his efforts to the contrary. "I'm waiting for you to tell me what the problem is. That was our agreement. That you not withhold information."

The way he'd withheld information from Theresa? Information he should have trusted her with. No, that was completely different from this situation.

"I know." Her voice was softer than his had been. "What are the effects of her medication on...fertility? Especially the teratogenic properties."

It came to him in a flash. Tanya was a young woman in her midtwenties. They'd asked the standard questions and taken blood test after blood test, checking for levels of certain things as well as pregnancy before the transplant and the steps leading up to it.

"She can't get pregnant." He qualified that. "She *shouldn't* get pregnant. Not right now."

"Then there you have it. If you want to know what's wrong and why she seems worried or upset. That's it in a—" she paused as if looking for the right word "—nutshell."

That made him smile, erasing his earlier thoughts about his childhood. "I see. So like I said, she shouldn't get pregnant right now. But that doesn't mean that she'll never be able to carry a child to term. But there are risks that come with pregnancy. And she needs to wait. She's on the largest doses of immunosuppressants right now, when the risk for rejection is at its highest. But we'll gradually wean her from some of those as her condition becomes more stable."

"So there's still a chance she could have children."

"Yes. But it won't be easy, and she can't just suddenly decide to get pregnant. It will have to be well-planned so we can juggle her medications and monitor her. Some of them have deleterious effects on pregnancy and on the fetus itself."

"That is very good news. Not the deleterious part—that means harmful, right?—but the fact that it can be done. I knew in general it was possible—after all there have been uterine transplants done—but I didn't know in this specific case…" She paused. "It took a long time for her to be willing to tell me this. She had to write it all down, since she's still on the ventilator, and she was visibly upset as she wrote."

He could relate to that. It would be a long time—if ever—before he felt comfortable enough with anyone to share certain things. And yet Kirsten had gained his patient's trust in, what…? Less than three hours? He was going to need to watch his step around her.

Kirsten pulled a piece of paper from her pocket and opened it to show him what Tanya had written. The ink was smeared in places, like something wet had dripped on it. He glanced at her.

"She was crying."

His gut contracted into a tight ball. "Damn. Why didn't she ask me this before the procedure? I could have put her mind at ease."

"She was worried about dying before the procedure.

Her survival instincts were hoping for a way out. An escape. And when the possibility of a transplant was placed on the table, she grabbed at it. Only now is she able to think beyond that, to the consequences of her decision."

He could relate to that all too well. At one time, Snow's survival instincts had given him a blatant disregard for anyone's well-being outside of his own. Empathy had been a hard commodity to find. It was there. Just submerged under the junk that littered his life.

His mom and Kaleb were two of the few people he cared about. Two of the few people he trusted. And now his mom was finally out of harm's way. His dad had put her in ICU for weeks. When she'd recovered and found he'd been arrested for what he'd done, she finally divorced his ass. Snow hadn't been in contact with the scumbag in over the decade he'd been behind bars. His mom had undergone counseling. And Snow? Well he'd been self-sufficient for a very long time. Counseling wouldn't help whatever was left of the damage his father had inflicted. And maybe that was for the best. It served as a reminder—a kind of cautionary tale.

"They're not permanent consequences. Maybe in a year we can start thinking in terms of having children." Too late, he realized his last phrase could have been construed differently from the way he'd meant it. "Tanya and her husband I mean."

She grinned, a cute dimple forming in her right cheek. "I knew what you meant. Us having children?

That would be a very bad match, I think. Besides, who knows where I'll be in a year's time."

He got hung up for a second on her saying they would be a very bad match, before moving to the last sentence.

"Are you thinking of leaving NYC Memorial already?"

"No. Not yet. We just never know where life will take us."

She was avoiding answering him directly. Maybe another hospital was wooing her. Or maybe she just wasn't happy here. Well, it was none of his business. If she left tomorrow, life as he knew it would simply go on unaltered. Except didn't he owe it to the hospital to be a positive force and not a negative one that created a toxic workplace? Maybe he should make more of an effort to be conciliatory and friendly—find a little of that misplaced empathy and put it on display.

"I do appreciate your help with Tanya. I'll talk to her about the having-children issue." He glanced again at the tearstained paper his patient had written on.

"Do you mind if I talk to her instead? It might be easier coming from me, since she and I have already spoken about it. If you can explain the steps she'll need to take, I'll make sure she knows."

That was fair. After all, Tanya had confided in Kirsten and not in him. And he knew himself well enough to realize that the pulmonologist presented a much more sympathetic face than he did. Snow was driven from task to task, moving to the beat of mental checklists that needed to be completed each day.

Feelings—and talking about them—didn't come easily for him. He shied away from them both with patients and in his personal life. But he had a feeling that Kirsten had no such problems. Neither had Theresa. She'd put in a whole lot more than she'd gotten out of their marriage. It's why, in the end, she'd decided he wasn't worth the effort. And he couldn't blame her.

Oh, he could for the affair. She should have just asked for a divorce and been done with it. She certainly had once she'd found someone else.

But he and Kirsten were colleagues and nothing else. So there was no need to worry about that kind of incompatibility. As long as his transplant patient was on the road to recovery, that's what he needed to focus on. That, and nothing else.

So as long as this particular problem was on its way to being solved, he could go back to what he did best. Treat his patient's physical needs while leaving the emotional side to someone else.

Someone other than him.

The cell phone that had been on his desk buzzed. He glanced at the screen. "Sorry, I need to take this."

"Okay, I'll talk to you later, then."

He nodded, picked up the phone and barked out his name. He listened for a second to the doctor in the emergency room, then stuck his head out of the door, catching Kirsten before she'd gotten halfway down the hall.

"Hey, Kirsten, could you hold up for a second?"

She turned with a frown, then headed back toward him.

His attention went back to the doctor. "I'll be right down. I'll have our new pulmonologist with me."

At least he hoped he would. Maybe she had another patient scheduled.

He hung up. "There's a case down in the ER. A lung-transplant patient from another state was visiting relatives here when he started having trouble breathing. Do you have time to go see him with me?"

"Yes, of course. Do you know anything else?"

They stood in front of the elevators. "Male in his thirties. Pulse ox isn't great, and it looks almost like a virus is attacking his lungs. At least that's what they're guessing. They want me down there in case it's the beginning of organ rejection."

They got on and Snow pushed the button for the first floor.

"And me?"

"I'd like another set of eyes and ears. Treating someone else's patient isn't the easiest."

Her eyebrows went up. "Or dealing with the doctors who treated them."

That got a smile out of him. "Are you thinking of any doctor in particular?"

Her eyes rounded as if in mock surprise. "Of course not. I don't ever have run-ins with other patients' doctors."

He laughed. "Somehow, I don't think that's true."

They came out on the first floor and he headed toward the emergency department with Kirsten close behind. The nurse at reception, a phone to her ear, pointed toward the first exam room on the left. One of the trauma rooms.

Snow pushed through the doors and found Dr. Lawrence standing next to a patient who had an oxygen mask over his face. "Thanks for coming. This is Randy Stewart. He came to visit his parents for a couple of days and started to feel a tightness in his chest."

Snow came over and greeted the patient. "Hi, Randy. I'm Snowden Tangredi, head of transplant surgery here at the hospital. Dr. Nadir is a lung specialist. So you're having a little trouble breathing, Randy?"

He nodded, breath coming out on an extended wheeze. A sound Snow did not like. "Just in the last two hours."

"Okay. I know Dr. Lawrence has already listened to your lungs, but I'm going to take another quick listen, okay?"

Using his stethoscope, he listened to the sounds coming from his lungs, frowning as he thought he picked up a slight sound almost like…

He motioned Kirsten over. "Can you listen for a minute and tell me what you think?"

Kirsten followed his lead and leaned in close, her eyes closed in concentration.

Snow studied her. Although he hadn't actually worked a case with her, other than Tanya's, he got the sense that she was nothing if not thorough. She'd gotten to the heart of the issue with Tanya, hadn't she?

It was one of the reasons he'd wanted her to come with him.

Her eyes popped open, finding his immediately. "I'm hearing some crackling."

"Yeah, me, too." He glanced at Dr. Lawrence, who nodded. "I did, too. If he wasn't a transplant patient, I'd say he was having an asthma attack."

Kirsten spoke up. "I agree. My asthmatic patients have this exact same sound."

What were the odds?

"Did you get ahold of Randy's transplant surgeon?"

"No, he's on vacation in the Bahamas. But they're accessing his records for us."

Randy lowered the mask for a second. "I had a checkup a month ago with my surgeon and everything was fine then."

"So you've had no problems before coming here for vacation."

"None."

"Where is home for you?"

"Montana." He wheezed again, but the sound wasn't quite as labored as his last breath had been.

Kirsten came up beside him. "Montana probably doesn't have the allergens there that we have here."

The pollution index had been high for the last week.

He sat on the stool and pulled over to the bed. "Did your doctor mention anything about the donor lungs? Any diagnosed problems?"

"No. The person had a traumatic brain injury from a traffic accident. Nothing involving the lungs at all. He was young, in his teens." Randy swallowed before reaching above the oxygen mask to pinch the bridge of his nose, as if fighting emotion.

He could very well feel conflicted. It was always hard discussing the donor. Transplant patients were always aware that their salvation came at the death of someone else. It was hard.

Kirsten came over and put her hand on his arm. "That teenager gave you a gift of life. I'm sure he would be happy to know that."

Even as he watched, the patient's hand dropped back to his side. "Thank you."

Kirsten had something that Snow didn't—that ability to somehow connect with a patient on an emotional level and reassure them. She'd done it with Tanya, when he hadn't been able to. Just another sign that he lacked some sort of empathy gene. Nature? Or nurture?

Hell, did it even matter? His dad had taken something more than Snow's ability to trust people with his deepest emotions. He had also screwed up his ability to relate to people in a visceral, instinctive way. Maybe partly because he didn't trust people enough to show vulnerability.

It made him good at being objective, gave him the means to look at things through a lens of science rather than a lens of feelings.

But Kirsten could go so far beyond that. And a part of him wished he could somehow tap that part of himself.

He couldn't, though. And that was all there was to it. He was also going to need to be careful around Kirsten. If she had a gift for unearthing emotions in others, might she somehow be able to dig beneath the rubble inside of him and find something he didn't want found?

Hell, he hoped not.

A nurse stuck her head in and handed him a tablet. "They just sent over the records from Montana."

"Great, thanks."

"And, Dr. Lawrence, I have a patient out front who's complaining of chest pains."

"I'll be right there." The other doctor threw him an apologetic look. "Can you take it from here?"

"Yep. We've got it."

We. Meaning him and Kirsten.

Well, he was the one who'd asked her to come. And it had been the right decision, despite the little part inside of him that warned him to keep his distance.

He flipped through the tablet, catching bits and phrases and sorting them into slots in his brain. Randy was right. There was no mention of asthma in the donor. But that didn't mean that it wasn't there. If he was a teen, he could have wheezed from time to time, but not enough to lead to a diagnosis. And the donor was also from Montana.

Setting down the tablet, he waited for Kirsten to finish saying something to the patient. Something that actually made the man laugh. He frowned, a spike of something going through him. Was he jealous? Jealous of her ability to be at ease around someone she barely knew?

Of course not.

He moved closer, waiting for Kirsten to look at him. "I'd like to run a test or two and if those show what I think they might, I want to give you a breathing treatment."

"So it's not rejection?" Randy's voice held a hint of fear.

"I don't think so."

"Thank God. I told my wife to stay at home with the kids. I haven't even called her to let her know I'm at the hospital. This was just going to be a quick trip to help my parents sort out the details of their wills." He paused. "I'm a lawyer, so I don't want to leave that kind of thing with just anyone."

"I can understand that." Just like Snow didn't want to leave the details of his past with just anyone.

Kirsten glanced at him. "So you *are* thinking asthma attack?"

"I do. Your thoughts?"

"The same. He said the tightness is easing a bit."

"Good news." Snow forced a smile. "So let's get you patched up and out of here. Unless you want to stick around for a while longer?"

Randy laughed. "No. I've seen just about all I want to see of hospitals."

"I can imagine. So while we want you to explore some of New York, a tour of the hospital isn't on most of the popular sightseeing routes."

"I'm okay to fly out day after tomorrow?"

"If this is what I think it is, then yes. But I do want you to follow up with your doctor at home. Sooner rather than later. They'll probably want to add a rescue inhaler to your regimen, although I hope this never happens again."

"I don't know how to thank you."

This time, Snow's smile wasn't forced. "Just live your best life and enjoy every breath."

"Thank you. I intend to do exactly that."

Kirsten should have felt better after her talk with Snow. Especially after treating Randy Stewart with him. The transplant surgeon had gotten the diagnosis exactly right. She should feel gratified that they'd been on the same page, and how easy it had been to treat that patient...together.

But as she walked from her office toward the elevator a half hour later, she was left with a nagging sense of unease. It wasn't due to the patient. It was the extra lock on the door to Snow's office. She'd made it a point to glance at the other office doors on the way back to her own office after the emergency case. No one else had anything marring the wood of their doors. His excuse had been that he sometimes slept in his office. But surely other doctors did, as well. Did he really expect someone to break in and disturb his sleep?

A chill went over her. Maybe he needed the extra lock for a completely different reason. Like not getting caught doing something he shouldn't.

Stop it, Kirsten. The man is not a drug addict.

Nothing in his demeanor indicated anything of the sort. He'd been completely lucid every time she'd seen him. But how many times had doctors hidden such habits?

Well, she didn't personally know any, but she'd heard the stories. And had been warned countless times in medical school not to start down that path.

She'd just pushed the call button for the elevator and gotten on when a hand stopped it from closing. Snow stood in the doorway looking more than a little bit intimidating. As if he'd heard her thoughts and knew exactly where to find her.

Ridiculous.

"I'm headed to lunch. Care to join me?" He stepped into the elevator and pushed the button for the ground floor.

She blinked. The difference between the Snow in his office and the one asking her to lunch seemed almost night and day. "Are you going somewhere close? I need to be back in an hour."

"There's a bistro that serves soup and sandwiches right around the corner—Sergio's. Have you ever been there?"

She hadn't been to very many restaurants, since she was still getting to know people, and she hated to eat at a restaurant alone. Lots of people did it, and she wasn't sure why she was so opposed to doing the same, but it made her feel even more isolated. Maybe she was just missing her dad. Or her former hospital. Whatever it was, the prospect of sitting down to a meal with another person was very appealing. Even if she hadn't gotten off to a very good start with the man who'd invited her.

"I haven't, but I would love to try it."

"Okay. And I promise not to talk shop."

"Shop?"

"To talk about work and patients."

Well, she couldn't imagine what else they would

have to talk about. "It's okay. I find work interesting. And I bet you've had some fascinating cases."

"I'm sure you've had your share, as well." He smiled. "But my stomach has been yelling at me for an hour. And I realize that I'm not the most friendly member of NYC Memorial's staff. I wouldn't want to be the reason you're thinking of leaving."

Thinking of leaving... Oh, what she'd said in his office about not knowing where she'd be in a year. So that's why he was inviting her to lunch. Great.

"Oh. Like I said, I'm not thinking of leaving right now. But if I were, it wouldn't be because of you or anyone else. It would be because it's what I feel I should do. So no need to invite me to lunch if that's what you're worried about. I'm a tough girl. I can handle doctors who 'aren't the most friendly.'"

He gave her a smile. One that carried at least a hint of sincerity. "It's not the only reason I asked you. It's later than I expected, and you've been a big help with Tanya, not to mention Randy. Her writing that list had to have taken up a lot of your time. I thought it might have been a simple thing, like the fear of organ rejection and not wanting to get her hopes up."

The elevator stopped, letting them off. "I was happy to be there for her. And for Randy. But I think Tanya realizing she might just have a future in front of her is what brought on the topic of children. She's finally able to look toward something not related to her illness."

"I guess I should be glad of that then. We'll hopefully get her weaned off the vent in another day or so."

She remembered something else. "I forgot to mention. Her pulse ox is actually up by another percentage point. So I think you can stop worrying on that front. They're also slowly reducing the settings on her vent, like you'd asked them to do, without any negative effects."

"That is very good news."

Maybe having lunch with him wasn't such a bad idea. It would give her a chance to see what he was like when he wasn't at work. And help her understand the need for the locks.

He's not a drug addict.

The repeated thought almost made her laugh. Since when had she become so suspicious?

They walked through the front lobby of the hospital, the ceiling there stretching up four floors. There were railings and chair groupings on each floor where people could look over the foyer, and a huge chandelier that rivaled the ones found in exclusive hotels. NYC Memorial was a beautiful hospital, she had to admit. Prestigious and influential. She didn't care about the prestige, though. She only cared about what was under its beautiful facade.

Kind of like she cared only about what was beneath Snow's attractive exterior. He seemed to genuinely care about his patients. And his instinct about there being something going on with Tanya had been right on target. So he was insightful. A very good trait in a doctor. Not all of them had it. A lot of times they were so focused on the physical signs of illness that they neglected digging deeper. But Snow had not needed to dig. He'd known something was wrong.

Not something she'd expect if his focus was anywhere other than his patients. That alone made her relax.

And she suddenly realized she was hungry, as well, as her stomach let out a loud burbling sound. Her eyes widened and she gave a little laugh when he glanced at her with raised eyebrows. "Okay, my stomach thinks this is a good idea, too."

"Glad to know I'm not the only one." He nodded at the traffic light in front of them. "We'll turn right here and then the bistro is two buildings down."

They were there in less than two minutes. There was no line of customers that she could see. At least not outside. Well, it was almost one thirty.

It had been just before twelve when she'd called him, and she'd actually been surprised he wasn't already out to lunch. She could have called his cell phone, but something inside had urged her to take the less personal route. Especially after his earlier comment about keeping his distance with patients. Besides, if he'd been out to lunch with someone, she hadn't wanted to disturb him. But, of course, then they'd gotten caught taking care of the transplant patient down in the ER. That had taken an hour in and of itself.

"Well, thanks for inviting me."

"It's fine. I could have eaten in my office or at the hospital cafeteria. I've just done that a lot lately and going off-site today was appealing."

"For me, too." She didn't add that since arriving, she'd been picking up food from the cafeteria and going back to her office with it, just so she wasn't sitting alone at a table.

Well, today she wouldn't be alone. And it would be the first time she'd gotten to eat at one of the local places.

They were greeted almost immediately and escorted back to a dim booth near the rear of the restaurant. The booth sported high backs topped with frosted glass partitions, giving the space an intimate feel. Maybe she'd spoken too soon about being glad to be off-site. But this was lunch between colleagues. It wasn't a date. So no need to feel awkward about it.

One of the waitstaff came over and greeted them. "What can I get you to drink? We have beer, wine, soft drinks and several types of lemonade."

She wanted a glass of wine, but since she was still working, decided against it. "I'd just like a cup of hot tea, if you have it, and a glass of water."

Snow added, "And I'll have a cola, brand doesn't matter."

"Great. I'll be right back with your drinks."

As soon as she left, Snow asked how she was settling in at the hospital.

"Okay, I think. It's much bigger than what I came from, so it's still a little overwhelming. As you could tell from my getting lost. Dr. Sabat has been a big help, and we've eaten a couple of meals together."

"Dr. Sabat?" He had a weird look on his face. "Kaleb is a nice guy, but—"

"Oh!" She realized what he must think. "No, I meant I've eaten with his wife, Nicola."

He seemed to relax back in his seat. "I keep forgetting that Nicola's last name has changed. They're both great people, and Kaleb and I go way back."

"From what Nicola says, they're head over heels in love. And they sure love that baby."

"Yes, I would say so, although I don't see as much of Kaleb as I used to."

"You said you go way back. Did you know each other in medical school?"

"Try elementary school in upstate New York." He smiled.

That surprised her. Somehow she couldn't picture him as a kid riding his bike with friends. "Wow, and you both ended up being doctors at the same hospital?"

He nodded. "Strange how life works. He was definitely a godsend when... Well, let's just say he was there at a time when I really needed a friend."

That touched her, and she wasn't sure why. He'd said Kaleb was a godsend when he needed a friend. So there'd been a rocky period in his life? It certainly sounded like it. That lock on his door crossed her mind's eye before she dismissed it.

She tried to think of a subtle way to get him to say more as he continued to talk. "So are your parents in the area?" he asked.

"No. My father moved back to Lebanon not too long ago. And my mom passed away ten years ago."

"I'm sorry, Kirsten."

The words were accompanied by a frown, as if he really was sorry. "It's okay. She could have used your skills back when we came to the States looking for a cure, though."

"A cure?"

"She was in the late stages of cystic fibrosis. She'd always said I was her miracle child, since she'd been advised not to get pregnant. I was an accident, but she said she felt like there was a reason for it. So it really made me feel for Tanya."

The waitress came back for their order. All she wanted was soup and half a sandwich, so she chose the chicken salad and potato soup. Snow opted for a turkey club sandwich.

"Your mom came over here for treatment?"

"A transplant, actually. But she didn't make the list in time. She died a year after we arrived. My dad decided we would stay, since I wanted to go through medical school. I did, and here I am."

"I'm sorry your mom didn't get what she needed." He glanced at her. "You're a pulmonologist…"

She answered his unspoken question. "Yes, my mom is why I went into this specialty. I'd like to think she would have approved."

"I'm sure she would have. She'd have really liked the way you helped Tanya."

"I didn't do much. Just listened." His words warmed her. Did he like the way she'd handled Randy, as well?

"It sounds like that's what she needed the most."

She smiled. "Don't we all, from time to time? Need someone to listen?"

Before he could answer, the waitress chose that moment to come by with their food. She placed their meals in front of them and asked if there was anything else either of them needed, then she slid into the background once again.

"So where did you live before moving to NYC Memorial?"

"I worked at a small hospital in Ohio. My mom was treated at one of the major hospitals there."

He nodded. "And you didn't want to work at the hospital where she was treated?"

"There weren't any open positions in pulmonology there when I started looking. But NYC Memorial had one. And it's okay. I think I needed a change of scenery, anyway. Once my dad moved…well, there was nothing keeping me anchored in Ohio. I thought maybe in a big city, I wouldn't be quite as…tied to needing a car for transportation."

She'd been going to say she wouldn't be as lonely—wouldn't have constant reminders of having her heart broken, of her boyfriend scooting out of her life as if she'd meant nothing at all—but she changed the wording at the last second. He didn't need to know that her immersion in her work was due to a failed relationship. Or that it was on purpose.

At thirty-two she'd only had one serious boyfriend and that was in medical school, where the pressures of studying and internship had taken a toll on them as a couple. She'd needed more from him in terms of emotional support and encouragement, whereas he seemed to handle the later parts of school by becoming laser-focused on the tasks in front of him. It had left her feeling wobbly and insecure. When she tried to talk to him about it, he sidestepped the subject time and time again.

And then, when they'd gone to separate hospitals, he'd walked away from her without so much as a backward glance. It had been a crushing blow. She'd tried texting him occasionally, and while he hadn't exactly ghosted her, his obvious indifference had made the wound fester until she finally deleted his number from her phone.

She decided she wasn't going to give another man the opportunity to turn his back on her like that. It made her decision to return to Lebanon that much easier.

But she had to admit that it was sometimes hard going home to an empty apartment, although she now valued her solitude, for the most part. But she did miss the camaraderie that medical school and the small hospital in Ohio had offered.

"Do you find you miss Lebanon? You said your dad went back there."

This is where it got tricky. She really didn't want anyone to know at this point that she was seriously thinking of going back there. She wasn't certain about it, but it had been rolling around in her mind for a while. What she didn't want to do was sink her chances at NYC Memorial by making that declaration to anyone. Because she might just end up at the hospital for a while.

"I do miss it. I grew up there and almost all of my relatives are there, except for a couple of third cousins who are in Philadelphia." Cousins she'd never met and probably never would. But her dad had made it a point to let her know their names and contact information in case she got into trouble. Not that she would call them.

"I imagine it's hard being away from them."

"Yes. But I love it in New York, as well. And I'm sure this will become 'home' with a little time and a couple more friends."

"Let me know if you need a tour guide for seeing the sights. I know a good one who's lived in New York his whole life."

She hadn't yet ventured into the touristy parts of the city, for the main reason that she'd hit the ground running as soon as she'd arrived. "That would be great. Could you give me the person's contact information?"

"You already have it." He gave her a smile.

She did? She didn't remember seeing that. Was it in the welcome packet or something? "I haven't looked through everything the hospital gave me yet, so I may have overlooked it."

"Actually, it's me. It's the least I can do for helping me out with Tanya. And for how unwelcoming I was when I called looking for you."

She frowned. "I talked to Tanya because I wanted to. And I was late, so I understand why you might have been irritated."

"That may be, but you're new here, and I was kind of rude. We can coordinate our next days off together and spend a morning or afternoon just hitting the high points. If you're okay with doing that."

There was something in his voice that sounded a little uncertain, as if he might think she really had a problem going with him. And, in reality, she might, given some of the tangled emotions he engendered in her, but what could she say? That she didn't want to see New York? Or that she didn't particularly want him as a tour guide? Because honestly, the thought of going from place to place with him held an odd appeal. She'd seen rare glimpses of a softer side of Snow and wondered what he might be like away from the hospital. Those imaginings worried her. Made her consider turning him down.

But going to see those sights on her own seemed almost as sad as sitting in a restaurant by herself. She could ask Nicola to go with her, but she had the baby and not a whole lot of free time, by her own admission.

So she let out a breath and decided to commit herself, before she could chicken out. But only for a day, in case it went horribly wrong. And it very well could. Except this wasn't a relationship or even a date, so what could it hurt?

"Okay. I'll take you up on your offer. Let me know when is good for you, and I'll try to sync my schedule with it."

Even as she said the words she hoped she wasn't making a huge mistake. One that could create problems with him in the future or with the hospital in general. But how could it? One afternoon did not a career break. Or a relationship make.

At least she hoped not.

CHAPTER THREE

HE WAS HAVING SECOND THOUGHTS.

Not about Tanya, whose demeanor had totally changed. She was throwing all of her energy into wanting to rid herself of the ventilator and seemed much more eager to start physical therapy, both of which were supposed to happen tomorrow. He had Kirsten to thank for that. Which is why he'd offered to show her the sights.

Right? The words at the restaurant two days ago had come out of nowhere. But when he'd asked her if she missed Lebanon, she'd gotten this funny look on her face and hadn't quite met his eyes. Was she that homesick? Homesick enough to leave NYC Memorial?

Why wouldn't she be? She'd said her family was all there. Snow didn't understand that kind of homesickness, since his family was at best dysfunctional, and at worst... Well, it's why he liked to lock his doors at night. His father had been out of the picture for a long time, but the habits he'd picked up from his time at home were not.

It's a compulsion. The words whispered through his

head, and he was quick to push them back out again. So what if he liked to lock his doors at night? So what if he'd asked for an extra lock on his office at the hospital? That didn't make it a compulsion. But he remembered his mom's hands shaking as she'd struggled to install a lock on Snow's bedroom door after a particularly bad night. He'd been seven at the time, and he hadn't quite understood why one of his mom's eyes was darker than the other. He'd learned soon enough, though, that even brand-new locks didn't always keep monsters at bay.

Hell! He hadn't thought about this in forever. Why now? Maybe it was Kirsten asking about the lock on his office door and frowning as she asked him if she needed one, too. He hoped she never did. Hoped she always felt safe.

Was that why he'd asked if he could show her some sights? Because he'd feel safer if she had someone with her, since she'd shared that she didn't know very many people at the hospital yet?

Ha! How funny was it that he, of all people, thought he could make her feel safe? He was never really sure if his dad's darkness was somehow inside of him. After all, his mom said that he'd been different when they'd first met. That he'd been charming and kind.

Well, Snow was pretty sure he couldn't be accused of being either of those things. But the other?

Damn. Well, he'd make sure she didn't get any funny ideas, not that she'd shown any interest in him. But he also remembered the shock he'd felt when she said that she'd eaten with "Dr. Sabat," and he'd thought she meant Kaleb at first. He knew his friend would never cheat on Nicola, so why had that weird feeling slithered through his gut, coiling there as if waiting to strike if his friend made one wrong move. Was it that darkness he worried about? Or simply because he'd been cheated on before? Just because Theresa had cheated, it didn't mean everyone did.

But Kirsten hadn't mentioned whether or not she was seeing anyone back at her old hospital or not. If she was, surely she wouldn't have agreed to go with him. Right?

Way to show your ignorance, Snow. Women and men can be friends.

With that thought, he went to see his next patient, making a note to himself to call Kirsten and let her know that he had next Wednesday off. If that didn't work, then maybe he could take a portion of one of his personal days and take her around then.

His phone buzzed and he glanced at the readout. He frowned at the coincidence that found his mind on Kirsten at the very moment she was calling him. "Hello? Snow here."

"Um, hi. I'm just checking to see how things with Tanya went today."

He stopped at a nearby waiting area and dropped into a chair, so he didn't have to walk and try to schedule things at the same time. "They went well. Really well. Thanks to you."

"Oh, I'm pretty sure she would have eventually gotten with the program with or without my help. She was just going through a momentary, er, *alhuzin*… How do you say it? A momentary depression, maybe?"

The ease with which that word in her native tongue slid out made him picture her in his mind. Were her straight black locks flowing over her shoulders before being caught in a ponytail partway down its length? Or was her hair loose and free, allowing him to…? Something shifted in his gut, and this time it wasn't a slithery dark sensation. But it was just as dangerous. And he needed to take it seriously.

"Yes, a momentary depression is the perfect word to describe it. But she seems to be looking forward to recovering now."

"And maybe having a baby of her own?"

"Yes. Maybe. We're certainly not ruling anything out at the moment."

"So, since Tanya is doing well, maybe I can ask your opinion on a patient of my own? She's a ten-year-old girl."

Ah, so this was the reason for her call, although he was pretty sure her interest in how Tanya was doing was genuine. "Of course. Is she in the hospital?"

"Not at the moment, but today was my second time seeing her over the period of a week. I'm suspecting something more is going on besides a chest infection. She's short of breath, even though I don't see any signs of bacterial pneumonia or a viral infection."

"That's a positive."

There was a pause. "It is, although ruling out simple reasons makes me suspect it might be a more complicated condition."

"Such as?"

"Right now, pulmonary hypertension is topping my list."

That stopped him in his tracks. Tanya's transplant had been due to primary pulmonary hypertension, but in a child? "You know that's a pretty uncommon finding in kids."

"Yes, and that's what has me worried."

He could imagine. Even though his specialty was transplantation, every time they could save a patient from needing one was a victory for the hospital and the patient, as well.

"Have you already set up another appointment with her?"

"No, I wanted to see what your schedule was like next week."

"That's funny, I was just about to call you to ask the same thing. I have next Wednesday off, if you're still interested in going to see what the Big Apple has to offer."

His suggestion was met with silence. Maybe she was checking her calendar. Or maybe she'd simply hung up on him. The latter didn't seem very likely. He hadn't done anything to make her mad. At least he didn't think so, not today. Then she came back on. "Yes, I can do Wednesday. What time?"

"I'll leave that up to you. I have the whole day off, so we can spend part of it sightseeing or all of it."

"And my patient?"

This time it was Snow who flipped through his appointments. "Can you do Friday, late morning?"

"I have a surgery first thing, but I should be done by about eleven. Can we make it right after lunch?"

He was tempted to ask her out to lunch, but he knew that was not a good idea. He wasn't even sure how smart it had been to offer to take her to see the sights on Wednesday. As he'd learned the hard way, there were consequences for every choice you made in life. His ex had suffered the consequences of his marriage proposal. The one that had ended in divorce. But he'd learned his lesson. From now on, he would make choices that only affected him.

"Yes, that will work. Say one o'clock?"

"One o'clock it is. And do you have a time preference for Wednesday?"

"How long do you think it'll take me to see everything?"

He chuckled. "In New York City? We measure sightseeing in terms of weeks, not hours."

"I guess I was thinking about just the biggest of the big. Like the Statue of Liberty or something like that."

"Okay, we'll put that on our list of things to see. That might be an all-day affair, in and of itself, though. Between that and Ellis Island, there's a lot to see."

"Sounds good." There was a pause. "And thanks for being willing to see my patient."

He smiled. "You were willing to see mine. I can't promise that same kind of breakthrough, however."

"Just a second set of eyes is all I need, Snow."

He liked it when she said his name, although he wasn't sure why. Everyone he knew shortened his name to Snow, since Snowden seemed stuffy, somehow.

"Well, you've got them. I'll see you Wednesday, then?"

"Yes, see you then."

They ended the call, and he set his phone on the desk, staring at it for a minute. He couldn't help but feel he was making a mistake by taking her around New York. He could always call Nicola and ask if she'd be willing to do it. But, like Kirsten said, Nicola and Kaleb had a baby at home and it didn't seem fair to pull her away from her family with the hours she was still putting in at work.

No, he'd do it. He'd just remind himself of his reasons and make sure his mind didn't wander outside of those preset parameters. As long as he did that, everything would be just fine.

Why had she worn a skirt on a sightseeing trip? Well, for one thing, it was cooler than pants on a hot day like today. And, two, because she pretty much lived her life in these same loose gauzy garments. She hiked up the white fabric to her knees yet again so it didn't drag on the ground when she stepped into Snow's low sports car, making sure she then tossed the fabric back over her knees once inside. Her low black espadrilles were super comfortable, too, and her sleeveless black top was loose and lightweight.

This was the first time she'd seen Snow out of his customary khaki pants and button-down shirt, and she had to say, he'd taken her breath away when he'd met her beside the car. Dressed in black jeans and a red polo shirt with his blond hair shoved off his forehead, he looked lean and fit, and far too gorgeous for comfort.

If she was smart, she would make up an excuse as to why she suddenly couldn't go. Like an emergency. It wouldn't exactly be a lie, because she was feeling a bit panicked about going.

She did her best to distract herself from stealing glances at him. At the way those long surgeon's fingers curled around the steering wheel, his thumb absently brushing across the leather surface. Because if she didn't, she was going to imagine that thumb stroking over her skin.

Yep, she might be in need of an emergency intervention. Had she learned nothing from her relationship with Dave? Yes, she had. That was part of the problem.

"So will the ferry stop at the Statue of Liberty first or Ellis Island?" It was pretty early in the morning, but Snow said if they left too late the line to get on the ferry at Battery Park would be very long.

He glanced her way, blue eyes surprisingly warm this morning. "The Statue of Liberty. I was able to get reservations to explore the platform, but the number of slots to climb to the crown are pretty limited. There wasn't enough lead time to try. And we'd have to climb the equivalent of twenty stories of steps to get to the top."

"Wow, that's a lot. I bet the view is amazing, though."

His thumb stopped stroking and his hands tightened slightly on the wheel. "Yes. The view is amazing even without the climb."

Had he taken someone special up there? Because his voice had had a funny timbre to it. Maybe he hadn't wanted to go up there with her. No, he'd said there were only a small number of people allowed up each day, which was understandable.

"I'll make it up there someday." She hoped, anyway. If her plans came to fruition, she might only be here for a couple of years before leaving for good. But no need to share that with him. Better *not* to tell him, actually. She hadn't even discussed it with her dad yet, although he would be thrilled if she came back home.

The problem was, her mom was buried in Ohio. Even though Kirsten knew her essence was not in those ashes, it would still be hard to leave the country, knowing she'd probably never be back to visit her grave.

A lump formed in her throat. As the only child, it would mean the grave would sit there all alone. Forever. Something far worse than eating alone at a restaurant.

She shook off a wave of melancholy. She was supposed to be here to enjoy the sights, not brood over things she couldn't control.

"Maybe you and Nicola can plan a day when her baby is older."

"Maybe." She forced her voice to be light and cheery. She was not going to spoil this day. Nothing like having him basically tell her this was their one and only outing. He'd as much as said he was doing it in appreciation for her help with Tanya. And because he hadn't been very friendly during their first interaction on the phone.

Why should his reasons matter? She barely knew him. And he didn't know her at all. It was already kind of him to have offered to take her in the first place.

It's just that it made her feel like some friendless charity case.

Well, she wasn't a charity case, but she was still basically friendless at this point, although she was starting to form some connections that looked promising.

Like with Snow? No, not with him. Maybe it was better to hurry and get this over with. "How far away is the ferry station?"

"About a half-hour drive in this traffic. Not far. Once we get on the ferry, the trip will be pretty quick. About five minutes to the statue itself."

"Wow. Somehow I thought it was farther out than that."

"Nope. Not far at all. Ellis Island is pretty amazing, as well."

"I bet." She'd heard of the island, but honestly hadn't thought she'd get a chance to see it. At least not anytime soon. Her hours at the hospital had been pretty hectic ever since she'd arrived to take Dr. Billings's place.

"Did you get to see the sights when you were in Ohio?"

"Yes, but my mom was so sick at first…" She took a deep breath and tried again. "She didn't get to see much at all of America."

He glanced at her again as he stopped at a red light. "I'm sorry, Kirsten. That had to have been a hard time for your family."

"It was. I know how lucky I am to have had her with us for as long as we did, but it still wasn't an easy time. My dad really held our family together during that time."

"That's great. Not everyone has that kind of luxury."

What luxury? Of having a dad? She guessed not. "I didn't think of it as a luxury at the time. In fact, my dad and I butted heads a lot."

"Yeah. That I can understand. But he was a good father?"

What a strange question. A shiver went over her at the implications behind it. She'd been very lucky in that her family had been a loving and nurturing one. She guessed not everyone had that. But the way he'd asked it… "Yes. My dad is a wonderful man. We have a very close relationship. At least we do now."

He nodded, but didn't look her way. "I'm glad."

And if she'd said he wasn't a good father? She blinked as a thought flickered in her head and then disappeared. She decided maybe she'd better move the subject away from her own life. "So are your parents both still living?"

"Yes."

The word came out quickly, and she waited for him to add something. Anything. She'd been looking at him when she asked the question, and was shocked by the sudden change in his profile after he bit out his answer. A muscle bunched in his jaw, flickering just like that lost thought from a few seconds ago. After the silence grew past the point of discomfort, she realized he wasn't going to expand on his answer. Maybe his family wasn't as close as she and her parents had been. As she and her father still were.

She swallowed. Her question had been innocent, but she suddenly felt she'd stumbled into an area that boasted a huge No Trespassing sign. "Sorry, Snow. I didn't mean to pry. I was just—"

"No. Don't be sorry." His shoulders relaxed and one side of his mouth quirked. "I deserved it. I pried into your family history, didn't I?"

She hadn't minded, because she had nothing to hide. Unlike Snow, evidently. There was a sense that his one-word answer had been loaded with a meaning she didn't understand. And it had nothing to do with language or culture.

"I didn't consider it prying. Still. I shouldn't have asked."

"Yes, you should have. My parents are still alive, but my father and I have no contact. Nor will we. My mom lives in Massena, actually. It's considered part of upstate New York."

"Upstate?"

"It means in the northern part of the state."

"Ah, I see." She couldn't imagine being estranged from one of her parents. It would take something drastic and terrible to have made her turn away from either of them. That earlier thought flickered again, getting a little brighter this time.

That extra lock on his door...

Surely not. Maybe it wasn't Snow who was hiding something and needed to keep people from discovering it. Maybe it had something to do with his dad. Maybe Snow didn't want him getting in his office. Except she didn't keep medication of any kind in her office, and she was pretty sure it would be against hospital regulations, anyway.

And she was probably reading way too much into all of this.

Snow pulled into the parking lot of a coffee chain. "I need a cup of coffee. Do you want something?"

"That sounds good. Some cream and a couple of sugar packets to go in it, please."

After placing the order and sliding up to the window, he handed her coffee across. She took a bracing sip, glad for the slight burn that trickled down her throat. It was going to be a warm day, but it always surprised her that coffee tended to cool her down rather than make her even warmer. Maybe it was the contrast of the beverage compared to the air inside the car.

Ten minutes later, they were pulling into the ferry station, and Snow found a place to park. There was already a line, but compared to what she'd been imagining, it wasn't too bad. They were just loading one of the ferries now.

"How many can it hold?"

"Several hundred passengers."

Her eyebrows went up as they got in line. "It shouldn't take us long to get on at that rate."

In actuality, they made it onto the ferry that was loading, although the line cut off a few people behind them. They went up the ramp to the boat and somehow managed to find a place near the railing, where they could see.

Then they were pulling away from the dock. A swift breeze blew into her face, and she was glad she'd scraped back her hair into a messy bun. It wouldn't have mattered if it had been neat, anyway, because most of it would probably be blown down by the time they got to the island.

Someone with a camera came over and squeezed into the space next to her, forcing her to move over until her hip pushed against Snow's. "Sorry," she murmured.

He leaned down, a hint of aftershave tickling her nose. "Not your fault." His voice was low, rumbling against her ear in a way that made her shiver.

She swallowed as unfamiliar sensations skipped through her belly, setting fire to whatever composure she had left. What would it be like to have this man whisper to her in a darkened room?

Not something she was ever likely to experience. And if she wasn't careful these ludicrous ideas were going to taint all of her future interactions with him. Was she in danger of developing a little crush on the handsome doctor? She hoped not, because that wouldn't be smart, given how aloof he was most of the time. And how secretive. While she'd shared quite a bit of personal information with him, the second she'd asked him to share something in return, he'd pretty much cut her off. Kind of the way Dave had cut her off at the end of their relationship. He'd gone from being her lover to immersing himself in his studies to barely answering her texts. For Kirsten, who was used to an open and warm home environment, that kind of attitude was strange and unfamiliar. But maybe it was just the American way.

Except she had known lots of other Americans in the ten years she'd been in the States. And while there were always some outliers, she'd met some incredible people. Like Nicola and Kaleb.

None of that mattered, however. Because letting herself fantasize about a man she worked with, a man she was likely to never see again if she left for Lebanon, was not a very smart idea. Because she would end up doing what Dave had done to her: walk away.

But you can look, can't you, Kirsten? And if you're leaving...

She was pretty sure she was already guilty of looking. But actually, her leaving might make it even easier. Because there would be no long-term commitments. No painful goodbyes. And Snow was pretty obviously not a warm and fuzzy, "forever" kind of guy. Even Nicola had mentioned yesterday that Snow was divorced and hard to get to know. She'd been surprised he was even taking her sightseeing.

So maybe Snow's attitude wasn't something she should take personally.

The person who'd squeezed next to her unexpectedly raised his arms to take a picture, and Kirsten jerked to the side, barely avoiding being elbowed in the chin. Snow must have noticed her evasive maneuver, because his arm went around her, and he edged her even closer. It wasn't with any kind of ulterior motive other than to help move her away from her annoying neighbor. It worked, and she found she could lean her head against Snow's shoulder. She rationalized it by telling herself it wasn't like she'd have to face him for the next twenty years. It might only be the next twenty months. Maybe less than that.

Then his thumb moved on her bare shoulder. Just like it had on his steering wheel. Just like she'd imagined him doing to her.

And boom! The thoughts she'd had while watching him drive hit all over again, skimming over her body and making her nipples tighten. Her knees went wobbly and she gripped the railing for support. Oh, Lord, she was going to have to learn to control herself. But unlike Snow, who seemed to be perfectly in control of his emotions and unaffected by her proximity, she wasn't used to having men pressed against her like this. Other than Dave, of course. She hadn't been in to casual dating, and he'd been her first real love. Her first time sleeping with a man.

She'd thought it would last forever, at the time. But evidently what she'd thought was a serious relationship hadn't been, at least not in his mind. They'd had some good times, but once they both left medical school and had started working in their prospective fields, it was like she'd been wiped off his slate of acquaintances. Added to that, their backgrounds were totally opposite.

His parents were divorced, and he had little contact with either of them, nor did he wish to change that. And he hadn't understood why she wanted to include her dad in every decision she made. It had caused a lot of friction between them. Maybe it was a matter of culture, but she didn't think so. They were just different. Too different. And to have it end after she'd bared her soul to him had devastated her, made her far less willing to share parts of herself with other people.

And yet she'd told Snow about her mom. About her

reasons for going into pulmonology. She wasn't even sure why she had. But she wasn't doing it again.

She was not going to get any ideas about Snow. And even if by some weird chance she came to care about him, they would fare no better than she and Dave had. He wasn't close to his family, by his own admission. And he was definitely not a very warm person. Or someone who shared things from his innermost being.

Not that she would. Come to care about him, that was. Because it wouldn't last. Even if she decided not to move.

Right now, though, none of that mattered. She wasn't looking for permanent things. Not even in her job at NYC Memorial. So she could sit back and enjoy being pressed close to someone who was very attractive. And if what Nicola had said was true, that he was hard to get to know, that could work in her favor. Because she wouldn't need to try to get to know him. Leaning against him was temporary. In a few minutes, even that would be over and they would go back to being two strangers.

But for now, she intended to be present in the moment and enjoy this outing. She would ignore those tiny warning lights that were flashing far in the distance. There was still a lot of time to make a detour around them. A lot of time to avoid the emotional sinkhole that might lie just beyond.

At least she hoped there was.

CHAPTER FOUR

SNOW HADN'T BEEN able to help himself.

That jerk had almost clocked Kirsten with his elbow and hadn't even apologized. What he should have done, though, was switch places with her rather than put his arm around her. Because when she'd laid her head on his shoulder...

Every protective instinct he had had risen to the occasion. Along with something else that had nothing to do with protection. Snow normally controlled every emotion that came into existence, only allowing them out after he'd examined them for any sign of irregularity. And the ones he'd had just now? They'd rushed out before he was even aware of them. Impulsive. Unexpected. Taking him completely by surprise. And that scared the hell out of him. Because what if one of them wrested control from him?

But the choice now was to nudge her away from him, and how was that being any less of a jerk than the eager tourist on her other side? The truth was, despite that fear, he kind of liked the feeling of having a woman leaning against him again. The most he'd done since his divorce was pass the time with a couple of women he barely knew. And they'd been the ones who'd pursued him, not the other way around. Unfortunately, one of them had been a nurse from a different department at the hospital who had sent him a barrage of text messages afterward, asking if he was interested in dinner. In a movie. In more of the same. "Just as friends, of course." Well, he didn't believe that, so he'd finally met with her and had a very uncomfortable discussion. It had worked. She hadn't texted him again. Nicola told him later that she'd spread some pretty nasty rumors about him to anyone who would listen.

He did not want to wind up in another situation like that. So he'd decided the best course of action was to stay as aloof as possible. And not talk about his past, if he could help it.

The boat docked with a gentle bump, and the tourist leaned over the rail, still snapping shot after shot of the Statue of Liberty, before finally moving away.

Kirsten's head lifted from its perch, leaving him with a strangely empty feeling. He uncurled his arm, noticing her face was pink-tinged.

"I'm sorry about that."

He smiled. "Again, not your fault."

It wasn't his, either, so why was *he* feeling so guilty? Ever since the nurse incident, he'd worried about sending the wrong signals, even though he'd gone over and over the events leading up to them sleeping together. The nurse had sat at his table at a hospital fundraiser and had made eyes at him all night. She'd asked him to dance when the music had turned slow. One thing had led to another and he'd left with her, only to regret it almost immediately afterward. Especially when those messages started hitting his in-box.

He did not want a repeat of that situation. Or the feeling of having no control over a situation.

Like this one? Maybe.

So why was he taking Kirsten on a sightseeing trip?

Maybe because she seemed lonely somehow...and hinted that she might not be at NYC Memorial for the long haul. And because he truly was grateful for the help she'd given him with Tanya.

They stood and joined the line to disembark. Maybe it was time to turn things back toward work. "So why don't you tell me about your patient. The one you want me to look at on Friday."

A tiny frown marred her brow. "Oh, um, I didn't bring her file with me."

"I didn't expect you to. I'm just interested in knowing some more about the case." *And shaking myself back to reality.*

"Oh, okay."

So she described what had happened on each of the previous visits along with the treatments she'd tried. "I'm not convinced anymore that it's a recurrent bronchial infection. Even a viral cause would either get better or worse, not just hang there indefinitely with no response to medication."

"You've ruled out neoplasms?"

A neoplasm was an abnormal growth of cells. While some neoplasms were benign, they could still cause inflammation that acted as a trigger for other symptoms.

They walked down the gangway and then down the long pier that separated New York from New Jersey. "No. I'm hoping to do that on Friday with an MRI." She stepped onto Liberty Island itself and stared at the towering statue in front of them. "Oh, wow. That's amazing. And huge."

With its pedestal half the size of the monument itself, the Statue of Liberty was an impressive sight. "It's something, all right. I'm sorry we won't be able to go all the way to the crown."

"It's really okay. I'm just happy to be able to see it at all." She turned back toward him. "Sorry. We were in the middle of talking about my patient."

"We can do that later. You didn't come here to talk about hospital stuff."

He needed to remember that. Even though he'd decided he needed to keep things professional, he was forgetting that not all women were like his ex, whom he should have been able to trust with his deepest secrets, but had never been able to get beyond the edges of the truth. Or even like the nurse down in Maternity. And Kirsten had shown no signs of being interested in him. Even putting her head on his shoulder had probably been an attempt at staying out of reach of that tourist. She hadn't meant anything by it at all. He'd been the one to haul her closer, for God's sake.

They worked in overlapping medical fields, so it was natural that they would get to know each other a little more than if they worked in separate departments. He just needed to find the line that separated personal and professional and do his best not to stray onto the wrong side of it.

They walked the distance to the sculpture itself. "The Statue of Liberty was actually placed inside Fort Wood, which had points like a star. It makes a perfect base."

"It does. I can't get over how big it is. Much larger than I expected."

He tried to see it through her eyes, which wasn't hard. Although he'd been here many times, its sheer size and presence still inspired awe. "It is big."

"So we get to go up into the...what did you call it?"

"The pedestal. And, yes, we have tickets. There are actually some interesting things housed in the building. We can either take the steps up to it or there's an elevator that goes most of the way."

"I think I need the exercise, if that's okay with you."

Perfect. He could use some time to regain his footing, anyway. "It's fine. I just wasn't sure with your..." He nodded at her skirt and shoes. She looked cool and comfortable, and far too beautiful.

And there he went again. Even more reason to take the slower route.

"It's kind of my go-to wear. And my shoes are almost as comfortable as tennis shoes. Now if my skirt was short, I might be going with the elevator, for obvious reasons."

Ha! Obvious reasons. Reasons he didn't need to be thinking about.

They wandered around the lower portion of the pedestal, and Snow pointed out different sights. "You'll see a lot more from the top of the building."

They trekked up the two hundred odd stairs that led to the center of the building. Snow frowned, then looked at his phone. "They used to have the old torch in here, I'm not sure... Ahh, they moved it to the new museum a couple of years ago. I should have looked to see. But this is what it looked like."

Kirsten came to stand next to him, looking at the image on his phone. "Oh, wow. Gorgeous. Why did they decide to replace it?"

"It was getting worn and the seals were leaking, letting water inside. After a while it wasn't feasible to keep trying to patch it up."

She glanced at him. "Sounds like what you do at the hospital. Replace things that can't be patched up."

"I never thought of it that way before." She had a point. "But the best course of action is to try to repair things so they don't need to be replaced."

She sighed. "It doesn't always work out that way, though, does it? Sometimes things just can't be repaired no matter how hard we try."

Like his childhood? His marriage? But in those particular situations, there were no transplants that would have allowed his dad to become a normal father, or that would have allowed Snow's marriage to live and thrive.

"You're right. Sometimes they can't be repaired."

She leaned back to look up at him. "I'm worried that my young patient might be one of those. I know children have transplants, too, but that's a lot of years to live with the immunosuppressant medications and the fear of eventual rejection. Or cancer."

"Yes, it is. But the alternative is death." That's exactly what had happened to his marriage. To his relationship with his dad.

"Yes. It is."

Was she thinking about her mom? He hadn't meant to put it quite so bluntly, but his thoughts had been chaotic over the last hour. "That came out a little harsher than it should have. And I'm sorry. Sometimes things just don't move quickly enough to save people."

She studied his face, her brow clearing. "You're talking about my mom."

"Yes."

"She just couldn't hold on until an organ became available, and at the end, she went on hospice care so they could keep her comfortable. It was no one's fault. It's kind of a crapshoot at times, isn't it? The whole transplant process."

"Yes, it's a matter of luck and timing."

Luck. Both good and bad. Good for the recipient, but terrible for the ones having to make heartbreaking decisions about loved ones.

Maybe she sensed his thoughts because she touched his hand. "I don't envy you your job, Snow. You're the patient's last stop. Their last hope. Most of the time, I'm not. If I run out of options, and they're still young and healthy enough, I can refer their cases to you and wash my hands of them."

Somehow, he doubted she washed her hands of them. Even when the patient wasn't hers, like Tanya.

"Except not everyone is eligible for a transplant." He turned over his hand and curled his fingers around hers. "And that is the hardest thing of all. Deciding who has the best odds for a successful outcome."

"Yes, it is. I remember the moment a doctor told my mom she was terminal. He wasn't very kind about it, just kind of chilly and detached, like he'd already handed her over to death. I vowed I would never be that kind of doctor. Except it's not that easy. If you allow yourself to feel everyone's pain…" Something shimmered in her blue eyes. "Well, I wouldn't be able to help the next patient or the one after that, if I couldn't get past my emotions. But it's hard. Really hard. There are just some patients…"

Like the one she wanted him to look at? For Snow, who was so used to controlling his feelings, he probably came across like the doctor who had told Kirsten's mother she was terminal. It wasn't intentional. And he wasn't trying to be cruel—or detached, like she'd said—but there was an element of self-preservation involved. Like there'd been during his childhood, when survival mode was the only mode under which he knew how to operate. Bits and pieces of that instinct still came out at times, and although he no longer feared for his life, deciding which emotions to pull out of hibernation was not an easy thing. He'd learned that during his marriage.

Sometimes it had been damn near impossible. Especially since there were times he still woke up in a cold sweat, thinking he heard something rattling his doorknob. He still locked his bedroom door at night to try to ward off those dreams.

Damn! Not something he needed to think about right now.

"Yes, you're right. It is hard." He released her hand, curling his fingers into his palms instead. "But being a doctor was never about being easy."

"No, I suppose not. But there are times when I relish the easy cases. The ones that I can solve and they stay solved. Those have happy endings."

"I think we all relish those types of cases."

She pulled her gaze toward one of the windows, seeming to shake away her thoughts. "So what are the views like up here?"

"They're great. Ready to see?"

"Yes. I'm definitely ready."

The sun was sinking low in the sky by the time they got through the Liberty Museum and visited Ellis Island. Back on the ferry once again, she realized she was exhausted, and despite her reassurances that her shoes were comfortable, her feet were a little more tired than they should have been. She slid her feet partly out of them and curled her toes before putting the shoes halfway on again.

"Hurting?"

"Yes, a little bit. I think they would have been tired even in tennis shoes, though. Sandals would have been worse."

"Probably. Especially on those stairs."

"Ah, yes, the stairs. Was I the one who actually suggested we go up them, rather than use the elevator?"

He grinned. "You were. Regretting it now?"

"Not exactly regretting, but wishing I was about twenty years younger."

His smile turned into a laugh. "You're not exactly ancient, Kirsten. You're what? Thirty? Thirty-one?"

"Thirty-two."

"Oh…so you *are* ancient."

She jabbed his arm. "That's not very nice." She knew he was joking, but it was more fun to pretend offense.

"No one has ever accused me of being nice."

Was he serious? Maybe. Hadn't she thought he matched his name, when she first met him? But she was finding that he had his moments. Like when he'd pulled her closer to help distance her from that tourist who was busy taking photos. "You're not so bad. Most of the time." She smiled to take away the sting. "Thanks for today, by the way. I had fun. I had no idea there was so much to see on the islands. At this rate, though, it will take me years to see all of New York."

"You have plenty of time."

She didn't. Not really. But she wasn't going to tell him that. And she was not going to ask him to go with her again. Once was enough. Why? Because she'd enjoyed today a little too much. "I'll start making my list of things to see."

"Well, at least you can check one item off of it."

"It's going to be hard to outdo what I saw today." She forced her feet back into her shoes as she spied the dock up ahead. In a few moments they would be getting off the boat and heading back to their normal everyday routines. She had to admit, there was a small part of her that didn't want today to end. And that wasn't good. Because everything came to an end, eventually. Everything.

The boat docked and everyone stood. The second she put weight on her aching feet, they protested and she realized the right one had gone to sleep from the way she'd been sitting. Her foot felt nothing. But she knew well enough that pins and needles would soon erupt beneath her sole, making her want to laugh and cry all at the same time. Yikes.

Snow, who'd been waiting for her to move forward, tilted his head. "Are you okay?"

"My foot's asleep."

As the crowd surged toward the exit, she realized she was in danger of getting caught up in the moving stream. Snow put an arm around her waist. "Hold on to me."

Just in time, because they were going whether they were ready or not. She snaked her arm around his lean hips and forced herself to move, leaning most of her weight on him and hoping her foot was landing flat. "Sorry. It has to be the way I was sitting. It'll wake up in a minute."

And it did. Seconds later, those familiar waves of prickles came every time she took a step. She groaned aloud in frustration.

He smiled down at her. "I take it it's waking up."

"Ugh. How can you tell?"

They somehow made it off the boat and Snow led her to a nearby bench. "Sit down for a second."

She did as he asked. "Thanks. Kind of embarrassing that I didn't notice it while I was sitting."

"It happens."

The sun was starting to go down and as Kirsten looked at the skyline, which had streaks of red appearing over the tops of the buildings, her foot was soon forgotten. "It's so beautiful. Sometimes life gets so busy, I forget to enjoy moments like these."

"Yes. Me, too."

Something in his voice urged her to look at him. And when she did, there was an emotion in his face that looked familiar. And terrifying.

Those light blue eyes were on her and not on the sky. And in those eyes she thought she saw...

Longing. Desire. Myriad things she'd been pretty sure she'd never see again before she left the country. And things she was positively sure she'd never see in Snow's face. Was he even capable of feeling those things?

Evidently, because there it was. And he wasn't trying to look away or brush it off as something else entirely. No. He didn't care that she'd noticed. Or recognized it for what it was.

Or maybe that was all in her imagination.

"Give me your foot." He reached his hand down.

Without hesitation, she lifted her leg and let him haul it onto his lap. His nimble fingers tipped off her shoe and set it on the bench next to his hip as her mouth went dry.

Was he going to—?

He palmed her bare arch, kneading the spots where her nerve endings had gone haywire. Except they weren't anymore. But something stopped her from admitting that fact or telling him that he didn't need to massage it. Because it felt wonderful. Heavenly, even.

She couldn't suppress the soft groan that slid out before she could stop it.

"Good?"

"Mmm…yes. I didn't realize how tired they were." She gave a nervous laugh when he shifted his touch to the base of her toes. "I'm not going to want to get up, if you keep that up."

He smiled. "No need to get up just yet. Neither of us are working tonight, so we don't have to go directly home, unless you're tired."

His thumbs were nudging pressure points on the sole of her foot, bewitching her and removing any desire to get up and get moving.

It was luscious. Her ex had never been a touchy-feely person, so there'd been no back massages, no little unexpected touches. Most of their physical connection happened in the bedroom. And for this to occur out in the open… She felt a little bit like an exhibitionist as she leaned her head on the back of the hard bench and gave herself over to his ministrations. Right now she didn't care who saw. And it wasn't like they were making out. Or anything else.

"Aren't your feet tired at all?"

"No." The one-word answer surprised her enough that she almost pulled away. Except he was now working on the base of her toes, moving the joints this way and that. It wasn't hurting anything to enjoy his touch. Like she'd thought earlier, she was not here in New York on a permanent basis. So she needed to soak up what she could while she was here. And if that meant a little bit of physical contact between her and the transplant surgeon, so be it. After all, she was a transplant herself. One that would soon be uprooted and planted somewhere else in a short period of time.

Why not just give in to what had been building for most of the day? She'd be lying to herself to say she wasn't attracted to him. She'd already reacted to his nearness. More than once.

But what about him? The difference between right now and her very first conversation with him was worlds apart. And she was pretty sure he'd been aware of her while they were talking about repairs and transplants.

She swallowed. Only one way to know for sure.

"Snow…" She whispered his name, half-hoping he wouldn't hear her. But he did. And when his eyes met hers, she saw that she hadn't been wrong. There was a heat burning in those pupils that surprised her. Ignited her.

His massaging fingers slowed, until they were no longer moving. Everything in their little bubble of space grew still as they stared at each other.

Then he finally lifted her foot from his lap and set it on the ground. She gulped, thinking she'd read him wrong, that he was going to get up and suggest they go back to the car. Then his arm snaked around her waist, just like it had on the boat. When he'd been trying to protect her. Only this time it was not protection she saw on his face.

This moment seemed inevitable, felt like they'd been hurtling toward it ever since they'd stepped foot on that boat.

And Kirsten couldn't stop it if she wanted to. And, Lord help her, she didn't want to.

When his fingers threaded in the hair at her nape and he tilted her face up, she was lost in a sea of blue. Her teeth came down on her lip, and his eyes flicked to her mouth. And then his head was descending in slow motion, and her world suddenly tilted on its axis.

CHAPTER FIVE

HE HADN'T MEANT to kiss her, had only meant to help with her foot. But then she'd said his name. The husky way it rolled off her tongue had made him come unglued, had pulled him toward her. And hell if her mouth wasn't every bit as soft as he'd imagined it would be. Her skin held a hint of salt from the spray of the boat trip. In trying to help her foot wake up, he woken himself, instead.

Pull away. Before it's too late. Before you're out of control.

The warning was already too late, because the second she started kissing him back, he was free-falling. Adrift in the sky with nothing tethering him to reality.

And right now, reality was the last thing he wanted to think about.

He bit her lower lip, and she shuddered against him, her arms looping themselves around his neck. He needed to take a step back, to make a decision. Get up and force himself to take her home. Or get up and take her back to his apartment to finish what he started. Because staying on this bench wasn't an option, unless he wanted to get them thrown in jail. Or maybe he should let her make the decision and take the choice out of his hands.

He leaned down and found her ear. "How anxious are you to get home?"

"Not anxious. Especially if I'll be there alone."

A wave of exhilaration crashed over him. It hadn't been his imagination. She was just as caught up in the moment—in him—as he was in her.

"You won't be alone, I promise. And I was thinking my place."

Her cheek slid against his, her arms tightening and holding her against him. "Your place it is."

"Can you walk?"

She leaned back and glanced into his face. "It's a little too early to be asking me that, isn't it?"

He laughed, catching her drift. "I was referring to your foot. But I've always liked a challenge."

Her face turned a wonderful shade of pink. "I wasn't suggesting… I thought you meant…"

"Oh, I know what you thought." He grinned. "So… your foot? Or would you rather I carry you back to the car."

"I can walk on it."

"Too bad. I was kind of looking forward to tossing you over my shoulder."

"You wouldn't!"

The way he was feeling right now, he wasn't too sure what he would do. But nothing about this felt ominous or truly dangerous to anything other than his own peace of mind.

Snow aimed a slow smile at her before taking her shoe and sliding it back in place. "Okay. No shoulders. At least not today." Then, taking her hand, he towed her toward the parking lot and his car. He hadn't set out on this trip with this endgame in mind. In fact, he'd tried to avoid this with every fiber of his being. But now that it was here, and she was just as into it as he was, he wasn't going to shy away from it. Even if he wanted to. And he definitely did *not* want to.

What about future text messages?

He wasn't sure how he knew it, but Kirsten wouldn't go that route. She hadn't been the one to initiate this— he had. And that should bother him on some level.

They made it to the car and headed out of the parking lot. He caught her hand in his and placed it on the gearshift. The sensuality of their hands together as they shifted from one gear to another made desire clutch at his innards. They stopped at a traffic light, and Snow pulled her toward him for a long, drawn-out kiss. A half hour had never seemed so long.

Then they were back in traffic. New York City definitely had a nightlife, so the line of vehicles was almost as long as it was during rush hour. He could see why some people chose not to have a vehicle, relying instead on public transport to get them where they needed to be. Kirsten had said that was part of the appeal of the city. Snow liked to drive himself, though, despite the inconveniences.

"Just a few more minutes, I promise."

She gave him a smile. "Don't worry. I'm enjoying the ride."

Something about the way she said that made his insides heat. Then again, it could just be him reading a secondary meaning into her words. He was tempted to find an empty lot and find out, but he really, really wanted to do this in his apartment, rather than in public. He wanted privacy. And leg room. And to enjoy her in small, sensuous bites. He could dissect all the feelings that went along with that desire later. But most of all, he wanted her naked, with her skin against his. Anything less than that would be…sacrilege.

A few blocks later, his apartment complex came into view. He pulled down a ramp, punched in his code and waited as the doors swung open. He'd rented this place six years ago, before he married Theresa. And after she left, he'd retained the apartment, although he'd thought about selling when they first divorced. But since not all of his memories in this place were linked to her, he was able to get past it. Besides, he already had his security measures in place, and to get something else… Well, it meant he had to make a decision about whether or not to cycle back through the measures he'd taken ever since he'd been out on his own. By keeping this place, he didn't have to make that decision. Could just pretend that it was easier to leave things as they were, than to have to deal with putting his past behind him, once and for all.

If he sat down and examined it long enough, he'd realize that no, he probably wouldn't have his extra locks removed. And that idiosyncrasy had played a part in the breakup of his marriage. A smaller part than the issues she'd had with his emotional availability, to be sure, but it all had jumbled together to make a huge mess of their relationship.

There'd been no saving it by that point. And maybe there'd been no saving him, by that point, either.

He found his parking place and pulled into it, shifting his car into first gear and turning off the engine. Kirsten had gotten quiet. A little too quiet. Maybe she'd changed her mind.

Hell, if she had, it was better to find out now than later. "Hey. Are you okay?"

"Not really."

His chest tightened, and he somehow forced the words from a throat that had gone dry. "Do you want me to take you home?"

"What?" Understanding dawned in her face. "No. I didn't mean that. I meant I didn't expect the trip over here to take as long as it did."

His muscles went slack with relief, and he laughed, swinging out of his car and moving around to open her door. "I'm afraid it's going to take a whole lot longer."

"What do you mean?"

He took her hands and looked into her face. "If you think we're going in there and moving through everything at lightning speed, you're very much mistaken."

She used his grip to tug him toward her. "I don't care what speed we move at. As long as we move." She nodded at the corner of the parking garage, where a small camera silently watched. "Because that thing is going to get a…how do you say it…? *Hadhar*… To see more than it wishes to see."

He loved hearing her say things in Arabic. "I think

eyeful is the word you're looking for. And you're right. It—or whoever is behind the scenes—is going to get an eyeful if we don't start walking toward the elevator."

Pressing his forehead to hers, he said, "There's a camera in the elevator, too, unfortunately."

"And in your apartment? Are there cameras there, too?"

She meant the words in a playful way, but his gut tightened for a second. Because there were. Only his cameras were very well hidden and could be turned off with the touch of a button. He was careful with how he phrased his answer. "No spying eyes in there. The only one watching you will be me. The only recording device will be in my head."

"I like that. So you'll be reliving it?"

"Will you?" He already knew his answer, but he wanted to know hers.

"You know I will."

He led her toward the elevator and pushed the button. Once inside, he used a special key that would take him to his assigned floor. Every tenant had one. It had been one of the features that had sold him on the place.

They arrived on the fourteenth floor, and got off the elevator. Snow curled his fingers around her hips and walked backward with her toward the door to his apartment. Once there, he unlocked the dead bolt and the doorknob, and pressed his thumb on the reader pad, then waited for that last security measure to release a lock. As they started through the entryway, he saw her eyes were no longer on him, but on the door they'd just come through.

"I didn't realize these big apartment blocks had so much security," she said.

"It varies from place to place." She didn't need to know that only his apartment had all of these measures. She was only here for a night. Not long-term, like Theresa had been. No need to explain anything. Or try. Not that his ex had bought any of his explanations.

"Got it." But there had been a tiny hesitation before she'd said that.

Time to get her mind back on other things. He slammed the door and reeled her toward him. "Still okay?"

"Oh, yes." She smiled, and whatever he'd seen in her eyes disappeared in a flash. "And now that we're alone…"

"All alone. Not even a pet fish to interrupt us."

"Mmm…I like that. Not the pet thing, but the no-interruptions thing."

His hands went to her shoulders and skimmed down her arms. Her blouse had no sleeves and the skin he encountered was warm and silky soft. She was addicting, in the best possible way.

He reached down and scooped her up, heading toward his bedroom.

Laughing, she said, "What about the tour?"

"Don't worry. You're about to get the most important tour of the house. There's a lot to see." He kissed her cheek, her nose, her mouth. "And even more to explore."

His bedroom door was open, so he walked in, then turned to push it shut with his foot. She stopped him.

"No cameras, right? So no need to shut the door."

He blinked. "Right. Just habit."

It was habit. One ingrained since childhood, when his mom had whispered for him to get into his room and lock the door. Leaving a door wide-open was hard. Even now. But he smiled and left it as it was, moving with her toward the bed. He set her on it carefully, smiling as she held her arms out to him.

He could shut the door later. It would be okay. It was actually the first time a woman had challenged him about his habit. Except for his ex. But even then, Theresa hadn't known the full reason behind it. She'd banged and banged at that door inside of his head, trying to get inside…to understand why he was the way he was. That had proved a disaster. Because the harder she pushed, the more he barricaded himself in. He wouldn't let a woman get close enough to try again.

And there was no need. Snow would honor the toast he and Kaleb had made a year ago—he was not getting married again. His buddy might have found his so-called soul mate, but he was pretty sure there wasn't one out there for him. And for his own peace of mind, he didn't want there to be.

Looking at the woman now sprawled across his bed, her eyes staring up at him as if waiting for his next move, all thoughts of Theresa—and the doors in his mind—fled as a wave of need coursed through him. The long white skirt emphasized her tanned skin and long slender legs. His glance went lower. "Let's get rid of these shoes, shall we?"

He leaned down and slid the black wedged heels off

her feet. There was a small blister on the outside of one of her big toes. He touched it. "Damn. Why didn't you tell me about this?"

She looked puzzled. "Tell you what?"

"That your shoes were giving you a blister."

"I didn't really notice it until the very end."

That didn't help. He felt like a cad for making her walk as much as they had. He sat on the bed and propped her foot across his legs. "We can put some lotion on that."

She straightened her leg, forcing it off his lap. "Later. The last thing I want to talk about is blisters or shoes or lotion."

He shifted at the waist, using his arms to lean down and bracket her into his space. "So, what do you want to talk about instead?"

"Don't want to talk at all," she muttered, taking hold of his polo shirt and pulling him down toward her. The kiss was hard and wet and full of so much promise that it made his throat tighten. Oh, to be able to just live in this moment for a lifetime.

Well, the lifetime part might not be possible, but living in the moment was definitely doable.

The kiss deepened, until it was teeth and tongue and the need to get closer to each other. When he pulled away, his breath was uneven, the area behind his zipper throbbing with need. And her face. Kirsten's face was flushed, and her lips had parted to reveal the edges of white teeth.

"Damn. How did you do that?"

"Do what?"

"Push me to the very edge of the world." He stood to his feet and took hold of her skirt. "Is there a zipper?"

"No, it's elastic."

He tugged, and like magic it rode the curve of her hips, and he waited until she lifted slightly before tugging it over her butt. White lace came into view. Lace that was wide across her hips and narrowed to play peekaboo with the area at the junction of her thighs. He wanted to pause there. But he needed to finish his task. The skirt.

After letting it drop to the floor, his fingers trailed up the outsides of her thighs, enjoying more of her silky smooth skin. But first, the blouse had to go.

The buttons were black, like the rest of the fabric, and he leaned over her, going by feel rather than by sight as each pearl fastener slid through its hole and displayed more curves hidden beneath it. This time the lace was black, matching the fabric of her shirt. He liked it. Liked that her bra was the opposite color of her underwear. It reminded him of the turmoil and contradictions he housed inside himself.

"You're beautiful, did you know that?"

She smiled up at him, her eyes bright, shining just for him. At least right now. "You're not so bad yourself." She sat up, her fingers going to his waistband. "But I think it's time to even up the playing field."

Pushing his shirt up his stomach, he leaned over so she could haul the garment over his head. Then it was on the floor, her fingers wandering over his bare chest, scraping down over his nipples in a way that made his

breath whoosh out on an oath. He somehow managed
to choke out, "That is not leveling the field."

Using his legs to push hers apart, he joined her on
the bed, his erection pressing into her belly with a need
that was hard to contain. He kissed her as one hand
skimmed up her side until he found her breast. It was
soft, her bra presenting it to him in a way that made his
mouth water. He did what she'd done to him a moment
or two ago, and gently scraped his thumbnail over her
nipple. Her moan shot through him, arcing right down
to his shaft and making it jump.

Hell, with the way his emotions were cascading out
of control, he was not going to be able to make this last
as long as he'd hoped. The horizon was moving toward
him at an ever-increasing speed. Soon he wouldn't be
able to stop it from slamming into him and dragging
him to a swift release.

Something about that niggled at the back of his
mind, a blinking red light that warned him to slow
down. But he didn't want to listen to it or anything,
right now.

He reached behind her and unhooked her bra, peel-
ing it down her arms and tossing it in the direction her
blouse and shirt had gone. Then she was bare, that
golden skin calling to him. He rolled over, pulling her
with him, until she was straddling his hips, sitting up
where he could see her, his gaze moving down her
throat, over those beautiful breasts, past her stomach
to the place where her legs parted for him.

Hard and throbbing and still struggling for control,
he reached back to his pocket and removed his wallet.

Took out a condom and threw the wallet onto his nightstand, missing and sending it sailing onto the floor. He didn't care. Nothing mattered right now except for getting the rest of their clothes off.

But he didn't want her to move.

He gripped her hips and rotated his pelvis into her.

Hell! Raw sensation rocketed through him, his mind teeming with tantalizing scenarios all ending with them finishing this right now, with their clothes still on. He repeated the act, letting himself fall a little further. Kirsten's eyes shut tight.

"No." Her word came out raspy and urgent.

He immediately sat up, that niggling at the back of his mind becoming a screaming, accusing siren.

"I'm sorry." His arms going around her to keep her from falling backward. "Did I hurt you?"

She got off of him and stood on the hardwood floor. "No. You didn't." Before he could figure out why she suddenly wanted to stop, her fingers went to her waistband and pushed her panties down.

"I thought you said—"

"I meant 'no' as in I want to feel you, and if you keep doing what you're doing—" she gave a visible swallow "—I'm not going to last very long."

Her meaning hit him, and the relief was so thick, he had to shut his eyes for a minute to get through it. Then he laughed, although it was shaky. "Damn. I was just thinking that maybe we could make it work without taking our clothes off at all."

"You thought wrong." She reached for the button on his jeans and undid it.

In a flash he was off the bed and shucking the rest of his clothes. He grabbed the condom package and opened it, rolling it over himself. "Okay, so no to the clothes. But yes to everything else?"

"Yes, to everything…and anything."

The words blazed over him, setting him on fire and storming his senses. To have that kind of trust, even though she knew almost nothing about him…

His throat clogged for a second. He would make sure that trust wasn't misplaced. Would make sure of her pleasure, even if it meant withholding his own.

He took her wrists and pulled them behind her, until they rested in the small of her back. Holding them there, he leaned down and kissed her, some weird feeling sliding up his spine and burrowing in the back of his head.

God, he wanted to do everything. Thoughts came in snatches that he struggled to catch hold of. "I want you on top. I want your hands like this."

"Okay." The word was breathless. Excited.

He sat on the bed, still holding her hands behind her, and she scrambled on top of him, until she was straddling him once again. He wanted to watch her. Wanted to see each movement of her hips, each expression that crossed that beautiful face of hers. Slowly he reclined on the mattress.

"Lift your hips, honey." He wasn't exactly sure how this was going to work, but hell if he didn't want to try.

She raised up enough to free him. Then, looking at him, she found him, shifted until she was positioned over him. Then she sank onto him in tiny increments, slowly enveloping him in a way he'd never felt before. There was a sensuality to her that came naturally. There was nothing artificial, nothing scripted. His fingers entwined with hers, staying right there with her as she started to move. He should touch her, make sure she came to completion first, but there was something in her face. Something that said she didn't need anything extra.

So instead of letting go of her hands, he used his hold to tip her forward until he could reach her breasts, letting his lips and tongue glide over her, hold her, suckle her.

Her breath came faster, and every once in a while a soft sound escaped, driving him wild. He'd needed this night. Needed to find a release he hadn't found in a very long time.

He released her nipple and lifted his head up so he could capture her mouth as she rose and fell faster, her movements becoming jerky and uncoordinated. God. He wanted to be right there with her. He plunged his tongue into her mouth, mimicking what she was doing above him. Suddenly she pulled away from him and sat up, her hips pumping, pelvis rotating each time it met his body.

Hell, she was pleasuring herself. "Oh, sweetheart. Damn, you are killing me."

Her face was intent, eyes tightly closed as she continued her movements. It was too much. He was going to…

She cried out, hips suddenly pumping hard, and he felt it. The pulsating squeeze and release on his shaft.

He erupted, driving into her with a groan, mind blanking out for a few seconds, all thoughts obliterated as he hung in space, lost in his own incredible pleasure.

Kirsten relaxed against him for a few seconds, before rolling forward to lie half across his body, breathing hard. He let go of her hands and wrapped his arms around her, holding her close.

He'd meant to bring her here, have sex with her and then drive her home. But that wasn't enough. Not right now. Maybe it was the stupor of his climax. Maybe it was the unbridled sex itself. But he wanted more. Wanted her again. As dangerous or stupid as that might be.

So he held her as his mind finally began to unravel, a delicious lethargy beginning to steal over him as he relaxed completely. He didn't ask her to stay, although the impulse was there, knocking on the door of his mind. He'd let her decide. He waited. Struggling to overcome the heaviness in his limbs, the satiation that was spreading through every cell of his body, until he finally gave in to it.

With one last tightening of his arms, he let his eyes close so the darkness could overtake him.

CHAPTER SIX

KIRSTEN ROLLED OUT of bed and gathered her clothes. Wow. Okay, so the not-being-able-to-walk thing was real, but it was more because her legs were so shaky that she could barely make them hold her up. A squeaked laugh came out of her.

He was leaning against the headboard watching her, hands behind his head. He looked totally relaxed. Totally at ease. And totally capable of walking unaided.

The thought of him sauntering naked to the bathroom made her mouth go dry.

"What?" he said.

There was no way she was going to tell him, so she just shook her head. "I didn't expect to spend the night last night."

"I'm glad you did."

That surprised her. She hadn't really thought the man housed any softer emotions. Even last night, he'd been all hard-edged and intense. And, actually, she was glad she stayed, too. Glad to see this transformation in him. She'd learned some things about him in the process. Her thoughts yesterday about how Snow and her ex were similar seemed completely off base now. They were nothing alike. Besides, she didn't need to worry about her heart being broken this time, because it hadn't been involved in what had happened last night.

And the sex had been…

Out of this world.

He'd woken and reached for her twice during the night and both times had topped the time before, which left her discombobulated, both mentally and physically.

Hence her uncooperative limbs. "I'm just going to jump in the shower, if that's okay."

One eyebrow went up. "Want some company?"

Her weak limbs somehow found new strength. She gave an internal eye roll. "As tempting as that sounds, I'll never make it to work on time if that happens." She reached for the doorknob and tried to twist it, but it didn't budge. She tried again, thinking it was just because she was shaky, but it still didn't move. A chill went over her. Hadn't she asked him to leave the door open last night?

"Why is this locked?"

His eyes went from warm and satisfied to cool and wary in the space of two seconds. He levered himself out of bed and came over to unlock the mechanism. And somehow not even his nakedness took the edge off her shock.

"Sorry," he said. "Force of habit."

Force of habit? Locking himself in his bedroom, when the rest of his apartment was already shut up tighter than a penitentiary?

She swallowed. Something about that didn't feel

right. She'd told them he could do anything to her. And he had, but there'd been nothing sinister about any of it.

But the locked door...

She'd reminded him that they were alone. And yet, despite that, sometime during the night, he'd gotten up and not only *shut* the door, but also *locked* it.

The chill spread to her bones. Anything personal she'd asked him had been met with short answers that told her nothing.

"Is there something I need to know?" First his office, and now his home.

He didn't meet her eyes this time. "Nope."

Another one-word answer, like when she'd asked about his parents. His later explanation hadn't been much more revealing. It was like he was withholding something. Something important.

He locked his bedroom door, even though he lived alone. Exactly whom was he expecting to try to get in?

Before she could stop herself a question came out. "Is someone *after* you, Snow?"

Maybe a disgruntled relative from a surgery gone bad? She'd certainly heard of that happening. And it would explain everything. Or almost everything.

The sudden pivot to face her came out of nowhere, causing her to take a step back. "What do you mean?" The wariness in his face had turned glacial, his jaw stiff, lips white. He might as well have been flash frozen.

Her idea didn't seem so ridiculous now. "I don't know. I've just never met anyone who lived alone and locked almost every door they had. I certainly don't do that. It just struck me as…odd."

Odd was the most neutral word she could think of. Because the other ones that were running through her head were things she wasn't going to give voice to.

"No one is after me."

He'd sidestepped her statement by answering her earlier question. So much for him not being like Dave. He'd evaded every question she threw at him as he was breaking up with her. She still had no idea what had gone wrong with that relationship. Had she been too clingy? Too ambitious? Was she horrible in bed? She had no idea, because he *wouldn't communicate with her*!

Well, fine. If Snow wanted to act like that, she had no horse in this race. But, something was going on. If he'd told her that New York could be a dangerous place to live, she would have accepted it at face value…but it took a special key to even get up to his apartment. And no one else at the hospital seemed to need an extra lock on their office door like he did. The hospital had pretty tight security. And cameras.

She made a decision. "Well, that's good to know. I think I'll skip the shower. Do you mind driving me home? I can catch a taxi, if not."

"Of course, I'll drive you." If anything, he looked relieved that she wasn't staying. Wasn't asking any more questions that he wasn't willing to answer. So much for his being glad that she'd stayed over.

Her perfect night had just imploded, and she wasn't even sure why. All she knew was that she needed to get home and clear her head before going to work. She definitely couldn't do that here. Not when her feelings for him had gone from simple lust to... She wasn't sure what these new emotions rolling around inside of her were. But she didn't like them. They spoiled everything she and Snow had done last night.

The sooner they could go back to being colleagues who worked together and nothing more, the better. All she needed to do now was figure out how to get there.

And how to forget the iciness of his demeanor when she'd asked about that lock on his door.

The look on Kirsten's face was going to haunt him for a long time. The shock when she'd turned the knob and realized she couldn't get out of his room had shifted to a flash of fear before the emotion disappeared. He remembered feeling that exact same thing as a kid, when his dad had rattled the doorknob to his room. The thought of doing something that made her afraid...

She'd asked why it was locked, and all he could think of to say was that it was out of habit.

It was.

But there were reasons behind the habit. Reasons he didn't want to explain, since she wasn't going to be in his life forever. And so the alternative was to clam up. She probably thought he was some kind of serial killer or something. She hadn't been able to get out of there fast enough.

All because of something he'd done.

Goddamn. This was why he didn't do relationships. Would never do them again. His past was his past, and not something he wanted to relive with every question. And he certainly didn't want someone to be afraid of him.

He'd tried sharing something with Theresa once, but the questions had kept coming in a never-ending barrage that had ended in cheating and divorce.

It was easier just to move through life without worrying about what others thought—when he himself didn't have to think about it. It was what it was, and he had no desire to change. For anyone.

Especially after what had happened with Kirsten.

Honestly? He should probably sit down and talk to her so that there was no weirdness between them.

No weirdness? How about sleeping together when they barely knew each other? How was that for weirdness? How about locking the door and scaring the crap out of her?

There was nothing normal about that.

Anger rose up in him in a wave. So what if he locked the damn door? He'd slept with two other women—women he didn't know very well—and it hadn't seemed to bother them. One had practically turned into a stalker afterward. So why was he suddenly so worried about what Kirsten thought?

Something inside of him, though, said that this time he needed to talk to her. To at least explain a little bit of what had happened to him. Before she got some crazy thoughts that weren't based in reality.

It boiled down to the fact that he didn't want her to be afraid of him. To think that he housed some kind of monstrous compulsion.

How can you be sure you don't?

His locked doors were a compulsion. He'd been able to admit that to himself a long time ago. But it didn't harm anyone. Or so he'd thought. Until this morning, when he'd looked into Kirsten's eyes and saw the size of her pupils.

Yes. He was going to pull her aside and talk to her. Maybe after they looked at her patient tomorrow. If she still wanted his opinion, that is. Maybe she wanted nothing to do with him now.

No, he had a feeling that Kirsten's patients came first with her, no matter how uncomfortable things might get with her personal life.

That could work in his favor, if he was careful.

A knock came at his office door, and he tensed. If it was Kirsten, he hadn't quite made a decision about how much to tell her.

"Come in."

It wasn't the pulmonologist who came through the door, though—it was Kaleb. Relief poured through him. He forced a smile. "Hey! I've haven't seen you around in a couple of weeks. How are Nicola and the baby?"

His friend came in and dropped into one of the chairs in front of his desk. "They're doing fine. I'm finally back at work after taking a week off to stay home and watch the baby while she recovered from RSV."

"I didn't realize she had that. No problems?"

Kaleb leaned back. "No, just fussiness and a lack of sleep. For both of us."

"You, fussy?"

"Ha! Funny. You try taking care of a sick baby and see how well you do."

"I can't see myself doing that. Ever." He changed the subject before Kaleb read more into the words than he should. "I saw Nicola around the hospital a couple of times, but just from a distance. She looked busy."

"Yeah, her schedule was more hectic than mine last week, which is why I was the one to stay with Cass."

"No lasting problems from the RSV?"

Kaleb adored his baby and Nicola. It was there in his eyes every time he talked about either of them. And Snow was glad for him. The pact they'd made may not have worked out for the facial reconstructive surgeon. In fact, it had seemed to backfire royally, as Nicola got pregnant after a one-night stand. But the pair was happy now. And despite Snow's doubts during the wedding itself, it didn't look like there were any problems in paradise. At least not yet. He was happy for them, even if that wasn't the path that Snow planned on taking.

Especially after what had happened with Kirsten.

"None, but that's not why I'm here."

"Okay." Snow had assumed his friend happened to be walking by his office and decided to pop in. Evidently not. "A patient?"

"No, you, actually."

"Me?" That surprised him. But if the man was here to tell him their toast had been a big mistake, he was barking up the wrong tree. It may have been a mistake for Kaleb, but it hadn't been a mistake for him.

"My wife actually sent me."

Maybe they were having a barbecue or a get-together and wanted to invite him.

"Okay, what's going on?"

"I think I should be asking you that question."

He frowned. "I don't follow."

Kaleb leaned forward. "You know I don't like sticking my nose in your business, right?"

"Uh, we've been sticking our noses in each other's business ever since we were kids. And I was the one who told you to go after Nicola, wasn't I?"

"Yes, you were. And you were right. Which is why I'm here."

"If you're going to tell me to go after someone, then you've got the wrong friend. There isn't anyone. I mean it."

Kaleb studied him for a minute. "Okay. I believe you." He waited another second or two. "Nicola ran into that new pulmonologist this morning…Dr. Nadif. They're friends. Anyway, she asked Nicola a kind of strange question. She asked what my wife knew about you."

What the hell? He picked up a pen off his blotter and turned it end over end. What had Kirsten told her?

The pediatric nurse's texts came back to mind. Had he read her that wrong?

"Why would she do that?"

One of Kaleb's eyebrows lifted. Great. So now Nicola and Kaleb both knew.

"It was nothing. And I really don't appreciate her going around telling people that we slept together." He stood up. "In fact, I'm going to—"

"Hey, hold on a minute." Kaleb held up a hand, stopping Snow in his tracks. "She's not. In fact, I didn't even know you slept together until this very minute. When *you* told me. Congratulations, by the way. That's exactly how Nicola and I started out."

This was just getting better and better. He dropped back into his chair. So Kirsten hadn't blurted out the truth...he had. But what else would he have thought?

"Sorry to disappoint you, but it was a spur-of-the-moment thing. It meant nothing."

So why were Kirsten's scared eyes branded onto his soul? It was the fact that she hadn't balked at anything they'd done. Not even when some of their foreplay had been passionate enough to sting. Because she'd dished out as much as she'd gotten. And there'd been no fear. No hesitation. It had been sexy and exciting, and he'd been imagining it happening again, even as she stood in front of his door the next morning wearing nothing but a smile. Except that smile had changed the second she tried to open the door.

Dammit!

"That's what I once said, too, Snow. But that's neither here nor there."

Which brought them back to the reason for his friend's visit. "So if she didn't tell Nicola about last night, then what?"

"She asked why your office door has an extra lock on it when no one else's does. She said she went around and looked just to be sure."

So he was right. It had bothered her every bit as much as he thought it had. "What did Nicola tell her?"

"Well, contrary to what you think, I haven't told my wife everything about when we were kids. It never came up. She knows we're friends and that you spent a lot of time at my house, but as far as some of the rest of it…"

"You could have told her. It's no big secret." Except it was. To him. And Snow was glad his friend hadn't said anything. He could only imagine the look of pity that would cross people's faces if they learned about his past. Or wondered if Snow might somehow perpetuate the cycle of abuse.

"It's not my story to tell. But Nicola thought maybe you should know about Dr. Nadif's question."

"Yeah, Kirsten asked me about it, too, and I avoided answering. I've already decided I need to say something to her." He dragged his fingers through his hair. "She got up this morning after we… Well, she found the door to the bedroom locked and got kind of weirded out."

Weirded out was one way to put it.

"You are kind of over the top as far as security goes."

"Yeah, I know. But I always figured it was my business. That it didn't affect anyone else."

His friend studied him. "And Theresa?"

"Well, even without the locks, that was probably destined to fail."

The locks were a symptom of something deeper. Snow was no psychiatrist, but even he understood that.

"I think you're probably right. I just don't want Dr. Nadif causing problems for you. You're a damn good doctor, Snow, but rumors—true or not—can twist things to make them seem far bigger than they actually are."

Yes, they could. He knew that from his experience with that nurse. And he could see how this could be made to look like something it wasn't. "Thanks for the heads-up. I'll talk to her."

"Good." Kaleb stood up. "You don't have to tell her everything. But you do need to explain enough to make her understand."

"I will."

They said their goodbyes, and Snow closed the door behind his friend, leaning against it, but not locking it. Why had Kirsten not just come to his office to ask him about it directly instead of going to Nicola? Well, she probably thought that his friend's wife knew more than she did. And he could see that it might be hard for her to come and ask him. After all, she'd already tried twice. Once when she'd asked about his lock on his office. And then again last night, when he'd evaded the elephant in the room, stepping around it and trying to pretend it didn't exist. Kind of hard when she was staring right at it.

So he wasn't going to wait until tomorrow to talk to her. He was going to have this out now. Before she asked anyone else besides Nicola.

He picked up his phone and found her number. His thumb hovered over the call button for a second or two before he finally took a deep breath and mashed it. It rang twice, and then Kirsten picked up. "Hello?"

He didn't want to go into the fact that Kaleb had

come to his office or that he knew that she'd gone behind his back and asked Nicola, when she couldn't get any answers out of him. Instead, he simply said, "Hey, do you have a few minutes sometime today to come by my office so we can go over your patient's chart before I actually see her?"

"Oh, um, yes. I have some time after lunch, if that works for you."

No hint of them going to eat lunch together. Not that he wanted to or was even going to suggest it. "I do. Say around one o'clock?"

"That sounds...doable."

Her slight hesitation wasn't lost on him. But she didn't mention last night, and he wasn't going to, either. Not over the phone, anyway. Was she afraid to meet in his office? He'd hate it if that was true, but who could he blame for that besides himself? There might not be anything he could do about what had already happened, but he could sure as hell try to change what happened in the future. Starting with giving her a choice of where to meet. "Would you rather we met somewhere else? We can always go sit on one of the benches outside."

"No. Your office will be fine. Besides, it'll be easier to look at her records on an actual computer rather than on one of our phones."

She had a point there. And her response sounded stronger this time. She was more sure of herself.

"Okay, I'll see you here at one, then."

"See you there."

He tossed his phone onto his desk and leaned back

in his chair. What should have been relief wasn't quite there yet. But hopefully that would come. Once he figured out how to broach the subject of what had happened last night and how to tell her enough, while sparing her the gory details of what his childhood had been like. Well, since he hadn't been able to find the fine line that divided the two, he was just going to have to do the best he could and hope like hell that she just forgot about what had happened and moved on to something else.

That little voice in his head reminded him of their conversation at the Statue of Liberty. Repair what was broken while it was still possible, so that there was no need for a transplant. He thought that was still possible, but he'd have to leave that up for Kirsten to decide.

With her computer tucked under her arm, Kirsten walked the distance from the elevator to Snow's office. Nicola hadn't shed much light on his behavior, but then again, Kirsten hadn't wanted to share everything that had happened last night and this morning. It was all too new and raw to do that. And although she liked her new friend, she didn't want to chance the news of their sleeping together getting around to other people in the hospital. Especially since she was already pretty sure she'd made a huge mistake.

Why?

Was she afraid people might think she was sleeping her way up the ladder? Well, that fear hadn't exactly stopped her from spending the night with the transplant surgeon, had it? And, good or not, that move could prove to be career suicide if it got around. She was still very new at this hospital, and she wanted people to take her seriously. Impulsive decisions like last night didn't exactly lend themselves to inspiring confidence in patients or co-workers. Sure everyone made mistakes, but she'd known it was a mistake before it even happened. And yet she'd done it, anyway.

She knocked on the door.

Half expecting to hear twenty or thirty locks being unlatched, she was surprised when he simply called for her to enter. She did, noting he wasn't at his desk.

"Over here."

She turned her head and saw him sitting on his sofa, his laptop parked on the glass-topped table in front of him. Shutting the door, she hesitated over the dead bolt. Did he want her to lock it? Leave it alone.

"It's okay, don't worry about it."

Great, he'd read her mind. She moved over to the seating arrangement, wondering how this was going to work if they were sitting on opposite sides of the table. So she perched on the very edge of the long sofa and placed her own laptop on the table beside his, then booted it up.

"Hey, before we start, I wanted to talk to you about something. I debated on just letting it go, but I don't want it to interfere with our working relationship."

"If it's about last night, don't worry about it. We can acknowledge it was a mistake that won't happen again." She didn't want to sit here while he dissected everything and then tossed it all in the trash. Ha! Hadn't she done almost that very thing?

"It is about last night, but not in the way you might think." He stopped, as if searching for how to begin. "You asked me yesterday about my parents."

Why did he want to talk about that, when it had nothing to do with what they'd done? "It's okay, you don't need to—"

"I do, because I don't want you to have the wrong idea about something." He shifted so that he was facing her. "I told you I don't have any contact with my dad, and I don't. Because he's in prison."

Shock filled her, knocking away any additional words she might have tossed out about mistakes and what had happened last night. "I'm sorry, Snow. I didn't know. I shouldn't have asked that question."

"Yes, you should have. We ask people all the time about where they're from, whether they have any siblings…what their parents do for a living. You can see how that might be a hard question for me to answer. Because when my dad wasn't drinking or doing drugs, he was using my mom as a punching bag."

Horror filled her. She'd thought all kinds of things. Even thought maybe he was in the witness protection program or something. But none of it came close to the reality of what he was telling her.

"Oh, God. I—I had no idea." Everything fell into place in an instant, and she felt awful for thinking it was Snow who had something to hide. That he had something to be ashamed of. She had a feeling he felt both of those things, though, and her heart ached for him. She felt awful for going to ask Nicola about him.

"I know. I don't tell very many people about it.

Kaleb knows because we grew up together, and because I rode my bike to his house during the worst of it."

His bike. She pictured Snow as a little boy pedaling as fast as he could, his fear propelling him to find safety. She swallowed past a knot of emotion that threatened to turn into tears. Tears he probably wouldn't appreciate.

"You were young when this started?"

"Yep. He's my actual birth father, not a stepfather or boyfriend who came along later. And he was there the whole time I was growing up." He shrugged. "You saw some of the residual junk from my past last night. You just didn't realize what you were looking at."

"The locks." She felt like such an idiot. All that talk about whether someone was after him or wondering if he was hiding some kind of nefarious activity. He had been. But he was hiding himself. Not because he was using drugs or had any kinky habits.

"Yes. When I was about seven, my mom came home from work and found me crying. My dad hadn't hit me. Not that time. But he'd come close, and I was scared. Anyway, my mom installed a lock on my bedroom door to help keep me safe."

Did he even know how that sounded? How could a mom leave her child in that kind of situation? Then again, she couldn't see inside the woman's head to see what her reasoning was. Maybe she couldn't get away. Or maybe she had no support system to help her. No one to turn to.

"But he's in prison now, you said."

"Yes. He is. But old habits die hard." He propped his ankle on his knee. "That first lock didn't keep my dad out, but when I was a teenager, I got a job at a locksmith and learned all about how they worked—how to install my own. I worked my way from simple to complicated, until I found a lock that included a steel bar that when turned fitted into a hole on the floor and top of the door frame. I realized I couldn't leave, because then my mom would be all alone. So I did my best to protect her. And me. Using locks."

"He's in jail now, so your mom must have turned him in."

"No, that was me, when my mom ended up spending a month in ICU. I told the police everything. Testified at his trial."

She couldn't imagine how hard that must have been. How heartbreaking for him and his mom. "How old were you when that happened?"

"I was seventeen and about ready to graduate from high school. I stayed with Kaleb and his family to avoid going through the foster-care system." He sighed. "So the locks became a habit. A symbol of safety and freedom. But more than that, I like installing them. And, yes, there's a neurotic element to it. I no longer *need* them. But they brought me comfort during a hard time in my life. And that's hard to let go of."

His eyes met hers. "I am very sorry, Kirsten, if I scared you by locking the door to my bedroom last night. I hope you know I would never knowingly hurt you, or anyone."

"I do." She decided to be honest. "It took me by surprise, and I'll admit a lot of thoughts ran through my head before I discarded each of them. I wondered if you were in the witness protection program or something."

"That's why you asked me if someone was after me."

"Yes." She'd also wondered if something from his past had been chasing him. Evidently it was—it just wasn't a physical presence.

"Feel better?"

She did about the reasons for the extra security, but not about why he had it. "I have to confess something. I'm embarrassed about it now."

"Okay."

"I asked Nicola about you. I didn't tell her about last night, but I did ask if she knew anything about you. About why your office door has a lock when no one else's does."

"It's okay. Kaleb already came to see me this morning to ask what was going on. He told me about Nicola. But I'd already decided to talk to you before he showed up at my office door. I was just going to wait until tomorrow to do it. It made me decide that I needed to address it sooner and not give you the watered-down version I'd planned on."

"So you didn't ask me to come here to talk about my patient?"

"I do. It just wasn't my only reason for meeting you today. And it kills two birds with one stone."

"Don't other women wonder why you have extra locks?"

He chuckled. "Well, maybe, but there haven't been

that many and they've never actually come out and asked before. No one else knows the whole story, except for Kaleb, obviously, but not too many others outside of my family."

Not even his ex-wife? Not that she was going to ask that kind of question.

So she was the first casual acquaintance he'd given this explanation to? Well, she had kind of freaked out about it, so maybe the other women he'd been with had been cooler about the whole situation.

Well, starting now, she was going to become one of those "cool" women. As glad as she was that he'd told her about his past—and as horrified as she was by what he'd gone through—it didn't change anything. Last night had been a mistake before his explanation, and it was still a mistake after it.

So no more asking questions or trying to figure him out. Because in the end, it didn't matter. They were colleagues at work and nothing more. The sooner she got that through her thick skull, the better off they both would be.

CHAPTER SEVEN

Snow came into the room and saw a dark-haired preteen flanked by a very worried mom and dad. He and Kirsten had gone over her chart yesterday after the discussion about his parents, and he had to agree with her. It looked like primary pulmonary hypertension might be at the root of the ten-year-old's lung issues.

"Hello, Gretchen, I'm Dr. Tangredi. I understand that you had an MRI done today."

The girl drew a deep breath before coughing into the crook of her elbow several times. The coughing could be due to her lungs, but it also could be a sign that her heart was starting to fail as it struggled to pump oxygen to the far reaches of her body. "Yes, I did. Kirsten thinks it will help us understand what's wrong with me."

He shot the pulmonologist a look. There was a debate in the medical field about whether patients should be encouraged to use a doctor's first name rather than their title. He guessed he knew where Kirsten stood on that particular issue. He found that he kind of liked it—it fit her. And he could see how, in pediatrics especially, it might help young patients connect better with their doctors—how it might take away a little of the fear for them to view their caregivers as people rather than someone who was there to poke and prod them.

"I agree with her. I looked at some of the other tests that have been done. Dr....I mean Kirsten asked me if I would mind coming in and giving her my opinion."

"She says I might need special care. More than she can give."

"You might." He smiled at her, remembering how Kirsten had said Snow was sometimes a patient's last hope. For some reason, he didn't want to let her down, if that was the case. "Let's wait and see what the results of the MRI are."

Kirsten stepped forward. "We should have them back by Monday."

The hard thing about having tests done on Friday, was that most of the time a doctor had to sign off on them, so not as much happened on the weekends unless it was a life-or-death situation. Gretchen wasn't quite there yet, but she might get there if they couldn't come up with a treatment plan that worked.

Try to repair, so that a transplant isn't needed.

Those words had come back to him a lot in the two days since Kirsten had spent the night. Telling her about his dad had done just that. It hadn't fixed all of the awkwardness between them—that would only happen if and when a time machine came into being so he could go back and undo taking her back to his place. But he did find himself more open emotionally than he had been. Her reaction had been nothing like Theresa's. Kirsten had shown horror, but she had pressed him for more information than he'd been willing to give. And for that he was grateful.

He turned to the child's parents. "So how is she at home?"

"She has a hard time catching her breath, even walking out to the bus stop in the morning. PE is impossible for her at this point. The school has made a special class in kinesiology just so she doesn't fail her grade. Homeschooling is an option, but she really wants to stay with her friends if she can."

"I can't blame her for that. We'll see what we can do to help her with that. Kirsten says she told you that there might be high blood pressure in the artery that connects Gretchen's lungs with her heart."

"Yes. I've been doing some reading online, but some of what I've found…" Her mom's voice fell away and her eyes filled with tears.

He knew how hard it was to stay strong and not worry about someone you loved more than necessary. He'd done that with his mom more times than he wanted to admit. The times when he was overcome with fear that his dad would kill her. Or him. He'd held all of those emotions in so she wouldn't see it in his eyes.

His glance went to Kirsten and he found her looking at him with…pity?

Oh, hell, no! That was the exact reason he didn't tell people about his past. But in her case he'd had no choice, really. Well, he had had a choice, but the alternative wasn't acceptable to him. Pity was better than fear, right?

He vowed no one would ever need to be afraid of him. And although he knew his demeanor didn't quite reach teddy-bear levels, he hoped he'd kept that promise.

Hoped he would always keep that promise.

"Reading things online is okay, but make sure you get your information from reputable sites, like the big teaching hospitals. And always feel free to ask us anything."

"Okay, thank you. And I do have a question," her dad said. "Is our daughter going to need a transplant someday?"

Well, Snow had said to ask him anything, hadn't he? "Some people with pulmonary hypertension will eventually need a transplant, but some cases can be managed for a long time on medication."

"And Gretchen?"

The child's mom spoke up. "Bob, let's not do this now."

His eyes closed for a second. "You're right. I'm just worried."

"Yes, we both are," she said. "Let's let them get the results of the tests from today, and we'll talk again. Just us."

Snow couldn't have said it better if he tried. And he really didn't want to scare their daughter unnecessarily, so it was probably a discussion they would have just between the grown-ups.

Kirsten smiled at them. "You wouldn't be normal

if you weren't worried. But I want you to know we're going to do everything in our power to keep Gretchen as healthy as possible. Maybe even enough to participate in PE within limits."

She'd said "we." Was she including him in that statement? Maybe not, but a warm feeling washed up his chest, anyway, despite the look he'd intercepted earlier. Maybe he'd even imagined it, but he didn't think so.

The girl made a face. "I kind of like learning about muscles."

Kirsten laughed. "Well, that's a good thing. I'll share a secret with you. Kinesiology was one of my favorite subjects in medical school."

"It was?"

She nodded. "Getting to know how so many things have to come together to get our arm to bend, or our legs to run, is pretty amazing."

Something else that was pretty amazing was watching the way Kirsten came to life when talking to her patient. Yes, she'd been informative and warm when she'd discussed things with Tanya—his patient—but on her own turf, within her own specialty, there was a special confidence that sparkled in her eyes. That sparkle had been missing when she consulted on his case.

"It's cool. We're going to do a project figuring out which muscles help us do what tasks."

The girl had taken three gulps of air in the course of saying that last sentence, a sign that breathing was hard work, and that she was getting tired.

Kirsten must have sensed it, too, because she said,

"Well, we'll let you get back to your day. Call me if you have any other questions."

While some doctors might have just said that without giving any real thought as to the actual words, he had a feeling that she knew exactly what she was saying and that she meant it. All of it.

He decided to follow her lead. "Yes, feel free to do the same with me, if you have questions about transplants and the process we use to decide when and if someone needs one."

He pulled out a card from his wallet and handed it to Gretchen's dad, since he was the one who held his hand out for it.

Once they'd said their goodbyes and the family had left the room, Kirsten glanced at him. "Thanks for agreeing to see her."

"Happy to do it."

She touched his hand, stopping where she was. He halted, as well.

"And thank you for telling me about the other thing. I promise I won't share the information with anyone."

He hoped that was true, although she'd asked Nicola about his background. What if someone came to her with the same type of question?

No, he didn't know why, but he believed her. He wanted to think that even if someone tried to pump her for information, she wouldn't share his story without his permission. Unless it was for a very good reason.

"Thanks. I appreciate that. It's not something that comes up in everyday conversation." Actually it had never come up in any conversation before. Except for with Kaleb's family. He still bought his friend's parents gifts for their birthdays and for Christmas. It was the only way he could think of to express his gratitude for them opening their home to a troubled kid. They hadn't known the extent of the abuse, either, until his dad went to prison, and he'd gone to live with them. His mother never talked about it with anyone, and back then, Snow had been afraid that anything he said would just get his mom in trouble with his dad. So being quiet had been his best bet.

She licked her lips, then said, "Maybe you can get rid of the extra locks one at a time."

Not happening. They didn't hurt anyone, and they'd been in his life for a lot longer than she had. Even Theresa had lived with that idiosyncrasy without too many complaints. It had been his lack of ability to connect emotionally that had left her cold.

Well, he wouldn't have to worry about that with Kirsten. They'd connected on a sexual level, but emotionally? Not so much. There'd been no need. There was still no need.

He decided to keep things vague. "Yeah. Maybe. We'll have to see what happens."

It was one way of saying "forget it, not happening," without actually saying the words.

"Okay. Thanks again. Do you want me to let you know what the MRI results are?"

"Yes, please. I'd like to keep up with the case just in case she does end up needing a transplant, even if it isn't right away. Maybe it won't be as bad as we think."

* * *

It was worse than she'd thought.

The right side of Gretchen's heart, as she'd suspected and noticed on X-rays, had disturbing changes. The walls had thickened and the ventricle itself had enlarged in an effort to hold and pump more blood with each beat. But it was already beginning to backfire, causing more strain on a heart muscle that was quickly becoming weary. She needed to call the family and let them know, but first she needed to talk to Snow and get his opinion. Again.

She didn't really want to do it by phone, though. So she headed for his office. Knocking, she noticed the lock was still there. But it wasn't like he could just pull it off and toss it. Taking it off would leave an ugly defect in the wood and would leave space to get a finger or two in that could unlatch the lock on the knob.

The door opened and there stood Snow. "You got the results back this morning, didn't you?"

"Yes. I was hoping you were here. Can we go somewhere to talk? Or are you busy right now?"

He glanced inside his office, but evidently decided— like she had—that meeting in a less private area would be better. "Do you want to go down to the foyer? There are a few seating areas off to the side. Maybe we can snag one of them."

"That's a great idea."

The hospital entryway always impressed her with its towering ceiling and chandelier. And despite its massive size it made everything look...welcoming.

They made their way to the elevator and headed

down. And then they were in the busiest area of the hospital, where visitors and patients alike hurried in and out.

Surprisingly, they were able to find a four-chair grouping in one of the far corners of the space and Kirsten sat down, setting her computer in front of her. "So there's probably still the possibility of managing Gretchen's condition with medication, but I want us to be on the same page as far as treatment goes."

They discussed the ins and out of the MRI results and Snow outlined the steps that they would need to do in order to be placed on the transplant list.

"I don't think we're at that point yet, but unless something drastically changes, she'll probably be on it within a year."

"I was thinking the same thing, but wanted to hear your take on everything."

"Do you want me there when you talk to the parents?"

"Yes, if you don't mind, since you can speak to the transplant side of the equation."

He nodded, leaning forward to look at her computer screen as if looking for something they'd missed. "It's not going to be an easy conversation. And I'll have to be honest and tell them that wait times are often horrendous."

"I know all about wait times."

"I know you do." He paused. "Is it hard?"

"Hard?"

"Treating patients who are sometimes in the same position your mom was. Sometimes worse."

"Sometimes." She sighed. Her mom's image still came up from time to time when she was talking to a patient. She wondered if that would ever go away. "It's harder in cases like this, when I know there aren't a whole lot of treatment options to slow the progress and when a transplant is a very real possibility."

Looking at Snow, who still struggled with issues from his past, she imagined he understood more than he realized. His trauma had lasted for a lot longer than hers had.

"What will you do if he gets out of prison?" The question came out before she could stop it.

"Nothing." He didn't ask what she was talking about. It was pretty obvious.

"And if he tries to contact you? Or your mom?"

"I think he knows better than that." Snow's face had taken on a hardness that actually had her worried for his father's safety, as ironic as that was. The boy who'd once needed protection from a monster might pose a threat to that very monster.

"I hope so."

"Sorry, I had no business asking that."

He nudged her shoulder with his. "It's okay. Believe me, I've asked myself that very question for more years than I can count."

"How long is he in for?"

"Twenty. So he still has quite a few years to go. He's been turned down for parole five times in a row."

That made her nervous. "So they still think he's a threat."

"Not very much chance of a man like that changing his stripes."

But people could change. She wasn't sure about people like his dad, but surely a person could change for the better if they really wanted to. If they worked hard, they could exchange their old habits for something better. Something that helped rather than harmed those around them.

Kirsten had changed as a result of her mom's death. Snow had asked if it was hard. Yes, it was damn hard, but the alternative was to turn her back on what had happened to her mother and pretend people like her didn't exist. She couldn't bring herself to do that.

So here she was in a hospital wing talking about a young girl's fate. At least Kirsten could play a part in advocating for her patient, to help make sure she got what she needed, even if what she needed most was a transplant. Getting her on that list in a timely fashion was crucial to giving her the best possible chance for survival. She was pretty sure Gretchen's parents would agree with her on that.

And if she couldn't make that happen?

She wasn't going to think about that right now. It was why she'd enlisted Snow's help. He knew how the system worked—he'd been playing the game for years.

Except this wasn't a game. It was deadly serious.

She went back to the subject they'd been discussing. "I hope your father leaves you and your mom the hell alone, then."

He looked surprised by the words for a second, then said, "Don't worry. I'll make sure of that."

By buying more locks for his mom's door? And his? Or by doing something more drastic?

Kirsten did what he'd done earlier and jabbed her shoulder into his arm. "Just make sure you don't wind up in jail yourself. You have a lot of people counting on you." In case he got the wrong idea, she hurriedly added, "Your patients, I mean. And your mom."

He smiled. "I knew what you meant. And don't worry. I made myself a vow a long time ago that I would be nothing like my father."

"From what I can see, you've kept that vow. I'm sure your mom is very proud of the man you've become. You said she lives in Massena? Is that how you pronounce it?"

"Yes, on both counts. It's where Kaleb and I grew up. My dad worked at one of the locks on the Saint Lawrence Seaway."

"Locks?" She had no idea what that was.

He smiled. "It's not like that lock on my bedroom door. It's actually a way that ships can travel between areas of a canal that have different water levels. The boats are held in a watertight box while water either fills or leaves the box until it matches the next stretch of canal. Then it's free to continue on its way."

Her face had heated at the reference to his bedroom, but by the time his explanation was finished, she'd pretty much forgotten about her momentary embarrassment. She was instead fascinated by how the ships moved forward.

"So, in a way, the boxes are a kind of lock. The ship is locked in, right?"

"Hmm…right. I'm not sure what the origin of the word is for this particular kind of lock."

She thought for a few seconds. "I don't know that we even have locks in Lebanon. I've never heard of them before."

"It's an interesting sight. You should try to visit one and see what happens."

"Maybe I will." It was one more thing to add to what she wanted to do before leaving the country. *If* she left. The thought of that wasn't quite as appealing as it once was. Because of Snow?

God, she hoped not. And she still had a while before she'd have to let the hospital know, if she decided to go that route. She'd also have to let her dad know so they could try to find a hospital that would accept her credentials. And although Arabic was her mother tongue, she'd learned a lot of technical words in English. She wasn't sure she knew what they all were in Arabic. Maybe she should start trying to review them.

She snapped the lid on her laptop closed. "I'll call Gretchen's parents and set up the meeting. Is there a time that's better for you?"

"I'll check." He opened his phone and scrolled through what must be his calendar. "I have patients to meet with the first part of the week, and, of course, if an organ comes available, I can't always promise I won't be in surgery."

"I know." She had a thought, since she was thinking about researching things for her possible move. "I'd really like to observe transplant surgery being done at NYC Memorial, if that's possible."

"Thinking of changing fields?"

"No. I'm pretty happy where I am. But it would be nice to actually see what goes on, so that I can explain things to my patients a little bit better. Especially if you're not around to help me do that."

"That makes sense." He studied his phone for another minute or two. "I have two patients that are close to the top of the list and are just waiting on an organ to be found. How about if I call you before the next one goes into surgery, and if you're free, you can come observe."

Excitement bubbled in her system. Because of the possibility of watching, not because it was Snow. "Really?"

"Yes, Really. I have one heart transplant patient and one heart-lung patient on my list."

"Thank you." There was something bittersweet in watching something that her mom had missed out on. But she liked to think that her mother would approve, if she knew. And it would be one more way that she could empathize and relate to her patients.

He stood. "Well, I'd probably better get back to work, but let me know when you schedule the meeting with Gretchen's parents and I'll do my best to be there, how's that?"

"That is all I can ask. Thank you again."

"You're welcome, Kirs. Happy to do it."

The shortening of her name made her throat tighten. Her mom had called her that. In fact, she was the last person to have called her Kirs. If anyone else had tried, she probably would have set them straight in a hurry, but somehow with Snow, it sounded natural. Right. She wasn't even sure he was aware that he'd done it. But she liked it.

"I'll see you later, then."

"Yes, see you."

He turned and walked away. Kirsten watched as he headed down the corridor, his steps firm and confident, his lanky form looking like he hadn't a care in the world.

She knew differently, though. He did have a care. Lots of them, in fact. And she wasn't sure that the man who had so many locks on his doors didn't have an equal number of them on his heart.

CHAPTER EIGHT

Surgery happened two days later.

Snow had gotten a call that a heart had become available for his heart patient three hours ago. It had just arrived, in fact, from a different part of New York. The team was getting everything ready in the surgical suite and he'd already met with the family. He checked in with Kirsten.

"I'm looking at around thirty minutes as a start time. Can you make it?"

"Yes, just tell me which suite and I'll be there."

He double-checked the number for the operating room. "Looks like it's number four. I'm heading down in a minute to scrub in."

"Okay, see you there."

He quickly reviewed the patient's chart, reminding himself of the game plan as he took the elevator to the surgical area. Then, scrubbing his arms with a little more vigor than necessary, he tried to figure out why he'd agreed to let Kirsten observe. But it would have appeared strange if he'd said no to her, when really, any of the staff with enough interest were usually allowed to watch as long as the surgeon agreed. There were only one or two who preferred to keep a "closed" surgery, one in which no one outside of surgical staff was allowed to watch. For those few, they usually stated that they wanted no distractions, and usually no music in the room.

Snow was also a no-music guy, although he wasn't as much of a hard ass about observers. The only time he'd closed a surgery that he could remember had been at the wishes of a patient who hadn't wanted anyone except for necessary staff to see her unclothed. He'd respected her wishes.

His arms still wet, he pushed through the doors to the surgical suite with his shoulder, then dried his hands with the provided sterile towels, finishing his routine. There was always an air of anticipation and nerves as he got ready to operate. There would be no second chances, if he made a mistake.

Unlike lungs or other organs, the heart was especially difficult, because if it refused to start, there was no going back, no fix, and the patient would die on his operating table. So far, every donor heart had cooperated with him. But he knew that with each surgery, the odds were growing that there would be a first time.

His gaze headed to the observation area, despite his admonitions to avoid glancing over. And just like Kirsten had said, she was there. She gave a little wave, which he acknowledged with a nod in her direction.

He again wondered about her being there. But why? Why her in particular? Was it because they'd slept together? Because she knew why he locked himself in his bedroom?

Actually, maybe that's why she *should* be here. So she could see that he was as normal as any other surgeon. He wasn't sure why that was so important, but it was.

He turned back to his team, which was already in place. "Is everything ready?"

The heart was there in its special container and the patient was already sedated and ready. They were just waiting on him.

He nodded for the recorder to be turned on and gave his initial remarks, including the patient's name, age and diagnosis. "Ready to begin."

The instruments were already placed in order of use on sterile trays and the surgical nurse was there, waiting on his first request.

They washed the patient's chest with surgical scrub and put the drape in place.

The first part of the surgery went like clockwork—he opened the chest and spread the ribs, exposing a heart that was enlarged and weakened by cardiomyopathy. There'd been no way to fix this heart, no medication that could reverse the disease process, just short-term patches geared toward getting the patient to this point in the transplant process. He took note of the implanted defibrillator and planned the timing of removing it. Everything had to be done in a methodical order. One mistake…

Damn. He needed to stop this before it became a self-fulfilling prophecy. He could feel Kirsten's eyes on him, even though she wasn't in the room. But none of that mattered. The only thing that counted was the patient, who was depending on him for life. For a fresh start. Someday that patient might be ten-year-old Gretchen, her family sitting in some waiting room hoping and praying that their daughter made it out of surgery alive.

He pulled his attention fully back on his patient. Preparing her for bypass was one of the most critical stages of the surgery, and he was well aware that he was about to take a beating heart and shut it off forever. Essentially, he was playing God. There was a scary solemnity to the act, and he paused for a second or two as he always did and weighed the risks and benefits. But this first actual look at the diseased heart proved what the MRI, EKGs and biopsy had told him. It was dying and carrying his patient down the river with it. It had reminded him of his dying marriage and the need to sever the link before it sucked both he and Theresa down with it. It had been the right decision.

And Kirsten? Was this the right decision? Yes, because he was simply letting her observe, not marrying her.

"Getting ready for bypass." He glanced at the perfusionist, who was sitting at a board, adjusting knobs and sliding relays. The man nodded at him. Okay, it was now or never.

With the tubing attached to the aorta and the vena cava, he shifted the job of oxygenating blood over to the machine.

"We're good," the perfusionist said.

Danny's job was as nerve-racking as his. Set up behind a table of controls, he looked almost like someone sitting at a mixing board at a recording studio. And maybe it was similar. And although it had nothing to do with sound, he had to get the levels perfect to give the patient the best chance at surviving. Maybe relationships were like that. If one element was out of whack, it could mean death. Or if one body part started to fail, it could mean the same thing.

Time to disconnect the heart.

Snow worked on detaching the organ from the patient, putting it in the stainless-steel specimen tray. A nurse whisked it away. Halfway there. He glanced at the clock. Two hours—right on time.

He sucked down a cleansing breath and clenched his fists twice, a habit he'd gotten into as he prepared for the second stage of his surgery—placing the donor heart into the patient. He'd already examined the heart once, but he gave it another pass as he got ready to put it in the chest cavity. He carefully reconnected it, and allowed the blood supply to flow through the tissues. Sometimes that was all that was needed to start the heart beating again.

Not this time.

It was okay. Sometimes the technique worked and sometimes it needed a little extra push.

"Paddles." The nurse handed the small unit to him and charged them to the correct specifications. Saying a quick prayer over the donor heart, he laid the paddles on either side of the heart.

"Clear!"

Snow sent the electrical charge through the organ and it spasmed, then was still.

Hell! Not what he wanted to see. A jolt of fear went through him and he tamped it down, then he placed the paddles a second time on the heart and shocked it. Stared at it. Willed it to come back to life in its new home.

It did. With big steady pumps that replaced the shallow strained movements of his patient's old heart. He closed his eyes for a second, sheer thankfulness spearing through him. Another life, saved. The energy in the room turned electric as the team began excitedly talking among themselves for a few seconds before settling back in to focus on the final stage of surgery.

He double-checked all of his sutures, looking for any and all leaks that might compromise the patient once they left this room. Finding none, he prepared to close the chest cavity. Sternal wires were used to put the sternum back together, and while some heart surgeons still used sutures or staples to close the surgical incision, Snow actually preferred glue, finding it made for a better scar.

And after that... Well, Kirsten was still up there, so he'd have to go speak to her once he was done, as well as the patient's family. But right now, his mood was one of elation, something he felt each time he had a successful surgery. It had been a little over four hours, and he was tired. But it was the good kind of tired. While his team sometimes went out for celebratory drinks, Snow rarely joined them. He preferred to sit in the dark of his office and unwind. It was one of the times he played music, a kind of "recovery" play-list that he'd made up specifically for surgeries, since he liked to spend the night in his office, in case there were complications.

He'd joined the skin edges together with the glue and left openings for the drainage tubes, so everything held together, just as it should have. He glanced at the monitors. The heart was still going strong. There could be some PVCs and arrhythmias as a result of postsurgical inflammation, but they'd keep a close eye on the patient for several days.

A long gauze bandage was applied over the incision to keep things as clean as possible and to protect the site.

"Okay, that about wraps it up. Good work, everyone. Let's hope for an excellent outcome."

Snow waited until the patient was wheeled out of the operating room and headed to recovery before he removed his gloves and surgical gown. Only then did he look up at Kirsten and motion for her to meet him outside the room.

He wasn't sure why, but he was suddenly glad he'd allowed her to watch. He had a few friends, but they were all in different fields. But from watching the way she dealt with Tanya, his earlier patient, and with Gretchen, she'd probably been holding her breath, too, when he'd tried to get that donor heart started.

Kirsten was waiting for him when he pushed through the door. She smiled. "That was…amazing. Truly amazing. But I can honestly say, I do not envy you your job. I don't think I could handle the tension of trying to start a heart and honestly not knowing if it will beat."

"It can be nerve-racking, no doubt. But every field has its own pressures. You just learn to deal with it." He nodded toward the hallway. "Want to walk with me so I can let the family know how things went?"

"Isn't that something you'd rather do alone?"

"If you need to leave, I'll understand. I just thought we could grab some coffee or something."

"I'd like that." They walked down the corridor while Kirsten's animated voice recounted all the things about the surgery that she'd found interesting. Now that the initial euphoria had worn off, Snow was feeling a bone-dragging tiredness that came from hours of double-checking each step before he actually performed it. From the adrenaline that had been pumping through his system nonstop to the sudden cessation of the hormone, he swung back toward the low end of the spectrum. Kirsten's voice was actually helping slow the fall in some weird way, becoming a buoy that kept him from being sucked too far down.

He went into the waiting room and a small group of people rose from their spots, the fear on their faces clear. He smiled at them before he ever reached them.

"Oh, God, she's okay, then?" The woman's husband, Mr. Fisher, was the first to speak.

"She did very well. Everything went as expected." No need to say the heart hadn't started right away. That happened from time to time, since the organ had had a shock of its own.

Chaos erupted as family members hugged each

other, some laughing, some crying as they all coped in different ways. He understood their reactions all too well. He'd had his own ways of coping. He still did, although the biting fear of abuse was long gone. He glanced at Kirsten to make sure she was still there.

She was. He wasn't sure why he'd suggested coffee. But he really wanted some. Wanted to drink it in his office to decompress. With her. Normally he preferred doing that alone with just his playlist going softly in the background. He'd sip at his coffee and kick up his feet, thinking of just…nothing. The after-surgery ritual was so strongly ingrained, he could feel it before it even happened.

"I'm going to go back and check on her in a moment. Once she's awake enough—" he nodded at her husband "—you can go back to see her for just a few minutes. Right now, what she needs the most is rest. But her new heart is working very well. It's strong, and her oxygen levels are great for a change. She should start feeling a whole lot better once the surgical wounds heal. She even mentioned wanting to do a five-K sometime in the future."

Mr. Fisher's eyes watered. "She loved to run. Did it every year until her heart started acting up."

"She'll have to be careful for a while, but there's no reason she can't take up running again." He patted the man's shoulder. "They'll come and get you as soon as she's ready for a visitor."

"Thank you. For everything. She would be dead without you."

"She has a strong will to live. That's what kept her going long enough to get the transplant."

He said his goodbyes and went back through the same door. He turned to Kirsten, who had been quiet through the exchange. "Ready for that coffee?"

"Yes. But if you don't want me to stay, I'll understand. I know some surgeons like to go off by themselves for a while."

"I'm normally one of them, but I could really use some company right now."

"Are you sure?"

"I am. If you're okay going back to my office, that is. A whole cafeteria full of chaotic conversations isn't exactly what I had in mind."

She hesitated.

Hell, maybe she thought he wanted something besides company. Or the lock incident had her nervous about spending time with him. "We can go somewhere else, if you'd prefer. I promise, all I want is someone to sit with."

"No, it's not that... Your office is fine. Or mine. Either one."

"Let's do mine, then." He wasn't sure why, but he needed to be on familiar turf right now. Just a place that he knew and understood.

"How about if I grab our coffees while you check on your patient. I'll meet you back at the office."

"I would really appreciate that." More than she knew. "I just take mine black."

She smiled. "Yeah. I remember from our trip to the Statue of Liberty."

That seemed like ages ago, but it wasn't. It had been less than a week ago.

He made a quick trip to Recovery, where his patient was awake, but groggy from pain meds and the aftereffects of anesthesia. And was still intubated at the moment.

"You did really well, Marilyn. I just talked to your husband about the possibility of you running a five-K. I told him that's a very real possibility now." The woman squeezed his hand to show she understood. "I'll come back by in the morning, okay? Your husband will be here in a little bit to see you. But we need to make sure you get some rest."

Then he was headed back to his office. Kirsten was already standing outside the door, holding two disposable cups with heat sleeves wrapped around each. "I hope you haven't been waiting long."

"Nope. Just got here." She handed him a cup. "Nothing but straight coffee in there."

"Thanks." Snow unlocked the lock on the knob, then, conscious of her eyes on him, he turned the key in the dead bolt. Then the door swung open, and he waited for her to go inside.

"Do you mind if I play some music?" Of course, that could be taken the wrong way, too. "It's on a loop that I run through, every time I do surgery."

"It's fine. How about I take one of the chairs, and you can stretch out on your sofa. You look exhausted."

"It's been a long day," he admitted. "I'll try not to fall asleep on you."

She frowned and stood just inside the door. "Are you sure you wouldn't rather be alone and take a nap?"

"Like I said, it would be nice to have company. As long as you don't mind staying."

"Of course not. I'll be happy to." She came fully into the room. "And if you do happen to fall asleep, I'll just let myself out."

He nodded, then went over to his computer and cued up his playlist. Soft jazz filled the space, the sound of a saxophone pouring over him. Sighing, he sat on the sofa, took a sip of his coffee and then held it on his thigh. When she sat down on a nearby chair, she was concentrating on something, her head tilted.

"What?" he asked.

"Your music. I like jazz," She said. "The Ohio Jazz Festival was one of the last places I went with my mom. It was very different, and we thought we'd just go to see what the music was like. We both ended up loving it. It was very different from anything we'd ever heard before. I went on a listening binge when we got home."

That surprised him. People either liked jazz or they didn't. There wasn't much in between. "I find it relaxing."

They sat for a few minutes in silence. He could feel his muscles beginning to unwind, the cramps working their way out of his fingers. One of the reasons he sat in his office rather than going home was because Theresa used to talk incessantly the second he arrived, even when he was so tired he could barely focus. And she expected him to carry his share of the conversation.

Yet, Kirsten seemed to instinctively know he needed

quiet. He wasn't even sure why he'd invited her back here, but he was now glad he had.

And when she kicked off her shoes and curled into a corner of her chair, head leaning on the back cushion, he couldn't quite take his eyes off of her. She made his heart do all kinds of things. But right now she made him feel restful.

She looked like she was totally into the music. Was barely moving, except to put one arm under her head. "Would you rather have the sofa?"

She didn't answer, so he looked closer and noted the slow rise and fall of her chest, the way she seemed totally at peace. It was then he realized he needn't be worried about falling asleep in front of her. Because she'd just fallen to sleep in front of him.

Sleep had never been further from his mind at the moment. All he wanted to do was sit and watch her, a strange longing singing through his veins that seemed to match the plaintive tones of the saxophone.

When he'd finished telling her about his father earlier, he'd felt a relief greater than any he could remember, and wasn't sure he'd ever feel again. And afterward, she hadn't avoided him or talked a mile a minute as if needing to fill every gap of silence, for fear he might bring up his past again.

No, he'd caught a few glances that he thought might be pity, but he hadn't been convinced of that. And she definitely hadn't balked at coming back to his office. Or falling asleep in front of him.

So with a sigh, he set down his coffee on the table

and stretched out on the sofa, turning on his side so that he could continue to watch her.

And as he did, something stole over him that he hadn't felt in a very long time: a sense of peace and rightness. Rightness in her being here. Rightness in confiding in her, even though he still wasn't sure why he had.

He wasn't sure what he was going to do about it, but that was a decision that didn't need to be made today. Or even tomorrow.

So for right now, he was content to simply lie on this couch and simply...be.

CHAPTER NINE

KIRSTEN CAME TO with a start. Blinking, she tried to pull her brain back from wherever it had been. Music played in the background, and she wasn't sure exactly where she…

Her eyes landed on the sofa and found Snow there, eyes open, watching her.

"Wow, I'm sorry. I was supposed to be keeping you company, not snoring away in your chair." Her eyes flashed to him. "I wasn't snoring…was I?"

One side of his mouth quirked up. "Do you want the truth, or…"

The thought that her snoring might have kept him awake was mortifying. "I am so sorry. I'll leave so you can—"

"I'm kidding. You didn't snore. But you did make these cute little snuffling sounds."

Her face turned hot. "Did you get any sleep at all?"

"No, but I don't always try to. Sometimes just stretching out in here is enough to get me back where I need to be."

A thought hit her. "Do you normally bring someone

back here?" Maybe he didn't like being alone, either. Kind of like she felt about eating at restaurants alone.

"No. It's normally too distracting."

"So you don't find me distracting." She wasn't sure whether to be flattered or insulted. Especially since seeing him lying flat out on that sofa was beginning to distract her. A lot. It brought back some memories of their night together. It was funny how that was now such a blur. Oh, the remembered sensations were there. In fact, they were doing a number on her now, but the actual events were just bits and pieces of them moving in time with each other, of straining toward the other, of...

And she needed to stop thinking about that.

"I think you know that's not true." As if he'd read her thoughts and needed to change the subject, he sat up. "So what did you think of surgery? I didn't get a chance to ask you much after the fact, since I needed to go talk to her relatives."

"Like I said, it was amazing. I knew the mechanics of it, but to see the damaged heart actually being lifted out of someone's body is a little disconcerting."

"It is. I think about that every time I do one of these. It's like I'm putting something to death."

"Sometimes in order to save something, you have to sacrifice something else. Something that is causing harm and might even result in death."

"I hadn't really thought about it like that. But it makes sense in a lot of areas and not just medicine."

Was he thinking of his dad? How he'd had to sacrifice him, in order to stop him from harming his mom?

"It's the right thing to do in those cases."

He met her eyes. "That doesn't always make it any easier."

"I imagine it doesn't. But if you choose to do nothing, then aren't you guilty of sitting back and allowing it to happen?"

His jaw tightened. "Yes, I guess you are. And sometimes you wished you'd intervened a lot sooner, and wonder if maybe you could have prevented—"

"Stop." She got up and went over to the sofa to sit next to him, putting her hand on his. There was no doubt what they were talking about now. "You were a kid. Making those kinds of decisions shouldn't have been left up to you. The fact that you were willing to do it at all… Well, you probably saved your mom's life. Who knows what would have happened the next time?"

She was sure he'd had this same kind of argument with himself time and time again.

"Those locks, Snow. I'm pretty sure you have PTSD from what your dad did, from what your mom went through."

This time he didn't say anything. She wasn't sure if he disagreed with her, or if he simply didn't want to talk about it. She couldn't blame him.

She put her hand on his cheek, turning his head until he was looking at her. "Please don't take that the wrong way. I can't imagine having to do what you did. I think you were impossibly brave. And you didn't back down, even though it meant your dad was going to prison. You asked someone to remove what was killing your family and to take it where it couldn't do any more harm. As a transplant surgeon, you of all people should get that analogy. You have to remove the cause in order to fix the problem. Maybe you went into transplant surgery for that very reason, without realizing it. Just like I went into pulmonology because of my mom."

He reached up and stroked her hair, a muscle working in his cheek. "You're pretty incredible, you know that?"

"I'm really not."

"I beg to differ." He leaned down and placed a light kiss on her mouth that made her want to curl her hands into his shirt and pull him closer. "And I think you're right. And you know what, it helps looking at it like that."

She smiled. "I'm glad. Because I think you're pretty incredible yourself."

"Do you?"

She nodded.

This time when he kissed her, it wasn't just some quick peck on the lips. It was a slow, drawn-out kiss that wound its way through her. Unhurried. Unwavering. Bringing with it a hum of emotion that she hadn't felt in quite a while.

She inched closer to him and cupped his face, wishing she could heal the hurt that he'd been put through all those years ago. But, of course, she couldn't. So she settled for showing him in the only way she knew how that she admired his bravery, his willingness to stay in a situation that wasn't of his making in order to try to protect his mom.

And she did admire him. In so many ways. She

wasn't sure when that had come about or why, but she cared about him.

There wasn't much time to dwell on that realization, though, because the kiss was deepening. His hands were beginning to wander as need erupted between them all over again.

And this time, Kirsten didn't want to take the time to go back to one of their apartments—she wanted him right here in this room, in the midst of the intimacy that was floating through the air. It seemed like a just conclusion to their conversation.

She found his shirt buttons with her fingers and undid them one at a time, pushing the garment away so she could touch his skin. God, she loved the feel of him.

Snow wrapped his arms around her and laid her back on the sofa, pressing her into the soft leather cushions. He surrounded her, his solid weight warm and welcome as he continued to kiss her. He lifted up enough to push up her skirt, and with her help, they soon had it bunched around her waist.

"I want you so much."

The heated words rumbled against her throat and matched everything she felt inside. She didn't care what the consequences were. Didn't care where they found themselves tomorrow. Right now, she just wanted him inside of her. In more ways than one.

She felt more than saw him taking out his wallet and retrieving a condom, heard the snick of his zipper being lowered.

Oh, God, this was going to happen.

And she wanted it. Wanted it more than she'd

wanted anything in her life. She was ready when he pushed aside her underwear and found her, sliding home in a rush.

She gasped, the incredible fullness feeling familiar and new all at the same time. She wrapped her legs around his waist, the fabric of his pants adding an element of sexiness as it rubbed against her inner thighs with each movement of his hips. He intoxicated her. Thrilled her. Made her want to stay with him forever.

When one hand slid under her shirt and found her breast, his thumb brushing over the peak, she remembered the way he'd brushed it over his steering wheel. How she'd longed to feel it on her skin. That trip seemed like forever ago.

She closed her eyes and let the sensations wash over her and through her, absorbing it into her brain. And her heart.

His movements weren't frantic, but there was a contagious intensity to him that pulled her along with him through space and time. She touched his face, tracing the planes of his cheeks, and when he lifted his head to look at her, she brushed her index finger along his lips. He opened and captured it, sucking it deeper, his tongue sliding along it in a way that brought an ecstasy of its own.

"Ah…" She couldn't remain silent, couldn't prevent herself from whimpering as nerve endings awoke and were teased and tantalized to the breaking point.

And when his hand edged between their bodies to find her, she pushed closer, head going back as the pressure grew, needing him so much. So very much.

Then like a dam bursting, the raging torrent inside of her broke free, and she gave a loud keening cry as pleasure crashed over her, dragging her along with it. Snow bit down on her finger as he plunged into her and strained for several long seconds. Then his weight settled back down on her all at once, and he allowed her finger to slide free, saying goodbye with a tiny kiss to its tip. His breath against the side of her neck was hot and unsteady.

"Hell."

She couldn't really think. Couldn't articulate enough to answer whatever his "hell" meant. Maybe he'd meant it was incredibly hot. It had been.

Although something made her wonder...

Then he was up and off her with a speed that shocked her, striding over to the door and turning both the locks.

She realized he'd forgotten to lock the door. She laughed, sat up and tried to straighten her skirt. "It's a little late for that, isn't it?"

He didn't crack a smile, didn't do anything except stand there with this grim look on his face. He could have been peering into the face of death, for all she knew. Except he was staring right at her. A shiver went through her.

"Snow?"

"Anyone could have come in here and found us."

The way he said that...

She yanked her shirt back down over her breasts, even as he disposed of his condom and zipped himself back in. Something was wrong. This wasn't just about the unlocked door.

"But they didn't."

He didn't respond, but she felt him withdrawing emotionally, like one of those motion pictures of an erupting volcano that, when rewound, shows everything being sucked back into the fissure before closing it up tight. As if nothing had ever happened.

Okay, so he evidently viewed this as one more mistake. Like the night they'd spent together. Only this time it wasn't the locks that bothered her, it was his behavior.

She swallowed. He reminded her of Dave, who had walked away from their relationship as it was dying on the ground. Or of that doctor who had given her mom the bad news about her condition being terminal. A total emotional detachment. That man had felt nothing for her mom, nothing for her family's pain. Or if he did, not a glimmer of it showed.

That's why Snow looked at her like she was death incarnate. Because he was about to do what he did with all of his transplant patients. Like he'd done with his father. He was going to remove her from his life, just like he did a diseased heart or a set of lungs.

You were never in his life in the first place, Kirsten.

Emotions had been high, and the sex had just happened. And Snow regretted it. It was there in his face, in the hands that were balled into fists.

Pain speared through her, although she wasn't sure why. They meant nothing to each other.

Except that wasn't true. She'd been scrabbling

around trying to grab on to an emotion right before they fell onto the couch together. And now, when she looked into her heart, she realized she'd succeeded in capturing it…was still holding on tight to it.

She loved him.

Horrified, she tried to release the emotion back into the universe, but it had already grown long tendrils that had wrapped themselves in and through her heart, refusing to release it.

Snow still hadn't said anything and panic was beginning to well up inside of her. He'd not only locked everyone out of the room, but he'd also locked them in. Together.

Well, she was going to save him the trouble of making up reasons why they couldn't see each other anymore or how this was a big mistake—which for him, it obviously was. And she wasn't going to text him or ask him why, like she'd done with Dave.

Walking over to him, she looked into his face. His eyes were back to the way they'd been when they'd first met.

Cool, unreachable.

Inside, that invasive plant that had taken over her heart was telling her to beg him to talk to her, to give them a chance. But why? They'd had sex on two occasions. Two. That was nothing in most people's books. And it certainly didn't add up to a relationship. Besides, she'd kind of been through this once before. The excuses. The emotional pulling back. And if you had to beg someone to let you into their life…

Well, it just wasn't worth it. So here she went…

"Hey, we may not agree on much, but I think we can both agree that this was a mistake, and I'm sorry. I swore to myself that it would never happen again after that first night." That was all true. But here came the part where she'd have to fudge things a little bit. "But here's where I give you an easy out. You were right about something. I *am* leaving NYC Memorial. It may not be tomorrow or next week, but it's going to be soon. Maybe even within a month or two. I'll be moving back to Lebanon to be with my dad...my family. So as soon as I wrap up my current caseload, I'll be out of your hair. No one will be the wiser."

The look of relief that crossed his face wasn't her imagination, and it sent another stab of pain through her.

"So you're leaving. I thought you said you weren't."

"Not exactly. What I said was 'who knows where I'll be in a year's time.' I wanted on at NYC Memorial to see if there were any cutting-edge lung treatments I could take back with me to Lebanon when I went. I wasn't sure when I came how long I would be here. But I'm thinking shorter is better at this point."

"Do *not* leave because of what we just did."

It would be hard to respond to that with anything that was less than a lie. Even if he hadn't turned into something as stiff and lifeless as that statue they'd visited in the harbor, her plans still included moving back to Lebanon. So wasn't this better in the end? If she'd loved him and he reciprocated, that choice would be so much harder. But thankfully he'd made it easy, had confirmed that what she was doing was the right thing.

"Like I said, my plans were always to go back. I miss my father, and the rest of my family."

He probably wouldn't challenge that, because he wouldn't be able to relate to a person actually having a father worth missing.

She realized the jazz that had been softly playing in the background was still going. Except the music didn't seem soothing anymore. It seemed mournful, and unbearably sad. But it was definitely fitting for saying this particular goodbye. And the hole he was going to leave was so much bigger than what Dave had left her with. She only hoped it would heal, given enough time.

He was blocking her exit, and if he didn't move, she was going to do something she regretted. Like cry in front of him.

"If you'll just unlock the door, I'll let you get back to your day." She forced a smile. "I'm glad your surgery went well."

He didn't say anything, just went over to the door and turned both of the locks, making a way for her to escape.

And that's what she did. With as much dignity and grace as she could muster. And then she was out of his office and would soon be out of his life.

As soon as she was gone, Snow went over to his desk and sat down behind it, turning off the music so he could have peace and quiet. It didn't work, because there was still a cacophony of noise going on inside of him that refused to be silenced. Kirsten's name was on a loop that repeated again and again and again.

What the hell had he done? He should have said something to her, should have been the one to apologize. Instead, he'd let her walk out of that door without a single damn word. Without a single argument.

She may have been planning to leave all along, like she'd said, but he could almost guarantee that the timing had changed because of what had happened in this room.

He'd overreacted about the locks. He knew he had. But when he realized he hadn't latched the door before they had sex, he had been horrified, furious with himself. Saying that anyone could have walked in had been true, but it was more than that. More than he'd been willing to say to her. And thank God he hadn't been able to put it into words, because she was leaving, anyway. It looked like he wasn't going to have to break his vow after all. And that was a good thing. Because he'd just seen firsthand what Theresa had complained about time and time again. When push came to shove—when it really, really counted—the emotions wouldn't come out. They were still bottled up inside of him. Because the specter of his father, of his past, was still holding him hostage in ways that he didn't understand.

Was it just the fear of becoming like him? He wasn't so sure anymore. But he'd held himself in check for so long, that he didn't know what freedom to express himself actually looked like.

It was safer this way, but that didn't mean it was any less painful. In fact, it hurt like hell. It was just that no one but him was able to see it.

So somehow he was going to have to figure out

how to work with her—or at least in the same hospital with her—until she was ready to hand in her notice and leave.

That would not be an easy task. But the possibility of her staying here forever would be even more unbearable. Because he was pretty sure—given what had happened so far—they would fall into bed again, if she stayed. It wasn't the cycle he'd originally feared being unable to break. But it might end up being almost as damaging to both of them.

So all he could do was avoid her as much as possible and pray that some cosmic being set the clocks on fast-forward. Once she was gone, things would go back to normal.

At least he hoped that was true.

Kirsten didn't invite Snow to the meeting she had with Gretchen's parents. Instead, she went to it alone, giving Sarah and Bob the results of the MRI and outlining some treatment options that she thought could slow the progression of their daughter's heart failure. But she also honestly told them that Gretchen's best chance for long-term survival, once the meds stopped working, was going to be a heart-lung transplant.

"Will she be able to do PE before the transplant?"

"Before the MRI, I might have said yes, but at this point, we don't want to put any further strain on her heart."

"So it's that bad," her father said. "What kind of timeline are we looking at?"

"I spoke with Dr. Tangredi earlier, and he thinks we've probably got a year and then she'll need a transplant."

Sarah's eyes closed for a second before reopening. "Gretchen is a strong girl. We'll talk to her, but I'm sure she'll want the transplant when the time comes. How do we go about that?"

"Snow…Dr. Tangredi wasn't able to be here today." She didn't tell them it was because she couldn't be in the same room with him right now. Instead, she went on, "I'll contact him and set up an appointment. He can give you a rundown on what happens once a transplant is a necessity. I think you already know, he's an excellent surgeon. One of the best out there. Gretchen will be in excellent hands."

"She's going to want you to be there with her through the process."

Kirsten smiled, even though her heart was breaking. "Of course. I'll be with her for as long as I'm at the hospital."

Unfortunately, that wasn't going to be very long. Not if she could help it.

She'd gotten a hold of her dad and told him the situation, leaving out the part about Snow and what had happened between them. But her father had always been able to read her like a book, and since they'd done a videoconferencing call, he'd been able to take one look at her face and see that something was wrong. He asked her not to rush into any decisions, that she'd only been at the hospital for a short time.

She'd replied that whether it was Lebanon or another hospital, she couldn't stay at NYC Memorial any longer. He didn't ask why, and Kirsten didn't volunteer any information, but she was pretty sure her dad knew exactly why she needed out of here. It made her feel like such a fool. First Dave and now Snow. Hadn't she once told herself that he couldn't break her heart, because her emotions weren't involved when they'd had sex. What a lie that had been. Because her heart was broken, and there was nothing anyone could do about it at this point.

Her dad told her whenever she returned home, she would be welcomed. He already had a house with three bedrooms, had just hoped he might need the two extras for a son-in-law and grandchildren.

At this point, she didn't see that happening, and she ached for the sadness that would bring her father.

Bob stood, dragging her thoughts back to the present. "We appreciate all you've done for Gretchen. Can you get us an appointment with Dr. Tangredi as soon as possible?"

"Yes, of course I will." She took a couple of prescription forms off her pad and scribbled the medications they would need. "Get these filled and start on them tomorrow. Let me know if there are any problems. One of them is to help regulate the pressure in her lungs and the other one is to help stabilize her heart. I'll let you know as soon as I get that appointment time with Dr. Tangredi."

She shook both of their hands, surprised when Sarah leaned in to hug her instead. Kirsten returned the hug, suddenly needing it with a desperation that surprised her. Then she let go and said her goodbyes. They didn't know this was probably the last time they would see each other, but she did.

As they walked away, she grieved not knowing what Gretchen's final outcome would be. But she'd told the truth. Snow was an excellent surgeon and if anyone could make this miracle happen, it was him.

As far as her own miracle was concerned, there was no surgeon in the world who would be able to fix her shattered heart. Even if there were a transplant that would fix the problem, she was pretty sure the new heart would crumble, too. And the one after that, and the one after that.

Until there were no more hearts left to try.

That was when she decided she wasn't going to wait a week or even a month. She was going to call Snow and ask for an appointment time and then she was going to take a personal leave of absence.

And go home.

Unfortunately, she ran into Nicola just before she reached the inner sanctum of her office.

"Hey, I was just looking for you."

"You were?"

"Yes, do you have time for a coffee? I could use some adult time. I love that baby of mine, but it's just come to the point that I..." Her words faded away as she stared into Kirsten's face. "Hey, what's wrong?"

Then and there, she knew she was going to lose it. She opened her office door and dragged her friend inside. Then she promptly burst into tears.

Nicola put her arm around her shoulder and pulled her over to the chairs that were in front of her desk, then waited until she sat down and thrust a tissue into her hands. "Now, spill. What is it? A patient?"

She shook her head, scrubbing the tissue under her eyes, so angry at herself that she couldn't see straight. How could she let herself get into a situation like this again? Once hadn't been enough to cure her? Evidently not.

Nicola leaned down and looked at her face. "It's Snow, isn't it? I should have known when you came to ask me about him. I'm sorry I didn't realize…"

"I didn't realize, either. Not until—" She shut her eyes. "It doesn't matter. I'm going back to Lebanon."

"What? When?"

"As soon as possible."

With that, she unraveled the whole story for her friend, telling her about Dave and how it seemed like history was repeating itself. How she'd come to care about a man who had no emotions.

"I'm sure that's not true. Snow has emotions. They're just…hidden."

The huge pause before she said that last word struck Kirsten as funny. She giggled. The giggle turning to a laugh that made its way back to tears. "I love him, Nic. But I just can't do—" she waved her hand in a circle and then placed it on her heart "—this. Not again. Please don't try to talk me out of leaving."

"I won't, honey. But please promise me you'll think long and hard about it."

"I already have. And every thought leads back to one of two places. With Snow breaking my heart. Or with me leaving. And I know that the only viable path—the only path where I can come away with any self-respect—is that last one." She reached over and hugged her. "Thank you for everything. I'll never forget how you helped me or gave me your friendship."

"I won't forget you, either, Kirsten. Even though I may not agree with your decision. Let me know if you need anything at all, you hear?"

"Thank you. I will."

CHAPTER TEN

SNOW WAITED FOR two days before deciding he'd call
Kirsten back. Her voice mail had been short and to the
point, asking him to please call Sarah and Bob Wil-
son to make an appointment to talk with them about
Gretchen's transplant process. It included their phone
number.

He hadn't called them back yet, either. He'd made
a huge mistake with Kirsten, but there was no way to
fix it now. He'd planned on pulling her aside after the
earlier meeting with Gretchen's parents that they were
supposed to have together, but she'd never called him
to give him a time. Evidently that meeting had already
taken place. Without him.

Not that he could blame her. Not after how he'd
acted the last time they were together.

He sat there and played with his phone, pulling up
her number and then sending it away.

What was wrong with him?

He'd had an emotional response to what Kirsten
had said to him that day in his office—after he'd told
her about his father. She'd even helped him to see why

he'd gone into transplant medicine. That response had driven him to make love to her, putting every ounce of feeling he possessed into it. The sex had been amazing, even with their clothes still on. And he realized then and there that he loved her.

Then he discovered he'd left the door to his office unlocked. But when he fixed it and then turned around to look at Kirsten, his father's voice sounded in his head as clear as day, the words every bit as smug and angry as they'd been that day: "This is what happens when you forget to lock your door, Snowden. Things get broken."

He remembered coming home from Kaleb's house when he was fourteen and finding everything in his room smashed to bits. His mattress had been slashed, clothing ripped apart and his game system had been lying trashed on the ground.

Too late, he realized that the same thing had just happened with Kirsten. The panic room he'd so carefully installed inside of himself was in ruins. Because he'd not only forgotten to lock the door of his office, but he'd also forgotten to lock the door of his heart. And Kirsten came in when he wasn't looking and tore down all of his defenses.

Except casting her in the role of villain had been wrong. So very wrong. Kirsten hadn't destroyed anything. And instead of recognizing that this might be the start of something better and even more beautiful, he'd stood there looking at her like she'd suddenly grown two heads. She hadn't. It had been shock. And the fear that he might mess everything up again, like he'd done with Theresa.

Guess what. He had. And when Kirsten had said she was going to leave, it was like a huge wave of relief poured over him. He wouldn't get the chance to mess things up, because there would be nothing here to destroy. She was leaving. Leaving his office. Leaving his life.

It was a good thing, right?

It wasn't. Because Snow had stood in this office over the last two days and tried to install an even bigger and better lock on his heart. He'd failed. Because all he could think about was Kirsten and how much he wanted her.

"Okay, Snow. Time to call her." Whether she left or not, it didn't change the fact that he loved her. And the only way he would truly be free was to stop bottling everything up inside of him, starting with this. He had to tell her how he felt. And let the chips fall where they may.

He found her number again on his contact list and stared at it for several seconds. Then he pushed the button. It didn't ring. Instead, a weird sound came through, along with a recorded message saying the number was either disconnected or no longer in service.

His mouth went dry, heart suddenly pounding in his chest. He was too late. She'd already left.

Surely not. She said she was going to get her cases all sorted out and it might take a while. But what if it hadn't taken that long. What if, like Gretchen's case, she'd simply passed them on to someone else.

He hung up, tossing the phone onto his desk. There was no way he was going to be able to find her in Lebanon. He didn't even speak the language and had no idea what city her father lived in.

Staring at the couch where they'd made love, his jaw tightened. So he was just giving up?

It would be the easier way.

Would a transplant surgeon really take that path? He'd always told his patients that the easiest thing to do was let nature take its course. But if they had the grit to take it to the next level, if they would get down in the mud and fight to make it happen, they might just come out on the other side a brand-new person. Transplant surgery was one of the hardest things a patient had to face. It wasn't "the easy way." It was damn hard. But if it worked, it was so very worth it.

Okay. So let's get down in the mud and fight, dammit!

The next step wasn't easy, but if his best friend could admit defeat and give in to love, so could he. Picking his phone back up, he called Kaleb.

"Hey, Snow, what's up?"

"I have kind of a weird question."

His friend went silent, and then he chuckled. "Is it about that pulmonologist that Nicola has been so chummy with?"

"Yes, why?"

"Just wondering why it took you so long to call."

A flare of hope went off in his chest. "Do you know where she is?"

"No, but I know someone who might. Hold on." He heard Kaleb call for his wife.

Nicola came on and didn't give him a chance to speak. "I'm telling you right now, do not mess this up, Snow. Or I'm personally going to come over there and kick your ass."

That made him laugh. "I'll do my best, which is why I called. I take it you know where she's at?"

"She's almost gone. She isn't leaving permanently, if that's what you're asking. But if you don't make it to the airport in an hour, you're going to have to wait for a week before she'll be back." There was a pause. "And that will probably be to pack up her life here. She didn't tell me why she's leaving so suddenly, but I suspect I'm on the phone with the reason right now, aren't I?"

He swallowed, knowing she didn't expect an answer to that particular question. "What's her flight number?"

"I thought so. And I'm not sure. All I know is she's headed to Lebanon and her flight leaves at seven tonight."

"Thanks, Nicola, I owe you."

"No, you don't. Just do the right thing this time, Snow. For both your sakes."

With that, he ended the call and got up from his desk, shoving his keys and phone into his pocket. And headed out the door.

Kirsten sat in her seat looking out over the terminal. Her flight would start boarding soon. She'd already let her dad know that she was coming home for a visit to do some thinking. As she'd promised, she was not making any hard-and-fast decisions, but whatever the outcome, she would probably not be going back to NYC Memorial. Although she hadn't made the break official yet—simply telling the hospital administrator that she needed a week of personal leave and that she'd handed her cases over to other doctors at the hospital—she couldn't see herself going back. To do so would just be inviting pain back into her life. And that was one thing she was no longer willing to do.

It had been surprisingly easy. Too easy to just up and leave Snow behind.

She amended that. The physical process was easy. But the emotional part had been pure unadulterated hell. Was still hell. She loved the man. But the reality was, he didn't love her. He'd proven that by not even trying to get in contact with her over the last couple of days. She'd canceled her phone service, so that she'd stop staring at it waiting for his call. She was cutting off points of contact, one string at a time. It would be hard, but she'd survive. If she could live through her mom's death, she could live through pretty much anything.

She swallowed. It wasn't the same, though. With her mom, there hadn't been a choice, there'd been no way to hold on to her and keep her here. With Snow it was different. She was making a conscious choice to leave him behind. And each and every day would bring the same choice: to call him or not to call. And with each don't-call decision she made, she had a feeling her heart would break all over again.

If she was in Lebanon, though, that decision would

be made easier because the distance would provide an additional barrier.

"Now boarding passengers for Flight 579 to Lebanon. We'll be starting with zone one and working our way back. Those in zone one can come on up."

She still had a ways to go, since she was zone four. After pulling her earbuds from her ears and wrapping them up to put in her bag, she stood, checking to make sure she had everything.

She didn't. But unless she wanted to kidnap Snow and stuff him in the baggage compartment, there was nothing she could do about that.

Glancing at her ticket to find her seat number, she jumped when someone tapped her shoulder. Turning, her heart leaped into her throat when the man she'd just been thinking about appeared in the flesh. No. That wasn't right. She blinked to make sure she wasn't imagining it.

God. He was still there. Still staring at her. She started to shake.

"Wh-what are you doing here? How did you even find me?"

He smiled, but it looked strained. "You once asked Nicola if she knew anything about me. Well, I took a page from your book and did the exact same thing. I figured if anyone knew where you were, it would be her."

"Zone two can begin boarding," the loudspeaker called out for the next group to come up.

He glanced at her hand. "What zone are you in?"

It was then that she realized he had a carry-on bag

with him. Her emotions tangled up into a ball that lodged in her throat. "What are you doing?"

"We don't have much time. And you have a decision to make." He let go of his bag and took hold of her hands. "I made a terrible mistake, Kirs."

She swallowed. Why was he putting her through this? "I know. We both did, and that's why I decided to—"

"No. My mistake wasn't in what happened in that office. My mistake was in not admitting then and there that I was in love with you. That I didn't want you to walk out of my office or out of my life."

"But you didn't." Her head was spinning so much that she wasn't quite sure what he was saying. Wait, had he just said...? "Say that again."

"Which part?"

Hope right now was as shaky as her legs had been after that first night she'd spent with him. "You know what part."

"Okay. I love you."

"Zone three is ready for boarding."

"But how? You sure didn't seem like you loved me that day."

"Because I was in shock. I never thought it could happen to me. And then I left my door unlocked and realized it wasn't the only thing I'd forgotten to lock. I'd left my heart wide-open. And you walked right inside."

She could understand that. Understand the fear that came along with it. But what if he suddenly decided he was going to take that padlock and put it on again, locking her on the outside while he hid inside.

"How do I know this won't happen again?"

"Zone four, please come forward for boarding."

The crowd had thinned considerably.

"I can't promise there won't be times when I struggle with things, with showing my emotions, but you have a habit of bringing them out in me even when I'm fighting my hardest against them. No one else has ever been able to do that. Except you. Besides, you'd call me out on it, if I ever tried to pull that kind of crap on you." He glanced to where passports and tickets were being checked. "I'm zone four, as well. So what'll it be?"

"What?"

"I bought a ticket for the same flight, but I'm in a different row. So we can talk here, or I can camp out in the aisle next to your seat and talk to you there."

"Do you even have a passport?"

He pulled it out and brandished it in front of her.

Kirsten couldn't believe this was happening. "What about your job? Did you even ask permission to leave?"

He gave that half smile she loved so much. "There wasn't time. I'm pretty much running on pure emotion right now. And it's actually pretty refreshing."

"That's great, but I have to tell you I'm feeling pretty discombobulated right now."

"Did I ever tell you I love it when you use that word?"

She rolled her eyes. "Give me your ticket."

He frowned. "Why?"

"Trust me?" Her hope had started to stand on its own two feet, its restarted heart now beating on its own.

He handed her the ticket.

She took both of them and walked up to the desk with them, knowing his eyes were watching her the whole way. The attendant at the desk asked if she could help her. "I have two tickets for Lebanon, but I won't be boarding today. Do you need the seat numbers?"

"Yes, thank you."

They made a note of the seats, and Kirsten walked back to where Snow was standing with their luggage. Then, in front of him, she ripped both tickets in half.

He smiled. "I take it we're going to catch a later flight. I do want to go. I want to meet your dad. And the rest of your family." He hesitated, and for the first time, she saw a hint of insecurity in his gaze. "That is, if you feel something for me, too. You haven't said it. That you love me."

She held up the torn tickets. "I think I just did." She wrapped her arms around his neck and kissed him. "Of course I love you. But I can't promise I won't ever want to move back to Lebanon."

"We'll sort that out later. But when we do, we'll make sure we have adjoining seats for the flight. I don't want to be separated from you ever again."

"Me, either." Kirsten looked at the now empty waiting area. "I'll need to call my dad and let him know I won't be on this particular flight."

"Will he be very disappointed?"

"No. He actually told me not to come. To settle whatever it was that was driving this decision first." She laughed, remembering how he'd tried to talk her out of coming home. "And he bought a house with extra rooms that he expects me to fill."

"What?"

"He wants grandchildren, someday, I hate to tell you. I'm pretty sure he knew I was running away from someone, even though I never told him about us." She looped an arm around his waist, letting him lead her over to the window. "You'll like my dad, Snow. He's a good man. A very good man. You remind me so much of him. You're stoic. A hard worker. But most of all you're a protector of those who need it the most."

Snow didn't say anything, but when she glanced up at him and saw a muscle working furiously in his jaw and his glassy eyes, she knew why. And this was one time she wasn't going to complain. Because Snow was learning to deal with his emotions, and she was going to let him take baby steps. All the baby steps he needed. Because that's what love did.

Arm in arm, they stood there as the doors closed on Flight 579 bound for Lebanon. The plane was pushed backward so it could turn to taxi onto the runway. They were still standing there when it took off, flying farther and farther into the distance until they could no longer see it.

Snow kissed the top of her head, and she smiled up at him, her heart so full she could barely contain her joy.

They'd almost lost each other. Might have been separated forever.

Except Kirsten now believed in miracles. Because she was standing next to the man who regularly made them happen.

EPILOGUE

"WE WOULD LIKE to introduce Dr. Snowden Tangredi and Dr. Kirsten Nadif-Tangredi. Please give them a warm welcome."

As everyone clapped, Kirsten walked up to the lectern. Snow loved everything about his wife's country. The food was crazy good. The people were ridiculously friendly. And his father-in-law was an amazing man, just like Kirs had said he was. Snow wasn't like him at all. Not yet. But he aspired to be like him, one day.

As his wife stood at the podium giving her portion of the lecture on innovative treatment plans for cystic fibrosis, he admired the curve of her back and her glossy black hair, which was pulled up into a tight bun. And when she turned slightly to the side to acknowledge the session's moderator, he caught sight of a slight curve in her abdomen that most would not take notice of. But he did. They'd discovered a month ago that Kirsten was pregnant. They were on their way to putting the first crib in his father-in-law's extra rooms. And he couldn't be happier.

Snow hadn't been sure about coming to the conference because of the pregnancy, but Kirs insisted she would be fine.

This was their second time participating in the International Medical Professionals Forum that was hosted here in Lebanon. And both times, Kirs had stood beside him as he spoke, translating his words into Arabic, so the audience could understand him. He loved hearing her converse in her native language and was working on learning it himself. And he loved meeting other specialists in his field. They had a lot to learn from each other.

Both he and Kirs had talked about joining Doctors Without Borders and helping in whatever ways they could. Her father had already said he would be happy to watch his grandchild whenever they needed him to.

And when they got back to the States, they promised Gretchen's parents that they would come to her birthday party. She'd gotten her heart-lung transplant last year and was now participating in PE, using her newfound knowledge in kinesiology to help her fellow students get the most out of their training. Her dream was to someday be a coach. Or a transplant surgeon. That had made him smile.

Snow looked out over the audience. Kirsten's dad was out there somewhere, although with the lights, he couldn't see him. It was obvious, though, that he was very proud of his daughter. Not only of her accomplishments in the medical field, but also of her as a person. A compassionate, loving, emotion-filled person.

It had been an adjustment getting used to everything—getting used to expressing himself. But he was learning.

The locks on his doors were history. Oh, not completely. They had what Kirs considered to be a reasonable number of safeguards. Even the extra lock on his office door had been taken off—the hole left where the mechanism had once been was covered with a red wooden heart, as a nod to his specialty. And to Kirsten.

And, hell, if he wasn't the happiest man in this room. Or at least tied for first place.

He had everything he'd never known he wanted but now realized he couldn't live without: a wife who loved him, despite all his faults, a baby who would be loved *by* him and a large extended family that was just as exuberant as his beautiful bride. And his mom, who'd welcomed Kirsten with open arms. Her healing had come years ago, and she'd thanked her new daughter-in-law—when she thought he wasn't listening, of course—for helping Snow find the healing that he so desperately needed.

Kirs glanced at him with a smile and spoke to the audience before translating it into English for him. "And now I'd like to introduce my husband, the love of my life and regular worker of miracles, transplant surgeon Snowden Tangredi."

He smiled as he made his way to the podium, stopping to give his wife's hand a quick squeeze as he passed her. His heart filled with love and gratitude. She may have introduced him as a "worker of miracles," but that wasn't true. Because the real worker of miracles was carrying his child. How did he know she could perform miracles? Because with a single kiss, Kirs had taken Snow's tragic, damaged heart and somehow made it brand-new.

* * * * *

MILLS & BOON

Coming next month

A FAMILY MADE IN ROME
Annie O'Neil

Lizzy drew in a quick breath. 'Are those…?'

'Public baths,' Leon said, his voice low to match the magical surroundings. 'Second century AD, they think. They would've been adjacent to what is now the palazzo.'

'And these other rooms, the tiles, the kitchen areas— those are all centuries old?'

'Around five hundred years,' he confirmed. 'The palazzo went through numerous renovations, of course, and as you can see…' he gestured to the walls soaring above them '…so has the rest of Rome.'

Lizzy shook her head in disbelief, leaning into Leon's hand, a movement that seemed so natural anyone around them would assume they were a couple. A movement that elicited a hundred questions for Leon, who knew they weren't.

'I can't believe we're seven metres below the rest of Rome!'

He laughed appreciatively. 'I couldn't either, when I first saw it. These elements of the palazzo were only discovered recently—and excavated this century—and the addition of the glass floors, so people can walk freely above the remains, is even more recent.'

'Palazzo Valentini…' Lizzy sighed. 'It sounds so romantic, doesn't it?'

Leon gave her hand a squeeze, and to his surprise received a small squeeze of acknowledgment in return. Tipping his head to give the top of her head a kiss, just as he would have five years ago, seemed the natural thing to do—so he did it. She leant into him again, then shot him a shy smile.

Perhaps it was being cloaked in the low lighting. Perhaps it was holding hands. Perhaps it was simply being with Lizzy. But standing amidst the remains of an ancient family's household, where lives had been lived and lost, filled him with a profound sense of longing.

What sort of history would the two of them leave behind? And, more to the point, what sort of future would they have?

He felt as if someone had taken the well-worn and very familiar carpet he'd been walking on his entire life, yanked it out from underneath him and—just like in this palazzo—uncovered metres and metres of memories and emotions to excavate.

Could he do that? Clear away the anger and the pain from his past to allow for a bright, loving future with Lizzy?

Continue reading
A FAMILY MADE IN ROME
Annie O'Neil

Available next month
www.millsandboon.co.uk

LET'S TALK
Romance

For exclusive extracts, competitions
and special offers, find us online:

f facebook.com/millsandboon

y @MillsandBoon

◉ @MillsandBoonUK

Get in touch on 01413 063232

For all the latest titles coming soon, visit
millsandboon.co.uk/nextmonth

MILLS & BOON

THE HEART OF ROMANCE

A ROMANCE FOR EVERY READER

MODERN

Prepare to be swept off your feet by sophisticated, sexy and seductive heroes, in some of the world's most glamourous and romantic locations, where power and passion collide.

HISTORICAL

Escape with historical heroes from time gone by. Whether your passion is for wicked Regency Rakes, muscled Vikings or rugged Highlanders, awaken the romance of the past.

MEDICAL

Set your pulse racing with dedicated, delectable doctors in the high-pressure world of medicine, where emotions run high and passion, comfort and love are the best medicine.

True Love

Celebrate true love with tender stories of heartfelt romance, from the rush of falling in love to the joy a new baby can bring, and a focus on the emotional heart of a relationship.

Desire

Indulge in secrets and scandal, intense drama and plenty of sizzling hot action with powerful and passionate heroes who have it all: wealth, status, good looks…everything but the right woman.

HEROES

Experience all the excitement of a gripping thriller, with an intense romance at its heart. Resourceful, true-to-life women and strong, fearless men face danger and desire - a killer combination!

To see which titles are coming soon, please visit

millsandboon.co.uk/nextmonth